My Fair Brady

Also by Brian D. Kennedy

A Little Bit Country

My Fair BRADY

BRIAN D. KENNEDY

BALZER + BRAY

An Imprint of HarperCollinsPublishers

For my parents, who always supported me and only *slightly* panicked when I annouced I was switching my college major from English to theater.

Thankfully, I think it all worked out in the end.

BECAUSE I KNEW YOU

I HAVE BEEN CHANGED FOR GOOD

—*Wicked*

One

WADE

I don't know if *all* the world's a stage. But as soon as fifth period lets out, our cafeteria certainly turns into one. It's not an ideal performance space—fluorescent lights lack the dramatic effect of a tight follow spot, and there's no twenty-piece orchestra ready to accompany anyone who wants to spontaneously break into song. But there's definitely an audience. People who are hungry for a good show.

"Just go over to his table."

"What would I even say to him?"

"I don't know. That you like his smile?"

"Yeah, that's not happening."

"Fine. Tell him his butt looks good in our school uniform."

"Oh my god. Stop."

Glancing over my shoulder, two girls I don't recognize stand behind me in the buffet line. They must be juniors because underclassmen eat the period before us.

"For the record," I say, "these khakis aren't easy to pull off."

When they realize I've heard them, their eyes go as wide as the plates on their trays. I smile, flipping on the charm as effortlessly as a light switch. "Oh, and I'd stay away from the wax beans if I were you.

They've probably been sitting out since I was a freshman."

It takes a second, but then they look at each other and laugh.

"Wax beans," one of them says. "So gross!"

It wasn't *that* funny. But sometimes . . . well, I don't have to try very hard to be liked.

Thankfully, a packet of soup crackers hits me square in the chest before my head can get any bigger. The girls laugh again, and across the buffet from me, Ava raises an eyebrow. "Hey, Prince Charming. I'd like to eat before my pizza gets cold."

I shoot the girls a conspiratorial wink and join Ava in line to pay.

"Flirting with girls," she says, shaking her head. "Are you really that desperate?"

"I flirt with everyone," I reply, a little too defensively. "It's my thing."

"Being the focal point of any room you walk into is your thing." Ava hands the cashier her student card, flashing an enthusiastic, camera-ready smile that says she enjoys attention just as much.

Once our lunches are paid for, we take a sharp right toward the exit. It's been two weeks since Valentine's Day, so I've had plenty of time to train myself not to glance over at our old table by now. But my eyes go there anyway, immediately landing on Reese. He's laughing and stealing a Tater Tot from Hannah's tray. My throat goes tight.

"Wade." Ava snaps my attention away from them. "Let's go."

Technically we're not allowed to eat outside the cafeteria, but since most students at Monroe Academy are chronic overachievers, the administration lets it slide. We're one of the top private high schools in Minnesota for a reason. People aren't skipping lunch to sit in their cars and get high. They're skipping lunch to sit in their cars and compare PSAT scores.

Having lunch in the prop room with Ava has been a nice change, actually. I like that it's just the two of us. When we reach the hallway outside the auditorium today, however, there are a few other students lingering around—freshmen and sophomores who should be in class right now. It's no secret that on the day the cast list goes up, the number of hopeful thespians who forget a textbook in their locker or suddenly have weak bladders increases by about 50 percent.

"You might have to hold my hair back." Ava tightens her grip on her tray. "When I vomit," she clarifies.

"Relax," I tell her, even though my own pulse is starting to race. "Mr. Z won't post the list until last period, like he always does."

Although Ava and I both know this to be true, we still sneak a quick peek as we pass by the bulletin board outside Mr. Zimmerman's office. Just in case.

Leaving the other vultures to circle, we head downstairs to the prop shop, which is a maze of shelves filled with relics from older shows. Like the umbrella from *Mary Poppins*, or a foam cutout of Greased Lightnin'. The prop master would be absolutely apoplectic if they knew we were eating greasy cafeteria food in here, on a tufted velvet sofa that was last used in a production of *The Importance of Being Earnest*.

"This is unbearable." Ava stares down at her untouched pizza. "You think anyone will notice if I skip the rest of my classes and lie facedown on the floor until the list goes up?"

"We need a distraction," I say. "Dream Role You'd Commit a Felony For?"

She leans back into the couch, her long black hair pooling behind her. "But our answers never change. You're just going to pick *Dear Evan Hansen* again."

I sigh, staring off into the distance. "That show not being licensed for high school performances yet is the greatest tragedy of my life."

"Maybe by the time we graduate from NYU you can star in the Broadway revival."

"Assuming we get into NYU."

"*When* we get in."

I smile, glad Ava's getting back some of her spark. Our early decision applications for NYU were both deferred, bumping us into the regular decision pool. It was a blow to my confidence, for sure, but I'm not giving up hope. I refuse to settle for Lachlan University, the small liberal arts college in Wisconsin that my parents have been pushing for.

"Your turn," I say, poking her in the side.

She takes a breath, considering her answer. "I don't know. Elphaba?"

"Liar."

She groans. "I don't want to jinx it."

Ever since it was announced that *My Fair Lady* was going to be our spring musical, Ava's been freaking out. Eliza Doolittle is her dream role. And the thing is, she's perfect for it. She has the beauty, the comedic timing, and the vocal chops. But she's also convinced that if she says it out loud, she'll ruin her chances.

"You know Mr. Z likes to cast his shows based on who's graduating," I say. "You have nothing to worry about."

"I'm hardly the only senior girl who auditioned. Hannah and

Ebony also read for Eliza at callbacks. So did Brittany Carmichael, and she's only a junior."

True, sometimes Mr. Z throws a curveball with his casting. It's how I ended up playing Captain von Trapp as a junior. But that's exactly why I'm not too worried about this year. You don't play the lead as a junior, only to be demoted to a supporting role your senior year.

And I'm sorry, but no one has better stage chemistry than Ava and me. It doesn't matter that I've been out since freshman year. People still like to cram us into a heteronormative box, which I'm not above using to my advantage when it comes to casting.

"Mr. Z had us read together at callbacks, like, five times."

"Three times," Ava corrects me. "But I also read twice with—"

She stops, averting her gaze.

"You're allowed to say his name," I reply flatly. "He's not Beetle-juice."

She looks back up. "I also read twice with Reese."

Okay, so he may not be Beetlejuice, and saying his name won't magically summon him to the prop room. But it does summon a slight tug at my heart. And the back of my throat aches, like after you've been crying for too long. For the past two weeks, I've gotten to know those feelings pretty well. But today's going to be my turning point. Once that list goes up and I see my name next to Henry Higgins, I can forget about Reese and finally get my senior year back on track.

"Reese will be cast as Freddy," I say. "It's a good training-wheels role for him."

I wait for Ava to agree, but she's suddenly distracted by her phone.

"What—" My voice jumps. "Did they . . ."

5

"No. It's just Ebony. She wants to work on our AP History project this weekend."

I feel bad about taking Ava away from our other friends at lunch-time. Once rehearsals begin, though, we'll be spending all our time together again. It will be awkward having to be around Reese. But that's another reason I'm hoping he gets cast as Freddy. Freddy and Higgins don't share a lot of scenes together.

Of course there *is* a chance I won't get Higgins. But if I'm being honest, I know I can do the role justice. And I really want it. Henry Higgins is a pompous ass—that's fun to play onstage. He's also misogynistic and classist, which is less fun. But the entire point of the show is that he's wrong for being that way. And it takes falling in love with Eliza for him to see his faults. There's something romantic about that.

Not the being classist and sexist part. The part about meeting someone who challenges who you are and makes you a better person for it.

I know certain people at this school—*certain people at my old lunch table*—would say I'm too shallow and self-involved to care about any-one other than myself. But I don't know how you can love musicals as much as I do and *not* be a hopeless romantic. Plays tend to be more realistic, therefore subtle. But in a musical every emotion is height-ened. Characters aren't hiding their feelings. They're projecting them out to the back of the theater.

That's why musicals are filled with some of the greatest romantic pairings of all time.

Tony and Maria.

Sandy and Danny.

Professor Higgins and Eliza Doo—

"Oh shit."

Ava's still glued to her phone. But judging from the way her mouth's gaping open, she's no longer discussing AP History.

"It's up," she whispers.

I grip the edge of the couch, goose bumps pricking my forearms.

Ava's eyebrows pinch together.

"What? Did something happen? *Why are you making that face?*"

She quickly closes out her texts. "It's nothing."

I have no doubt Ava's going to be standing behind a podium someday, accepting her Tony Award. But I also know when my best friend is lying to me.

"Someone texted you the cast list, didn't they?" I ask accusingly.

"What? No."

It doesn't matter how good the news is, you're not supposed to ruin this moment for anyone. Sure, sometimes you see the list and you're dealt a blow so crushing it feels like you'll never recover. But when the opposite happens? When you first see your name next to the part you so badly wanted? Nothing beats that feeling.

"You know something," I say.

"Wade. I swear." She sets her tray on the cushion. "Ebony just said the list was up and everyone was freaking out."

"Freaking out in a good way? Or . . ."

"I don't know!"

We stare at each other for a moment, too scared to even breathe.

"Okay," I finally say. "Let's do this."

Good actors know the importance of milking a dramatic moment for all it's worth, so when Ava and I walk upstairs, we pause just before entering the hallway. The buzz of noise around the corner is like Christmas morning, hitting the top peak of a roller coaster, and waiting in the dentist's chair for a cavity filling all wrapped into one.

Ava grabs my arm, giving it a squeeze. "Hey, whatever happens out there, it's only one show. We have a lifetime of auditions in front of us."

Only one show? Okay, she *must* know something. Unless it's just her nerves. She's going to be devastated if she doesn't get Eliza. Which is why I can't wait to see her face when she realizes it's her name at the top of that cast list.

When we finally round the corner, there's a crowd of people standing in front of the bulletin board. Some are jumping up and down, feigning surprise at being cast in the role they were not-so-secretly coveting. And some are hiding their disappointment behind congratulatory hugs and plastered-on smiles, proving my theory that the best acting happens offstage, before rehearsals begin.

Maybe it's just my imagination, but as Ava and I push our way forward, the crowd seems to part. Heads turn, staring at us with knowing looks.

My heart catapults against my rib cage as we finally make it to the front. Since Ava's shorter than me, and at the perfect eye level for the cast list, she lets out a short gasp before I can lean in close enough to read any of the names. My heart catches in my throat. But then I see who's at the top of the list.

Eliza Doolittle: Ava Mehta.

I knew it. I *knew* she had nothing to worry about. I'm so excited for her that it takes me a second to process the name listed under hers.

Henry Higgins: Reese Erikson-Ortiz.

The smile drops from my face. My stomach immediately follows. Ava turns around to say something, but her words don't register. There's just this humming in my ears. No—not a humming. A name.

Reese Erikson-Ortiz.

My ex-fucking-boyfriend.

Two

ELIJAH

I get that porn isn't going for authenticity, but something always feels off about scenes that are set in a locker room. Two guys are usually standing there, fresh from the showers with only towels around their waists. They'll look each other up and down—slowly, head to toe—before striking up a conversation.

"Hey, saw you pumping iron out there."

"Yeah? That's not all I'd like to pump."

Unfortunately, the dialogue's always that bad. Not that I watch enough porn to know—but I *am* a sixteen-year-old who's familiar with the internet. Anyhow, it's hard for me to suspend my disbelief for this particular fantasy. Because who looks at other people in the locker room? Who *talks* to people? Who spends time doing anything other than trying to get out of there as fast as you can before anyone notices you?

"Shit, Dombrowski. Your nipples are big enough to be on a pepperoni pizza!"

Okay, so I guess the rest of my classmates do those things. The entire locker room erupts into laughter as everyone stops to look at Jake Dombrowski's nipples.

"Whatever, Caleb," Jake replies. "Your mom hasn't complained.

She keeps asking for the meat lovers' supreme. *Extra meat*."

I'm almost certain Jake is making a thrusting motion with his crotch. But I can't bring myself to look. My cheeks are burning as if it were me they were talking about.

"Boys, boys, boys," says a voice I know all too well.

Connor Goldfarb.

Cute, funny, fearless Connor Goldfarb, who makes everything look so easy.

"I heard Caleb's mom took one look at Jake's meat and went vegan."

This gets more laughter. Which always surprises me—that straight guys find Connor funny. I know we've progressed as a society, but when you think about a group of sophomore boys, you have to assume there's still plenty of aggressive, hyper-masculine bullshit. Not when it comes to Connor, though. He's somehow found a way to transcend homophobia.

Quickly pulling my gym shirt down over my head, I hurry out into the gymnasium and wait. Coach Walker has us playing badminton this week, which calls for teams of four. If I get my timing right, I might be able to work my way on to Connor's team. One round of badminton won't turn us into friends, just like us both being gay doesn't automatically make us friends. But I have to start somewhere.

As soon as Connor exits the locker room, he's ambushed by Callie Navarro and Brooke Martin. Callie wears her long brown hair in braids, and Brooke keeps her shorter blond hair pushed back with a knotted headband. Despite our unflattering maroon gym shorts, they still manage to look fashionable.

So does Connor, of course. With his curly chestnut hair. And his constantly rosy cheeks. And his white socks, which he pulls up all the way to his calves. He seems so confident in everything he does.

I wish I could be more like that.

As they move to pick out rackets, I hurry over before anyone else can join their team.

"I can't get over it," Connor tells his friends. "*Wade Westmore* as Colonel Pickering. His senior year. He must be crushed."

"But Colonel Pickering's a lead role," Brooke offers.

"It's all dialogue—he only gets *one* duet. Besides, Colonel Pickering is basically an old grandpa who smells like butterscotch."

I clear my throat, but my voice still comes out warbled.

"Hey. Mind if I join your team?"

Connor gives more of a shrug than a verbal confirmation, but I grab a racket anyhow and join them as they make their way over to one of the nets. Connor and Callie take one side, me and Brooke the other.

"Rehearsals are going to be so awkward now," Callie says.

"Do you think they'll get back together?" asks Brooke.

Connor tosses the shuttlecock up, only to catch it in his hand again. "No way. Reese dumps him, then *also* gets the starring role? There's no coming back from that. Which is fantastic news for me. Because I'm single and ready to tingle."

"You mean mingle," says Callie.

"No, babe." Connor waves his racket over the general direction of his crotch. *"Tingle."*

Even though I don't really know what they're talking about— something to do with the spring play, I guess—I can't stop the corners of my mouth from tugging into a smile. I don't want to seem like a creep, but the way they talk, the way words effortlessly fly out of their mouths, it's all just so . . . funny.

I *wish* I could say whatever I was thinking without overanalyzing it first. But my brain doesn't work that way. Instead, the only thing I've ever been good at is retaining useless trivia knowledge. Unlike humor, which is subjective, facts are either right or wrong. I guess that's why I like them so much. Once you learn a fact, that's one less thing you can be wrong about.

Plus, I figure if I amass enough information about things, it'll eventually come in handy when one of those facts pops up in a conversation.

Next to me, Brooke lets her racket hang at her side, not even attempting to look active. "I do feel bad for Wade, though."

"Are you serious?" Connor's perfectly sculpted eyebrows push up. "First of all, you never have to feel sorry for someone *that* good-looking. Their life's going to work out just fine. Second—"

Coach Walker's whistle blows. "I want that shuttlecock out of your hand, Connor."

"Sounds pervy when he says it like that," Connor replies, smirking.

Callie sticks out her tongue. "Shuttlecock tease."

"The other reason I can't feel bad for Wade," Connor continues, finally making his serve, "is that he has a speaking role. I refuse to pity anyone who has lines to say."

Callie groans. "I can't believe we're stuck in the chorus again."

"At least I don't have to be a Nazi this year," Connor says as we volley back and forth. "Talk about a bummer on your acting resume."

"Ugh." Callie swings her racket. "Being an extra *sucks*."

As the shuttlecock comes back across the net toward Brooke, she just stands there, not moving as it hits her in the chest.

"Oh, Brooke. Baby!"

"We didn't mean it like that!"

Connor and Callie both run up to the net. Connor sticks his fingers through the little squares as though he's trying to coax a wounded animal from the back of its cage. "We were being ungrateful. Don't listen to us."

"You're going to have so much fun doing costumes," Callie tells her. "They're really amazing for this show."

Brooke slowly makes her way up the net. She touches her fingers to theirs, and the three of them share a moment. I'd say it was annoying, but I'm actually jealous. Callie, Brooke, and Connor are bonded in a way that I'm not with anyone.

Last year I joined the Quiz Bowl team and made one friend. Micah and I were both freshmen, and both kind of quiet. After a few weeks, we started hanging out after school to do homework together. I thought we were getting close. But when I mentioned I was gay, he suddenly lost interest in me. He never said why, but I could tell I made him uncomfortable.

Eventually I just stopped showing up to Quiz Bowl. Micah's family ended up moving to Colorado over the summer, so I guess I could've rejoined the team this year. But I wasn't very good at it to begin with. I always froze under pressure.

Coach Walker's whistle blows again. "Don't make me separate you four over there."

Right. As if we could ever be four. Instead of three plus one.

If I wanted to be a part of their group, I'd have to stop being quiet.

I'd have to come up with something funny or interesting to say. They probably think it's weird that I haven't said anything since we started playing, but that's always been my default. I'd rather say nothing at all than say something to make me look foolish or wrong. People have enough reasons to laugh at me. I don't need to give them more.

And, yeah, I don't know much about this play they're doing. But I do know who Wade Westmore and Reese Erikson-Ortiz are. Everyone does. It shouldn't be difficult for me to be a part of this conversation.

"Speaking of costumes," Callie says, starting her serve as we get back to playing. "How hot is Reese going to look as Professor Higgins?"

Connor sighs. "I just love a man in a top hat and cravat."

The shuttlecock starts heading my way. This is it. My chance to finally say something. "Did you know," I reply, returning the serve with surprising ease, "that a top hat once saved Abraham Lincoln's life?"

The shuttlecock flies over the net, landing halfway between Connor and Callie, neither of whom moves to hit it. All three of them are staring at me now, as if they suddenly realized there was a fourth person on their team.

I know I should explain the rest of the story: a bullet pierced his top hat, tipping him off to the sniper who was trying to assassinate him. My tongue's too thick, though. Heat starts creeping up the back of my neck as I wait for Coach Walker to blow his whistle again, hoping he can save me. But the whistle never comes.

"Random," Connor finally says, twisting his mouth into a smile.

The three of them laugh. And while it doesn't feel like they're laughing at me, exactly, I don't think they're laughing *with* me, either. When gym class ends, I change back into my school uniform without saying another word. I don't want to humiliate myself further.

I tried—that's something to be proud of. But it's hard to feel good about a failure.

Walking past the auditorium on my way to my locker, there's a small cluster of people by the bulletin board in the hallway. Mom's probably waiting for me in the parking lot already, so I can practice driving home. But my curiosity gets the best of me. I move closer to see what everyone's looking at.

It's the cast list. I'm surprised by how many names are on it. A second sheet of paper, even longer than the first, is for the stage crew. I knew theater was popular at Monroe, but I never realized it took this many people just to put on a show.

"Did you audition?" a girl asks, looking directly at me.

"What?" I laugh. "No, I just—" My cheeks go warm, as if I've been caught doing something bad. I shake my head and hurry off to my locker.

When I finally exit the school a few minutes later, the February air hits my lungs like an icy punch. (Trivia fact: lungs are the only organ that can float on water.) I shove my hands into my jacket pockets and look for Mom. But standing on the sidewalk, all bundled up in their puffy coats, are Connor, Callie, and Brooke.

Before I can look away, Connor glances in my direction.

Without thinking I raise my hand.

Fuck. What's wrong with me?

Connor nods. A warmth blossoms in my chest, defrosting some

of the chill. Okay, maybe we're not friends yet. But he's also not ignoring me?

Instead of walking away, my mind wanders back to the cast list. I never rejoined Quiz Bowl because I didn't like the performance aspect of it. But what if I could be a part of something that didn't require me to be seen?

I take a step forward, letting my mouth speak the sliver of an idea that I'm still trying to formulate in my head. The idea that if I don't say out loud right now, I never will. "Hey, um, do you know how I can join the stage crew?"

Connor's eyebrows notch up. "You were supposed to sign up during auditions."

Brooke gives him a sideways glance. "It's not like anyone's being waitlisted for the crew. I'm sure he could still join."

I look at Connor like I need his approval.

He shrugs. "You should talk to Mr. Z."

"Okay," I say, trying to hide my smile. "Maybe I will."

"Cool," Connor replies.

Not wanting to kill the moment, I leave before I can do anything to embarrass myself. Unfortunately, Mom's here now. Parked in front of the curb at the end of the entrance way. Stepping out of the car, she gives me a wave as she makes her way around to the passenger side.

Be cool, Elijah.

Be cool, Mom.

"Who's that?" she asks, as I climb into the driver's seat.

"Mom!"

"What?"

"They can hear you."

She looks in Connor's direction. Like, right at him. "I'm sorry. But it'd be nice to finally meet some of your friends."

Connor's not my friend. Not yet. But if I join the stage crew, and we start spending more time together . . . who knows.

First, though, I have to concentrate on getting out of here. After adjusting my mirrors, I place my foot on the brake and take a breath. I don't know why driving's so hard for me. It's been a month since my birthday, and I still don't feel ready to take the test. I know all the rules, but as soon as I'm behind the wheel, my nerves take over.

Shifting gears, I take my foot off the brake and press the gas. But our car doesn't go forward. It goes back. Right up over the curb.

"Fuck!" My entire body cringes.

"You have the vehicle in reverse," Mom replies calmly.

I'm gripping the wheel so tightly my knuckles are white. I can't bring myself to look in the rearview mirror, because I can't bear to see the expression on Connor's face. As I shift into drive and take my foot off the brake, there's a loud screech of metal against the curb. Like the last shred of my dignity being dragged away.

Three

WADE

Once you're lucky enough to get cast in one of Mr. Z's productions, there are three non-negotiable rules you're expected to follow:

If you're not five minutes early to rehearsal, then you're already late.

Phones have no place on the stage. (Unless they're a prop.)

We're all family here.

Yes, our third rule sounds like a slogan for Olive Garden. But it really is true. The spring musical is intense. By tech week—when we add in all the technical elements to the show—you'll be spending more time with your fellow castmates than you do your actual family. And since you'd never date someone you're related to, choosing to date someone you do theater with is—or in my case, *was*—a really big mistake. Because now that rehearsals are in full swing, it's impossible to avoid Reese.

"He's literally in every scene that I'm in," I complain to Ava, who's sitting next to me in the auditorium. "At least when we did the read through yesterday, we were on opposite sides of the room, you know?"

Ava nods, absent-mindedly chewing on a strand of her hair as she studies the highlighted lines in her script.

"And it's not like I can't be professional. Acting's all about inhabiting a character. If I can pretend to be a naval captain who's in love with the governess of his seven children, then I should be able to act like it's not awkward for me to be standing onstage next to Reese, right?"

"Right," Ava says.

"It's just . . . how am I supposed to look at him and not think about what happened between us? Not to be dramatic, but getting dumped was probably the most humiliating experience of my life. And now everybody else in the cast is going to be thinking about it, too."

"Don't worry about everyone else. Just worry about yourself."

Ava's trying to be supportive. But the way she says it—her casual, distant tone—makes it feel like she doesn't really understand the gravity of my situation here. Which, yeah, kind of sucks. But I shouldn't complain; I've been asking a lot from her lately.

"Do you think it's too soon to try out my Cockney accent?" she asks, finally giving me her full attention. "I'm nervous people will laugh."

Ava might be nervous, but I can also see the spark of excitement in her eyes. She's waited four years to have the starring role. It's finally her moment.

"No one's going to laugh," I assure her. "You've been working on that accent since the show was announced."

"Practicing in my bedroom is different. You know some of the white girls in here are just waiting for me to screw up. Anything to justify why Eliza should've gone to one of them."

Ava's right. I should stop complaining about my problems—I've sucked up enough of the attention in our friendship. After reassuring her that she's going to be great, I pull her in for a pre-rehearsal selfie.

"Make sure you're working your angles," I remind her. Ava elbows me in the ribs, but then points her chin down like I taught her to.

While Ava goes back to studying her lines, I open my Instagram. The lighting in the auditorium's not the best, but I can always adjust the brightness to make our faces pop. The harder part is picking which photo we look best in.

Ava peers over my shoulder. "You're not going to post that one, are you?"

"Yeah. Why not?"

"Wade. My eyes are half-closed."

I take a closer look. *Oops. Shit.* How'd I not notice that?

As I start scrolling through the other options, I become aware of a presence in the row in front of us. I look up, and my heart immediately twists. Short black hair, light brown skin, school tie still knotted in place. Why does Reese always have to look so good? Even his earring—which I still find *so* hot—seems to catch the light.

"Want me to take one for you?" he asks.

Selfies look more spontaneous. Even if you have to take a dozen to get the perfect one. But I hand Reese my phone anyway—because I'm not sure what else I'm supposed to do. After not talking for three weeks, he's suddenly acting like everything's normal again? My ribs tighten. *Did he really get over me that quickly?*

As Ava and I lean in together, I can only imagine how strained my smile is.

"Cute," Reese says, looking at the photo before handing back my phone.

Cute? I look like I'm sucking lemons.

"So, um, hey . . ." Reese crosses his arms, making my eyes go straight to his biceps. "Should we talk before rehearsal starts?"

Ava closes her script. "I should check if the costume shop wants me to start wearing my rehearsal skirt yet."

I shoot Ava a pleading look, but she hurries out of the row, leaving me alone with Reese. I try to hold his gaze, but when I look at him, I see the person who got the role I wanted. The person who dumped me. The person . . . I still miss. Reese is talented, funny, and infuriatingly hard to stay mad at.

"I wanted to congratulate you, but . . ." he trails off, licking his lips. *Lips I used to kiss.* "Well, I didn't want to sound like an asshole."

My reply comes out too wounded. "Why would that make you an asshole?"

"Uh, because I know you didn't want to play Colonel Pickering?"

Hearing him say that only cements how real this is. Leading roles are not why I do theater. *Theater* is why I do theater. The rush of stepping out onto the stage, knowing you have an audience's attention, knowing the show will never be exactly the same two nights in a row. Nothing beats that feeling—no matter how many lines you have.

But yeah, I wanted to go out on a high note. And after busting my ass in shows for the past three years, I guess I was starting to think I deserved it.

"I'd congratulate you on *your* role," I tell Reese, "but you probably wouldn't think I was being sincere."

He laughs. Which almost kills me. Because for a split second, it feels like everything is back to the way it used to be. Like the past three weeks have been a bad dream I can finally wake up from.

"You could still say it," Reese tells me. "If you really mean it."

I wish I could mean it. I really do.

But at least I know how to fake it.

"Congratulations," I say, forcing a smile. "It's a great role."

"Thanks. I appreciate that."

The look on his face is more sad than appreciative. Like he's disappointed we even had to have this conversation. Disappointed in *me*, still. And if I take a moment to consider whether or not he might be right—no. I can't go there yet. "Rehearsal's starting soon," I say, reaching for my script. "I should probably—"

"Don't you think we should talk about it?"

I let go of my script. "Talk about what?"

He looks at me. "You know what."

No, actually, I don't. Am I devastated Reese broke up with me? Of course. But there's nothing for us to talk about. It's not like we have a chance of getting back together. Not after what he said to me in the cafeteria. In front of everyone at the theater table. On Valentine's Day.

You'll never be a good boyfriend, Wade. Because you'll never love anyone more than you love yourself.

My throat gets tight just thinking about it again. I wish I could say Reese was the only villain here. But he never would've said that to me if I hadn't fucked up first. I shouldn't have tried to surprise him with all those flowers. It was too over-the-top. And it doesn't matter that my intentions were good. I hurt Reese, which is something I regret.

But once he said those words, there was no taking them back. Which is why I have no interest in discussing it now. What's left to say? He thinks I'm a horrible person and wants nothing to do with me. Message received.

"Look . . ." I pause, trying to keep my voice even. "We both want this show to be good. And whatever personal feelings we have toward each other, we don't have to let those get in the way of rehearsals."

Reese studies me as if he's trying to decide whether or not he can trust me.

"Yeah. That works for me," he says finally.

I shift in my chair, less relieved than I hoped. This wasn't how rehearsals were supposed to go. This wasn't how *senior year* was supposed to go. Not getting cast as Henry Higgins was disappointing enough. But not having Reese in my life anymore, and having no one to blame for that except myself? I never imagined my last few months of high school could be so miserable.

Reese opens his mouth to say something else, but he's interrupted by the sound of Gretchen, our stage manager, striking her handheld xylophone to get everyone's attention.

"We're going to start with attendance in just a moment," she announces. "If you need a pencil, there's a box of them onstage. Please don't use pen to make notes in your script. I repeat: *no pens*. I've said it twice now, I really hope no one gives me reason to say it a third time."

And everyone thinks actors are the melodramatic ones.

"Guess that's our cue," Reese says.

As the rest of the cast starts gathering in the front of the auditorium, the energy in the room only grows more palpable. Everyone's eager to get onstage and start putting this show together. I wish I could feel that excited, too. But I can't. Not while things are still this bad between Reese and me.

"Wait," I say, surprising myself.

When he turns back around, a hollowness settles in my chest. I don't want to remember Reese as the person who dumped me in the cafeteria. I want to remember him as my boyfriend. I miss him walking up behind me in the hallways to wrap me in a bear hug. I miss what a messy eater he was—and how it was kind of cute. I miss the texts we'd send each other when we were supposed to be paying attention in class.

"I just . . ." I pause, searching for the words I probably should've said weeks ago. But those words still won't come. So instead I say, "Have a good rehearsal."

Silence hangs between us. Reese gives me a quick head nod, but his voice comes out flat. "Yeah, you too."

As he takes off to join everyone else, I close my eyes and take a breath. I don't know why those words are so hard for me to say. Because I *am* sorry.

Sorry for what I did to him.

And even sorrier for what I did to myself.

Four

ELIJAH

What the hell was I thinking? There's no way I can join the stage crew. I'm not even in the auditorium yet and my stomach's already more twisted and knotted than a balloon animal. I've spent the past ten minutes hiding in the lobby, guessing the plots of previous shows based on their posters.

Fiddler on the Roof.

Easy. A guy plays his fiddle on his rooftop, pissing off his neighbors.

How to Succeed in Business Without Really Trying.

Hmm . . . I'm guessing generational wealth and nepotism?

Joseph and the Amazing Technicolor Dreamcoat.

Well, I hate to stereotype, but this is clearly about a homosexual man named Joseph, who's very proud of his rainbow-colored coat.

Coming up blank on a show called *Brigadoon*, I check my phone. Rehearsal started two minutes ago. I don't have to peek through the doors to know how many people are in there. I could hear them all laughing and talking over one another until someone started playing the xylophone to quiet them down.

The xylophone seemed a bit much, even for theater kids.

I look toward the hallway. It's not too late to back out. I haven't actually committed to anything yet. However, Connor told me about talking to the director last Friday, and I already chickened out on the first rehearsal yesterday. This is the closest I've come to making friends since Micah. If I turn around now, I'll just go back to listening in on other people's conversations again.

Taking a deep breath, I open the door and brace myself for whatever comes next. Thankfully, no one seems to notice me as I sneak in. They're all too busy getting up from their seats as a white girl with a clipboard and T-shirt that reads *Is that your prop?* yells at them from the stage.

"We have a lot to get through today. So let's hurry, please."

I look for Mr. Z, the director, but he doesn't seem to be here yet. Not wanting to be the only person left standing in the auditorium, I follow everyone else as they make their way to the stage. Maybe I can hide in the back and blend into the crowd.

"Okay," Clipboard Girl says. "Everybody circle up."

Shit. So much for blending.

I search for Connor, but people are moving in on either side of me, locking me into the circle that's taking shape. "Since we're all getting to know each other still," Clipboard Girl says, "we'll start with the Name Game."

Hold up—*game?* My shoulders tense. Normally, I don't mind games. I've even been known to get a little competitive at Trivial Pursuit and Scrabble. But that's when I'm playing them in the privacy of my home, with just my parents.

A fair-skinned girl with a ponytail and impossibly bright smile starts us off. "Brittany," she says. And just when I think that's the extent of the game, she gracefully extends her arms, lifting herself up on her tiptoes, like a ballerina. "Balanced."

To my horror, everyone repeats this move together.

"Brittany. Balanced."

Brittany points to someone else and the game continues. I try to keep my head down. If I don't make eye contact with anyone, they can't pick me. Hilarious Hannah passes it to Loud Lexi, who passes it to Juicy Josh, who passes it to—

The theater goes silent. I look up. *Fuck.* Juicy Josh is pointing right at me.

"I'm . . . um . . ." My cheeks burn. I try swallowing, but my throat's too dry. "Elijah," I finally manage to choke out.

I wait for everyone to repeat my name, but they're all just staring at me. This has quickly turned into my worst imaginable nightmare. Next to me, someone whispers, "You have to add your adjective."

I look over to see who's talking to me. It's Reese Erikson-Ortiz. Okay, *this* is my worst imaginable nightmare. If Connor Goldfarb's out of my friend league, Reese is from a different galaxy.

"Just say the first thing that pops into your head," he tells me.

The only thing popping into my head right now—besides a deep, endless scream—is a list of nouns. *Eggplant. Email. Exoskeleton.* When I finally land on an adjective, I'm so excited I shake my hands and blurt it out.

"Elegant!"

Everyone in the circle mimics my hand shaking. "Elijah. Elegant."

Yeah, that was the opposite of elegant. It's mortifying, but at least it's over now. Before I can point to someone else, however, Clipboard Girl comes back to the stage and stares directly at me. "Sorry. Who are you?"

I open my mouth, though I'm not sure how to respond. Was she not listening? Is she really going to make me repeat that I'm Elegant Elijah?

"You're not in the cast," she says, scanning her clipboard. "What are you doing here?"

"Oh. Um . . ." All eyes are on me again. "I was hoping to talk to the director. About joining the show?"

Her eyebrows pinch together. "Did you audition?"

"I'm not an actor!" I don't mean to shout it. But the Name Game was terrifying enough, I can't imagine performing in front of an actual audience. "I wanted to be on the stage crew," I add, a little more softly this time.

Clipboard Girl still looks confused. "The crew doesn't attend warm-ups."

Wait, so I just embarrassed myself for nothing? This is definitely a sign I should've gone home after school today.

As the rest of the group continues their warm-up, Clipboard Girl has me follow her into the auditorium, where she switches out her clipboard for a massive three-ring binder. "What's your name?" she asks, pulling a freshly sharpened pencil from the messy bun in her hair.

"Elijah."

"*Full* name."

"Brady. Elijah Brady."

"Do you have any experience working stage tech?"

I bite my lip, wishing I had a different answer to give. "No."

It's subtle, but I think she's giving me the side-eye. "Okay. Was there a particular area of the crew you were interested in?"

Connor said something about costumes. That's where Brooke's going to be. "Um, the costume team?"

The side-eye becomes less subtle.

"Can you sew?"

"No."

She sighs, thumbing through the pages in her binder. "I guess we could use another person on the lighting crew. You'll need to fill out this contact form first, though."

I take the paper from her. "Oh. Well, I'm not actually sure I—"

"Look, if I let everyone pick which crew they wanted, it'd be chaos. Had you signed up at auditions like everyone else, you could've ranked your choices and maybe gotten your second or third pick." She pulls another pencil from her bun and hands it to me, barely pausing to breathe. "I'm Gretchen, by the way. Your stage manager."

I was going to say I still wasn't sure if I even wanted to do the show, but now I'm too scared not to.

"Okay, Brady," she says, adding my page to her binder.

"Oh, no. That's not . . ."

"That's not what?"

I swallow my words, not bothering to correct her.

"If I knew people would be joining the show after auditions, I would've made extra photocopies of the script ahead of time." Her tone's not rude. Just efficient. "The rest of the crew's downstairs. Check in with Szabo. He's the head lighting tech."

I didn't even know our theater had a basement. There are a lot of people down there, too. After narrowly avoiding getting run over by a garment rack, I overhear two girls who are sitting on the floor, untangling black electrical cords.

"I heard he might drop out of the show."

"Wade? Shut up. He wouldn't."

"No. But he'd *tell* people that. For the attention."

"Oh. Totally."

The girls stop talking when they realize I'm standing there, listening.

"Um . . ." I shift my weight. "I'm looking for Szabo?"

"Green room," one of them says, pointing farther down the hallway.

Contrary to its name, the green room isn't actually green. Although there is a lumpy olive-colored sofa in there. Three guys are currently sitting on it, sharing a bag of microwaved popcorn and a two-liter bottle of Dr Pepper.

"Sorry," I say, even though I'm not sure what I'm apologizing for. "I'm looking for someone named Szabo?"

The guy in the middle—who's white, with shaggy dark hair and a backward ballcap—looks up from the well-worn copy of *The Kite Runner* that he's reading. "I'm Szabo."

"Oh. Hi. Gretchen told me to come find you. I guess I'm part of the lighting crew now?"

He gives me a casual nod. "Cool. Welcome to the team."

The guys on either side of him introduce themselves as Rhodes and Yang, and it finally dawns on me that everyone must be going by their last names. "I'm Brady," I say, but it comes out sounding more like a question.

"Do you know anything about hanging lights?" asks a voice behind me.

I spin around. Leaning against the wall—with her arms folded

31

against her chest and a blank expression—is a tall, lanky girl with medium brown skin. She's wearing black Doc Martens and a flannel shirt over her school uniform.

"Um. No."

"That's Navarro," Szabo says. "You can start by shadowing her today. She'll teach you everything you need to know."

Navarro uncrosses her arms, taking off down the hallway without waiting to see if I follow. "We don't have a light plot to work off yet, so we can't do much in the catwalks. I'd like to test some of the Fresnels, though. And I could always use help sorting gels."

I have no idea what any of that means. But soon we're in a freight elevator that I also didn't know existed and moving on to other topics.

"You can call me Summer, by the way. I use she/her pronouns."

"Elijah. He/him."

"What made you want to join the crew, Elijah?"

"Uh . . ."

Her question catches me off guard. I can't tell her the real reason: that I'm halfway through sophomore year and still don't have friends. I have to be cooler than that.

"A lot of people end up here after they didn't get cast in the show," she tells me. "And no offense, but you can always tell who secretly wants to be an actor and is only doing this to earn brownie points with Mr. Z."

"I *don't* want to be an actor," I assure her.

Summer smiles. But only slightly.

"Good. You're one of us, then."

"One of us?"

"A techie. Part of the crew."

"I mean, I still haven't—"

The elevator jolts to a stop. The door slides open along its track, slowly revealing the backstage area.

"Just stick by me," Summer says. "I'll show you what to do."

I glance over at where the actors are still warming up. Connor and Callie seemed so unapproachable in gym class. But here, they're just two people pretending to toss an imaginary ball around in a circle.

Summer takes off again, leaving me with two options: give this a real shot, or go back home and stop trying. I already survived the Name Game. How bad could the rest of it be?

I take a step forward, ready to find out.

Five

WADE

"And this over here is the Royal Opera House," Gretchen says, pointing to a strip of red spike tape that stretches across upstage left. "You won't be able to step through a wall during a performance, so please don't make a habit of doing it during rehearsals."

Once we're done getting our bearings, Mr. Z stands at the apron of the stage, lowering his bifocals to get a better look at us. "Okay, gang. We'll begin by creating a tableau vivant."

Only Mr. Z would use the phrase "tableau vivant." And only anyone who's acted in one of his productions before would know what it means. As Gretchen meticulously scribbles notes, Mr. Z arranges us around the stage, building the picture he wants for the opening of the show.

"It's a cold, rainy night in Covent Garden," he reminds us. "The opera has ended and you're in your best gowns and formal wear, trying to catch a taxi without getting wet. Unless you're one of the costermongers—your next meal might depend on making a sale, so staying dry is a luxury you can't afford." He pauses, a hint of a smile settling across his lips. "And remember, it's 1912. No ridesharing apps yet."

Everyone laughs. And it's not just a bunch of actors kissing ass in hopes of getting a little extra stage time—we all genuinely like Mr. Z.

Well, we all *used* to like him. I'm still finding it hard not to feel bitter. Mr. Z's a good director—he's won multiple state theater championships for our school. And he's clearly passionate about teaching his students. I'm sure he had his reasons for casting the show the way he did. I just wish I knew what they were.

"Which brings us to our leads," Mr. Z says, gesturing to Ava. "Eliza Doolittle, the lower-class flower girl who uses her determination and wit to infiltrate high society and become a proper lady."

Ava grabs the sides of her rehearsal skirt, performing a curtsy.

Mr. Z turns toward Reese. "Helping her achieve that transformation, of course, is Henry Higgins—our uptight phonetics professor. He's a bit of a prig. But thankfully we have the next two months to discover some redeeming qualities in him."

Everyone laughs again and Reese eats it up with a wide grin. I force a smile, waiting to see if Mr. Z will say something about my character, too. But he just returns to directing people where to stand.

I can't ignore the sting it leaves. I swear, I don't always need to be the center of attention. But I also don't want to be an afterthought. I love acting too much. And I've worked too hard to become skilled at it. Much like how my brothers must feel when they pitch a no-hitter or score the winning goal, I take a lot of pride in being able to memorize a script, learn complex choreography, or sustain a note I'm projecting to the back of the auditorium.

And the payoff—connecting with an audience? Making people

feel something? My body vibrates just thinking about it. It's like there's this energy onstage. A kind of magic, almost. One I've never felt anywhere else.

Acting makes me feel loved. By the audience, and honestly—by myself. When I'm acting, I can finally believe I'm good at something. Only . . . now that I don't have the lead, or even a solo, I'm starting to wonder if I was wrong. Maybe I'm *not* that good.

"Perfect," Mr. Z says, taking a step back to admire his creation. "This is where we begin our show."

After Gretchen finishes marking our positions, Mr. Z has us move on to blocking out the rest of the scene. Since this is only our second rehearsal, and everyone's busy writing notes in their scripts, no one's expected to put much effort into their acting yet.

That doesn't stop Ava from trying out her Cockney accent, though. And while it might not be flawless, she carries herself across the stage with so much confidence, you'd think she's been doing this for weeks already. I smile just watching her.

That smile, however, fades when I look down at my script. Normally, I would've practiced my lines a million times before rehearsals began, but for this show I didn't see the point. It's hard to get excited about a character who's wholly unremarkable. Colonel Pickering doesn't serve much purpose other than being a gentleman to Eliza, even though she's in a different social circle than him. Which is nice, I guess. Except "nice" isn't very fun to play.

When Reese makes his entrance into the scene, my breathing shallows. He hasn't been performing for as long as Ava and I have, but he's naturally charming and charismatic. It's hard not to be drawn to him. Especially now, as he seems to be doing a decent job. His shoulders are pushed back, his British accent is smooth and crisp, and the winning smile on his face doesn't betray any first day jitters.

I grip my script a little tighter. That's how I would've played Higgins, too. Uptight, but aloof. Cocky, but magnetic. My jaw clenches as I watch him say those lines now. *The same lines I read at callbacks.*

"Wade," someone says.

I look toward the house. Gretchen stares back at me.

"It's your line," she says.

My ears burn. I hold up my script, but everything blurs together. I can't find my place until a finger—Reese's—drops in front of me, pointing me in the right direction. "Thanks," I whisper, my mouth going dry.

As we continue the scene, I try to match Ava and Reese's energy, but everything comes out flat. I've never felt self-conscious onstage before, but now everything I do feels like it's not good enough. Did Mr. Z not cast me as Higgins because he knew I couldn't handle the part?

"Excellent," Mr. Z says, once we reach the end. "Ebony, that gesture you made when someone bumped into you—really good, let's keep that. And Ava and Reese . . ." He pauses, placing his bifocals on top of his head. "If you can maintain that chemistry until opening night, we're in for an exciting show."

His words hit me like a stage weight. *I'm* the one who's supposed to have good chemistry with Ava. Not Reese. And the worst part is, I can't exactly argue with what he's saying. I don't know why I didn't see it at callbacks—maybe because I couldn't see past my own ego—but their playful confidence pairs well together.

Before we can try running the scene again, it's time for a rehearsal break. As people refill their water bottles and catch up on gossip, Ava takes a seat at the edge of the stage with Ebony and Hannah. Ebony grabs a strand of Ava's hair to braid, while Hannah shows them something on her phone that they all laugh at.

I should go over there and join them. They're my friends, and we haven't really spent time together since things blew up between me and Reese. But instead I walk past them, heading straight toward Mr. Z.

It's like watching a trainwreck.

Except I'm the train, chugging my way to disaster.

"Wade," Mr. Z says, picking up his mug.

"I'm kind of struggling with my character," I say, not wasting any time. "I was just . . . I was wondering if you had any notes for me? Like, was there something in this character that made you think of me for the role?"

Translation: *Why didn't you cast me as Higgins? Was Reese really better?*

Mr. Z takes a sip of his tea, which is always lukewarm from sitting out so long at rehearsals. He's been around theater kids long enough to know what I'm really asking, which is probably why he's taking his time coming up with his answer.

"Colonel Pickering is a distinguished older gentleman," he finally says. "Don't be afraid to commit to that."

My nostrils flare, I try not to grimace. He wants me to *commit*? Is he serious? That's all I've done the past three years. I've auditioned for every show. Memorized thousands of lines. Spent countless afternoons and weekends rehearsing my ass off. And look what it's earned me. A supporting role.

I nod, pretending to be thankful. Really, though, there's a fire brewing in me now. I'm angry and motivated, ready to show him how committed I can be. I turn around and jump back on to the stage, but just as I start to run over to where I was standing before, someone steps in front of me.

The last thing I hear before we collide is—

Six

ELIJAH

"Fuck!"

The stage light slips from my hands, missing my foot by about an inch as it hits the floor with a clatter. Everyone's heads turn in my direction, causing a tiny bit of bile to rise at the back of my throat.

"Hold," someone yells. "Nobody move."

My body's frozen—I couldn't move if I tried. Once I recover from the initial shock, I look up to see who I ran into. No—*who ran into me*. Broad shoulders, skin that's never known a blemish, and a swoop of floppy dark hair that's just begging to be flipped back in slow motion.

Wade Westmore.

"What happened?" the stage manager, Gretchen, asks as she makes her way over to us. When she sees the equipment laying at my feet, her eyes grow wider. "Do you know how expensive those are?"

Wade and I look at each other. He opens his mouth, but no words come out.

"You shouldn't even be onstage right now," Gretchen says, in a tone that's not exactly scolding, but pretty close. "Not during rehearsal."

"I'm, uh . . ." There's a waver in my voice, and I can feel my eyes start to water. If I cry in front of everyone right now, I'll have to transfer schools. Preferably to another country.

"It's my fault," says a voice behind me.

Summer walks out onto the stage calmly, with her arms folded over her chest. "I forgot to explain the rules to him. Won't happen again."

Uh, that's definitely a lie. Summer told me I shouldn't be on the stage when the actors are rehearsing. But I'm sorry, it looked like they had taken a break. And it's not my fault Wade came running out of nowhere.

"What about this light?" Gretchen asks, pointing to it.

There's a crack in the glass and one of the shutters is now dented and bent. But Summer just shrugs. "It was already busted. We were planning to use it for parts."

Gretchen places a hand on her hip, exhaling slowly. "Sorry if I yelled. But let's try to be more careful, okay?"

I nod. And as Gretchen leaves, I turn to Summer. "Was it really busted?"

"No. But now I'll have a good excuse to take it apart and fix it."

As I crouch down to pick the light back up, two shoes come into view. "Um, are you okay?"

I glance up. Wade Westmore is towering over me. Charismatic, popular, and impossibly good-looking. I try to swallow back the lump in my throat. Of all the people to run into, why'd it have to be someone like him?

I realize I'm staring and quickly look away. My eyes land on

Connor and Callie, who are huddled next to one of the curtains, giggling. I have no proof they're laughing at me. But at this point it doesn't matter. I've given them more than enough material.

"Hey," Wade says. "I asked if—"

"Don't worry about it," I mumble, standing back up and exiting the stage.

Hauling the busted light over to the freight elevator, I'm relieved when the door slides open right away. I step in and jab the down button repeatedly. But the door's too slow; Summer follows me in.

"Don't sweat Gretchen," she tells me. "Stage managing's a hard job. She has to act that way, otherwise people would never listen to her."

"This isn't working," I say, setting the light down.

"I told you," Summer replies stubbornly. "I can fix it."

"No. *Me.* I'm not working." I close my eyes, pushing back the tears that are dangerously close to spilling out. I don't know what I was thinking. There's a reason I don't have friends like Connor does. I'm not the right kind of gay.

I mean, that's bullshit. There's no "right" way to be gay. Except at this school, it kind of seems like there is. Everyone wants to be friends with the hot gays, like Wade or Reese. Or the funny ones, like Connor. Nobody's interested in getting to know the quiet, slightly awkward, clearly accident-prone gays.

"Thanks for showing me around," I tell Summer as we finally come to a stop. "But I won't be joining the lighting crew after all."

As soon as the elevator opens, I'm out of there, making my way toward the green room so I can grab my backpack and go home.

"Um . . . " Summer calls after me as I enter the door at the end of the hallway. "That's not the way out."

It's too late, though. The door clicks shut behind me. Under the hum of fluorescent lights, tall metal storage units stretch out before me, their shelves packed tight with junk. It looks like someone's basement. And they're badly in need of a garage sale.

Not wanting to go back out and face Summer, I walk down one of the aisles, examining its contents. Old typewriters. A collection of mismatched saucers and teacups. Fake wedges of cheese made from spray-painted foam. (Trivia fact: the average American consumes about forty pounds of cheese each year.)

Turning the corner at the end of the row, I stop in front of a large velvet sofa.

I take out my phone and check the time. If I call Mom to pick me up early, I'll have to explain why I'm not doing the show anymore. I know my parents—they'll say I didn't give it a fair shot. Maybe it's better if I pretend to attend rehearsal for a couple days before breaking the news to them.

The sofa smells like moth balls, but I lie down on it anyhow. At least it's quiet down here. As much as I want friends, I have trouble shutting off my mind when I'm in a group. *What's everyone thinking? Did I say the wrong thing?*

When it's just me, though, I can relax. And, really, being alone isn't as lonely as it sounds. Not when you have your phone. Or . . . shit, a driver's license test you should be studying for.

I pull up the DMV app on my phone and start one of their practice quizzes. Before I can get more than a few questions in, the door clicks open and voices carry into the room.

"But our break's half over."

"We still have time."

"Wade . . . "

I freeze, clutching my phone.

"Ava, please. I just—I can't be up there right now."

"Fine. But we'd better not be late."

The sound of their footsteps grows closer. Jumping up from the couch, I consider saying something. But then I'd have to talk to Wade again. I've already embarrassed myself in front of him once today; hiding seems like a better option.

Moving behind the nearest shelving unit, I squat next to some vintage suitcases as Wade collapses onto the couch with a groan. His friend, Ava, sits next to him. "It's only the first day of blocking," she says, placing a hand on his knee. "You don't have anything to worry about yet."

Wade laughs, but there's an edge to it. "Easy for you to say. Your chemistry with Reese is already off the charts. I mean, wow. Maybe you two should try dating."

Ava frowns, pulling her hand away. "Wade, I love you. And as your best friend, I wish Reese hadn't dumped you and got cast in the role you wanted. But as an actor, I'm not going to feel guilty for doing my job."

Wade doesn't say anything for a moment. He just sits there, sulking.

"Sorry," he finally says. "I didn't mean that."

So Wade Westmore *can* apologize. Just not to me.

"I know this isn't easy for you," Ava tells him. "But you're still a great actor. You don't have to question that."

"Not as good as Reese, apparently."

Ava sighs. "It's not about being better; you know that. Sometimes it's just about timing."

"But that's exactly why this is so fucked up!" Wade sits up, suddenly energized. "It's *my* senior year. Reese wasn't even into theater when he met me. He was a soccer player, and I taught him how to act. I mean, sure, he had natural talent. But I helped him refine it. I was even helping him prepare for the audition before he dumped me!"

Wow. Someone thinks highly of himself. Though after what happened earlier, that shouldn't come as a surprise.

"Am I wrong?" Wade asks.

Ava's voice is tentative. "Do you want the honest answer? Or the friend answer?"

"The friend answer. Obviously."

"You're right," she tells him. "And I'm sorry."

"Thanks," Wade replies. But his voice is dull, like it didn't actually leave him feeling any better. For a moment, I almost feel sorry for him.

Repositioning myself to get a better look at him, I grab on to the shelving unit. Except, in doing so, I accidently bump my foot into a tambourine sitting on the bottom.

Fuck.

"Hello?" Wade asks.

I hold my breath, waiting to see if they'll go back to talking. But Wade gets up from the couch and starts making his way over to me. In a panic, I grab the first thing in front of me, so I can at least look like I have a reason to be here.

Wade rounds the corner, stopping when he finds me. We lock eyes

45

for the second time today, and his eyebrows pinch together, like he's trying to place where he knows me from. Which, I'm sorry . . . *are you serious?*

"I, um, didn't realize anyone was in here," he says.

I nod, not trusting my voice to come out in anything other than a squeak.

"Were you . . ." he pauses, scratching the back of his head, "eavesdropping on us?"

I happened to overhear his conversation. Which, okay, is pretty much the same thing. But I was in here first. And technically I'm still a member of the stage crew. So I think that gives me more authority than him, at least in this room.

"I was working in here," I reply. "For the show."

His eyes move to the object I'm holding.

"Funny, I don't recall a scene where Eliza plays the ukulele."

"I . . . I'm reorganizing."

I return the instrument to the shelf and start moving a few other items around. I can still feel his eyes on me, though, and I have to concentrate on not letting my hands shake. I'm not used to talking to people like Wade.

"You could've said something when you heard us come in," he says.

"Right. And you could've apologized upstairs."

It comes out in a mutter. But the point was made.

"Apologize for what?" His brow creases, like he's actually confused. "Wait, are you serious? You think *I'm* the one who ran into *you?*"

"You came out of nowhere. I couldn't have run into you if I tried!"

"Are you kidding me? You weren't supposed to be there."

"I thought everyone was taking a break," I say.

"We were."

"So what's the big deal, then?"

His eyes pop, incredulous. "You were in *our* rehearsal space!"

Their rehearsal space. Not mine. As if I wasn't already fully aware that I don't fit in here.

My bottom lip quivers as the tears I've been fighting start building up again. I never should've shown up today. I'm not used to putting myself out there. And now that I have, now that people are fractionally aware of me, I can see that I've made a mistake. I should've stayed invisible. Because people who are invisible don't have to worry about getting their feelings hurt.

Someone clears their throat. It's Wade's friend, Ava.

"Awkward timing," she says. "But we need to be back upstairs now."

I blink. I only have to stay strong for another minute until they leave, but Wade's still staring at me, and I can already feel the first wet tear streaming down my cheek. I wipe it away, turning my head so I don't have to look at him.

"I'm—" Wade stops.

And then, he does the most gentlemanly thing I could ask of him right now: he leaves without saying another word.

Seven

ELIJAH

When Mom picks me up and has me practice driving home from rehearsal tonight, she doesn't badger me with a million questions like she normally would. That's the upside to being a not-so-great driver, I guess.

As soon as we get home, though, I know something's up. The kitchen smells like garlic bread, and Dad—who's wearing his *Trophy Husband* apron and uncorking a bottle of wine—greets us with an eager smile. I don't have to glance at the stovetop to guess what's for dinner.

If you ask me what my favorite meal is, I'll tell you I don't have one.

If you ask my parents, they'll say it's fettuccine Alfredo.

To be fair, fettuccine Alfredo is pretty delicious. And I'm sure we had it for dinner one night and I said as much. But I don't ever recall saying it was my *favorite*. My parents just invented that. And now, whenever there's something worth celebrating—like when I finally got my learner's permit—Dad makes it for me.

Which means they're turning my first day of rehearsal into An Event. Dread pools in my stomach. I broke a light and cried in front of Wade Westmore . . . not really the "events" I want to be celebrating.

"So?" Dad asks, loading up my plate. "How'd it go?"

"It was good." And then, because I know that won't be enough information to satisfy them, I add, "They put me on the lighting crew."

Dad's face perks up. "That's a complex part of the show, kid. I bet they don't let just anyone work on lights."

No, actually, they do. I'm proof.

"Don't forget to ask when tickets go on sale," Mom says. "I want good seats."

Mom and Dad were disappointed when I quit Quiz Bowl. I think they worry about me spending so much time by myself. And I'm sure they won't be thrilled when I don't follow through with this, either. They just want to be proud, supportive parents—which is nice. But I'm sorry, they're already being way too embarrassing about this. It's the stage crew, not a National Merit Scholarship.

"You know . . ." Dad twirls strands of fettucine around his fork. "Back in the day I dabbled in a few theatrical productions myself."

The way he says *dabbled*, it's like he's talking about trying LSD once. And yes, I do know. He's told me multiple times.

"After dinner, I'll see if I can find my old yearbooks. I even had a speaking role once. Rusty Charlie in *Guys and Dolls*."

Mom almost spits her wine back out. *"Rusty Charlie?"*

"He was a gambler," Dad says.

Mom raises her eyebrows, shooting me a look. "If you say so."

Despite being in a bad mood from everything that happened at rehearsal, I find myself smiling. Dad's sunny disposition and eternal optimism often make him an easy target for Mom and me, and our more cynical outlook. Dad's an overgrown Boy Scout who thinks

49

everything happens for a reason. Mom and I both know that shit happens, and there never needs to be a reason—only bad luck.

"Are your friends in the show?" Mom asks.

Speaking of rotten luck.

"Uh-huh," I say, remembering that she saw me talking to Connor the other day.

"Are you going to invite one of them on your camping trip?"

I can feel their eyes on me, waiting for my answer. I shift uncomfortably in my chair. Much like how fettuccine Alfredo is apparently my favorite meal, my parents also decided that what I really wanted when I turned sixteen this year was to go on a father-son camping trip. I think it was their gentle way of making sure I don't celebrate my birthday alone.

Camping with my dad wouldn't be so bad. Except they suggested that I invite a friend along. After Micah and I stopped hanging out, my parents didn't stop asking about him until he finally moved away. I thought maybe I'd have another shot at finding a friend with Connor—we're both sophomores, both gay, both involved with the show. But today, I totally blew that up.

"I've been reading up on insulated sleeping pads," Dad says. "Maybe we can check some out at the store this weekend."

I clear my throat. "Or, you know, we could just wait and go camping once it gets warmer. Like this summer, maybe?"

Dad frowns. "But your birthday was in January. You don't want to wait that long."

"There could be a snowstorm," I say. "Think of how guilty you'd feel if my birthday present put me in a hypothermic coma."

"Spring break's not until the end of March," he reminds me. "And we're renting a camper cabin. Besides, it's supposed to be an adventure. That's the whole point of this trip—to do something memorable so you'll never forget the year you turned sixteen."

Based on how things have been going for me so far, I'm not sure there's anything I want to remember about turning sixteen. Dad might be hanging on to his old yearbooks, but he actually *did* stuff in high school.

"Just remember," Mom says, "the only condition for this trip is that you have to get your driver's license first."

I love how she says that like it's a threat. As if I haven't put off scheduling my test for that very reason. (Well, that and the fact that I'm still a terrible driver.)

"He'll get his license," Dad says. "He can do anything he puts his mind to."

"Did you do something different with this sauce?" I ask, changing the subject. "It's even more delicious than usual."

When school gets out the next day, my plan is to do homework until it's time for Mom to pick me up. I figure I'll keep up the ruse that I'm on the crew until the end of the week. Being a failure is embarrassing enough. I at least want my parents to think I tried.

While changing out my books at my locker, however, someone comes up behind me and taps my shoulder. I spin around. Summer's holding a bound manuscript, which she thrusts into my hands.

"Here. Gretchen's sorry she couldn't get this to you sooner."

It's a copy of *My Fair Lady*. I stare at it, surprised they still want me involved.

"Actually, I'm not—"

"Don't worry about yesterday," she says, cutting me off. "Actors are showboating narcissists. That's why the crew sticks together."

As Summer turns to leave, I'm unsure if I should follow her or not. She did cover for me yesterday. And she was nice enough to try to make me feel better. I guess I can always quit the show next week.

When we arrive in the green room, Szabo says he wants to work on something called the lighting plot today. So far it looks like that mostly consists of sitting on the couch with Rhodes, Yang, and a bag of Starburst.

"The conservatory's going to be a challenge," Szabo says, looking at his script. "We have to make it look like the light's coming through the foliage."

"*Foliage?*" Yang asks.

"Tree leaves," Szabo explains.

"I know what foliage means," Yang replies. "It means Ava Mehta will *never* talk to you if you keep using vocab like that."

Szabo's cheeks turn pink, but the conversation doesn't slow down long enough for anyone to dwell on it.

"Ooh, can we get an effects projector?" asks Rhodes.

"Too expensive," Yang says, bouncing a tennis ball off the wall.

"Fine, how about some gobos then?"

Summer scoffs. "Only if you want it to look tacky."

I have no idea what they're talking about. But it's fun to watch them tease each other. And even though they're all upperclassmen, and I'm the only sophomore, it's less intimidating than playing the Name Game in front of everyone.

Szabo snatches the tennis ball from Yang. "Let's make a note to go through our Roscos and check which shades of green we have."

"There's a shit ton of emerald from when we did *The Wiz*," Summer says.

Rhodes looks at her. "You're positive about that?"

"It's Navarro," Szabo says. "She can still recite the cues from our last show."

Yang grabs the bag of Starbursts. "Fuck, Rhodes! You ate all the pink ones?"

"What? I saved you the yellow."

Yang extends both middle fingers.

"That reminds me," Szabo says. "What's your favorite candy?"

It takes a second to realize he's looking at me.

"It can't be chocolate. Or anything that melts. No sticky fingers on the light board."

"Oh. Um . . ." I try to think of what I like, but my mind goes blank. I guess this is why I end up eating so much fettuccine Alfredo.

"Twizzlers?" I finally say.

"Excellent choice." Szabo pokes Rhodes in the shoulder. "Write that down. Twizzlers for Brady." He looks back up at me. "Tech week gets stressful. We like to stock up on everyone's favorites and keep a secret stash in the control booth."

They would do that for me? I bite my lip to keep from smiling. Only an underclassman would act like this is a big deal.

As we leave the guys to their lighting plot, Summer starts educating me on the different kinds of stage lights. "Most people will tell you ellipsoidals are the sleeker, sexier light. But most people are wrong. Fresnels are clunkers, but they have a good wash."

I'm not sure I'm retaining much, but Summer seems excited to have someone to explain stuff to. At least I think she's excited. It's hard to tell when she delivers everything in her dry, matter-of-fact tone.

"Next week we'll go into the catwalks. You're not afraid of heights, are you?"

I tell her I'm not, which is true. But the part I leave out is that I'm not planning on being here next week. At least I don't think I am?

"It's a lot to take in," she says. "But you'll get the hang of it."

"You seem to know more about lights than anyone else," I reply. "How come you're not the head tech?"

"I did the fall play, *The Crucible*. Puritan hysteria just felt more my style, you know?"

I can't tell if she's joking or not. But it's cool that she doesn't seem to care either way. I wish I could be more like that.

By the time rehearsal ends, I can't believe two whole hours have passed already. Back home, I would've just done homework or played on my phone. This seems more fun.

As the actors start spilling out into the auditorium, Connor and Callie make their way over to Brooke, who was downstairs with the rest of the costume crew. Maybe if I stick with the show, instead of quitting, they'll eventually start hanging out with me, too.

Impossibly enough, after a minute, all three of them walk over to where Summer and I are standing. But they can't be coming here to see me. I mean, it couldn't be *that* easy. Could it?

Callie smiles as though she's excited to see me, which is how I know this can't be real.

"What do you want?" Summer asks coolly.

I swallow a nervous laugh. *Oh god. Please don't let her make me look worse in front of them.*

Callie rolls her eyes. "Can you tell Mom and Dad I'm going over to Connor's to study?"

Hold up—*Mom and Dad?*

"You can't just text them?" Summer asks, crossing her arms.

"They trust you more. You're the good daughter."

"I'm hardly—" Summer pauses, shaking her head. "Fine."

It finally clicks that Szabo referred to Summer as "Navarro," which is also Callie's last name. I should've connected those dots sooner.

"I didn't know you had a sister," I say, looking at Callie.

"She's *always* had a sister," Summer replies, storming off suddenly. I don't know if it was something I said, or if Summer and Callie really just hate each other that much. Right now, though, I have other things to worry about.

This could be my chance to connect with Connor. A do-over from my embarrassing mishaps yesterday. The lighting crew has been pretty nice so far, but Connor and I are in the same grade. I need to start interacting with some of the underclassmen in the show.

"How was rehearsal?" I ask, stopping them before they can leave.

Connor looks at his friends. "It was . . . good."

"Neat." I clench my jaw, trying not to visibly cringe at my word choice. I don't know why making conversation is so hard for me. It's what normal people do. And look, I've seen theater kids do their warm-ups now. You can't crawl around the stage making animal noises and still act like you're too cool for everyone.

"Well . . ." Connor shrugs. "We really do have homework to get to."

I grip the straps of my backpack, not ready for my second chance to slip away. I don't want to be the kind of person who doesn't have anyone to invite on a camping trip for his birthday. And unlike Micah, Connor won't be weirded out because I'm gay.

"Me too," I say. "So much homework. I'll probably be studying all night."

I'm being obvious. But I don't know how else to do this. Is there a casual way to convince people to be friends with you? Because up until now, waiting for other people to take the initiative hasn't exactly worked.

As we continue to stand there, it's clear an invitation to join them isn't going to happen. "Um, anyhow . . ." I say, trying to keep my voice upbeat. "Have a good night."

I turn to leave. But before I'm out of earshot, Connor snickers.

"God. Way to finally read the room."

I stop. And even though I shouldn't, I turn back around and look at him. Connor's rosy cheeks turn a darker shade of red.

"Sorry, I didn't . . ." He pauses, the expression on his face changing from embarrassment to pity. "Look, Elijah. You seem like a really nice guy. And, uh, not to be conceited . . . but I think it's kind of obvious you have a crush on me. Which is *so* flattering. But sadly, not reciprocated. I just didn't want to lead you on, you know?"

My face goes warm, probably turning my cheeks as red as his. *A crush?* I was just looking for a friend. Even if I liked Connor—*which I don't*—I never would've tried to act on it. I know my place in the social hierarchy of this school.

Which, actually, now that I think about it, is sad. But that's just how things work. Obviously, someone like Connor would never go for someone like me. I mean, he doesn't even want to be friends, let alone *boyfriends*.

Before I can tell him he's mistaken, I sense someone behind me.

"Hey, there you are."

Out of nowhere, Wade Westmore appears at my side. My body tenses. And if that wasn't confusing enough, he puts his hand on my shoulder—like, *on purpose.* "I hope you're still free to help me run lines."

When I don't respond, he gives my shoulder a squeeze.

"Uh-huh," I somehow manage to spit out.

What the fuck is happening? I don't know what kind of face I'm making, but Connor's expression is one of complete and utter shock. I used to admire how funny Connor was. Until I realized *I* was the joke. So it's hard not to take some pleasure in this moment.

"I, um . . ." Connor pauses, composing himself. "Sorry. Can I just say what an inspiration it was to have you play Captain von Trapp last year? I mean, as an out gay actor, it's nice to know I won't always be the comedic relief. I could still play the romantic lead, you know?"

Wade bristles, probably at the reminder that he doesn't have the lead role this year. *Talk about not reading the fucking room, Connor.*

Wade forces a smile. "Cool. Thanks for being a fan."

No way. Connor Goldfarb being called out as a fanboy. It's too much.

Wade keeps up his charade as we leave the theater. But once we're out in the hallway, his arm drops from my shoulder, causing the smile to drop from my face.

"Why—why'd you do that?" I ask, still in shock.

He shakes his head, letting out a huff. "I heard what he said to you. You shouldn't let him treat you that way."

"What way?"

"Like he's better than you."

I study his face, trying to get a read on him. He sounds sincere. But after our last interaction, I have to wonder if this is some kind of game. Unless he's just clueless about how high school actually works.

"Okay," I say. "But why do you *care*?"

He shrugs. "I felt bad about yesterday. I didn't mean to make you—"

"Drop a stage light?" I offer.

". . . cry."

Oh. I'd be embarrassed, except my mind's still stuck on how Connor was acting around Wade, falling all over him. Is it really just Wade's good looks? Or is it something more than that? His personality? His . . . unchecked sense of confidence? I mean, Wade had the nerve to run into me and then act like *I* was to blame.

Maybe if I had as much confidence as Wade, I wouldn't have to go looking for friends. They'd come find me.

Unfortunately, much like driving a car, being confident doesn't come easy to me. I need, like, a learner's permit. Or someone to teach me. Wait—*could that work?*

"Anyhow," Wade says. "We should be even now, right?"

Looking up at him, I'm reminded of what Summer said: actors are showboating narcissists. If I want a teacher, shouldn't I try for the best?

Wade's already seen me cry. What do I have to lose by asking?

"Actually," I say. "Maybe there's something else you can do for me."

Eight

WADE

This techie may as well be holding an empty bowl of gruel as he stares up at me with his pleading eyes. I probably shouldn't have gotten myself involved, but I felt bad about what happened yesterday. I hate seeing people cry.

"I was wondering if . . ." He trails off, his Adam's apple bobbing up and down. "Could you help me become more confident?"

I laugh. Not to be mean—it's just . . . not what I expected.

"I'm sorry," I say. "But I'm not sure how I would even—"

"You taught Reese how to be a good actor, right?" he presses.

My stomach twists at the mention of Reese's name. "When did I say that?"

"I overheard you." He looks down. "In the prop room."

So he *was* eavesdropping. I knew it.

"I was thinking you could teach me how to be . . . well, popular." His eyes grow even more desperate as he looks back up. "By giving me some pointers. And, like, maybe a few lessons."

I take a moment to really study this kid. Messy reddish-brown hair that covers too much of his face. A smattering of freckles across his nose. Terrible posture. He could use some help, sure. But this is almost too comical.

"So, wait—" I try not to smile. "You want me to be the Henry to your Eliza?"

His eyebrows inch together, as though he doesn't know what I'm talking about. "You mean from the play?"

I close my eyes. "It's a musical. Not a play."

"Oh. Sorry. I haven't read it yet."

My eyes snap back open. "You're kidding."

"I just got my script yesterday."

"But you've at least seen the movie?"

He stares blankly at me. "Um . . ."

Wow, I'm almost tempted to help him now. Because anyone who hasn't experienced the full glory of the eight-time Academy Award–winning film starring Audrey Hepburn and Rex Harrison is clearly at a disadvantage in life. But I have enough problems of my own to deal with.

"Look," I say. "I'm sorry for everything that happened yesterday. Really. But I can't help you with this. Popularity's overrated, anyhow. You should just . . . I don't know, try believing in yourself more."

His shoulders drop. "Seriously? *That's* your advice?"

"What? It's true."

"I could've found that on a poster in the guidance counselor's office."

If he wasn't so rude, I might laugh.

"Never mind," he mumbles.

I shake my head as I watch him leave. I swear, the techies get weirder every year.

★

Returning to the auditorium, I check to see if Ava's still here. She's sitting in one of the back rows, applying a fresh coat of lip gloss.

"Hey," I say. "Up for an after-rehearsal milkshake at Flamin' Joe's?"

She scrunches her nose. "I can't."

"Come on. My treat."

"I would, but I have a FaceTime date with Drew."

Drew. Her boyfriend. Who drinks protein shakes at lunch and would probably bleed Gatorade and Axe Body Spray if you cut him.

"You can't FaceTime with him later tonight?" I ask.

"He goes to bed early when he has weight training the next morning; this works better for our schedules." She grabs her coat. "Sorry, I have to get home before he calls."

It sounds like this works better for *Drew's* schedule. I can't say that to Ava, though. She already thinks I haven't given him a fair chance. And maybe I haven't. But Ava's my best friend—of course I'm going to have high standards for her boyfriend.

"Rain check?" she offers with a smile.

"Yeah. Rain check."

I could go to Flamin' Joe's without Ava, but the thought of sitting at a table by myself is too depressing. The milkshake was just a stalling tactic, anyway. What I'm really trying to do is avoid facing my parents at dinner, where they'll undoubtedly ask how rehearsal went.

As soon as I arrive home, my nostrils are hit with the smell of garlic and spice. The crockpot's out on the counter, but the kitchen table is empty. Mom and Dad are nowhere to be seen.

A muffled cheer travels up from the basement.

Right. It's game night.

I make my way downstairs, stopping in the doorway of our rec room, otherwise known as my parents' "sports cave." There's a seventy-inch TV, a beer and wine fridge, and enough college sports memorabilia to rival a frat house. Except, instead of taping their posters to the walls, everything's nicely framed. Only the best for my brothers.

"Wade," Mom says, glancing my way. "We thought you'd be home later."

I shrug. "Everyone was tired by the time rehearsal let out."

"Get some good acting done today?" Dad asks.

"Yeah, I guess." I wait to see if they'll press me for more details, but their eyes remain glued to the hockey players gliding across the screen. One team has yellow and navy jerseys with a large *M*— the University of Michigan, Brett's team. Not to be confused with the gold and navy uniforms my oldest brother, TJ, wears when he plays baseball for Notre Dame.

"Did Brett start again?" I ask.

"Sure did," Mom replies gleefully.

There's a whistle and Dad throws up his hands. "C'mon! What was that?"

"Elbowing," Mom says.

"That wasn't elbowing. This ref has it out for our guys."

"Watch the replay." Mom turns to me again. "There's chili in the crockpot. I can fix you a bowl if you want."

"Actually, I'm just going to eat in my room."

"You don't want to see your brother play?" Dad asks, finally looking at me. "We could move up a ranking if we win tonight."

Whenever my parents talk about my brothers' teams, they act like it's something the whole family is a part of. *We* could move up a ranking. *We* could make the playoffs this year. When it comes to theater, though, it's always "your" rehearsal, "your" show. Not that my parents haven't been supportive—they've come to plenty of performances. But it's not like they have a "Broadway cave" or hang any of my posters on the walls.

"I should get started on homework," I say.

They nod, returning their attention to their son who's on the TV, instead of the one standing in the same room as them.

After fixing myself a sandwich, I head up to my bedroom and crack open my Spanish workbook. But conjugating verbs only reminds me of Henry Higgins trying to teach Eliza to lose her Cockney accent.

I let out a sigh. Maybe my parents would care more if I had the lead role. They seemed really proud of me last year.

Turning on my twinkle lights, I flop onto my bed and pull up the Broadway playlist on my phone. It doesn't matter what type of song it is, belting out even the most heart-wrenching show tune always leaves me feeling better afterward.

As I scroll through the playlist tonight, however, my heart's not into it. Switching over to Instagram, I get a rush from all the notifications on my last post. But as I stare at the strained smile on my face in the picture Ava and I took before rehearsal, the rush fades, leaving behind a dull ache.

I start going through my older posts. There are a lot of Reese and me. Ice skating during winter break. Wearing our *Book of Mormon* costumes at Ebony's Halloween party. Eating Sweet Martha's cookies at the state fair. My smile isn't forced in any of those. Because when I was with Reese, I actually felt wanted.

Scrolling all the way back to last spring, there's a post of me on opening night for *The Sound of Music*. I'm in the makeup room, dressed in my captain's uniform with my hair slicked back. Reading through the replies, I smile when I get to Reese's.

Okay. We see you, Captain von Thirst Trapp.

Reese never would've auditioned for that show if I hadn't started flirting with him first. I don't regret dating him, though. Reese and I were together for almost a year. Except for Ava, he probably knows me better than anyone else at school. He got to see *all* sides of me. Not just the good ones I post on Instagram.

A heavy feeling settles in my stomach.

What if no one else is willing to put up with me?

My twinkle lights start to blur as I blink back the tears pooling in my eyes. I can't change what part I'm playing in the musical. But that doesn't mean I have to give up and let the rest of senior year be a bust.

Staring at Instagram, I imagine a post of Reese and me, back together on prom night, grinning as we gaze into each other's eyes. I already know the perfect caption: *Can you believe we almost screwed this up?*

Nine

WADE

"What about this one?" Ava asks, nudging me with her foot as we sit in the hallway.

I look up from my Spanish workbook. The bell's going to ring soon, and I still haven't finished my homework from last night.

"I like the beaded bodice," she says. "But I'm not sure I want that much tulle."

"Pretty," I say, glancing at the bubbly blond girl on Ava's phone. I don't mean to sound uninterested. But it's about the hundredth dress she's asked my opinion on this morning. I reached my saturation point a while ago.

Ave wraps a strand of hair around her finger and sighs. "You know what? Screw this website. They only use skinny white models. There's *one* girl with a darker complexion—and she's Italian at best. At this point, I'm just going to attend prom in my bathrobe."

"You have plenty of time," I tell her.

"Not if I have to make alterations. Or what if I don't like it, and I need to return it and start all over again? Maybe I should order a couple of dresses. My parents would kill me. Unless I had them delivered to your house?"

"You're going to look fabulous," I tell her. "You always do."

"Thanks." She manages a smile, but it fades when she looks at me. "Sorry, this is probably the last thing you want to be talking about right now."

I turn my gaze back to my workbook. "I haven't thought much about it, actually."

Ava's been my best friend since middle school. She knows when I'm lying. *Of course I've been thinking about prom.* Mainly how Reese will no longer be my date for it.

"I know you're still getting over the breakup," Ava says. "But when you're ready, boys will be throwing themselves at you. You remember my cousin Shoba, right? She said there's a lot of gay guys at her school. We could do a deep dive on her Instagram account?"

It's nice Ava's looking out for me. But I'm not interested in going with anyone else. I already had prom night all scripted out. I wanted it to be like the end of a musical, where there's this big, emotional finale—the kind that gives you goose bumps and makes you leap to your feet for a standing ovation.

Reese and I would both win prom king—him junior, me senior. And for our celebratory dance afterward, we'd share the biggest, gayest kiss possible in front of the entire school. Just thinking about his lips on mine again makes my heart race. I mean, talk about a show-stopper. I can't think of a more perfect ending to senior year.

"Babe!" Ava jumps up.

Drew walks toward us, greeting her with a kiss. *Ugh.*

When it comes to straight guys, Ava could do a lot worse. Drew has curly blond hair and a thick wrestler's build, making him a great candidate for prom court as well. And while Drew has never made much of an effort to be friends with me, he's also never been an outright jerk.

"Sup, Wade?" he says, looking over at me.

"Hey." I give him a little wave, then immediately put my hand back down. Masculinity's a bullshit social construct, and I don't usually feel the need to conform to it. But talking to Drew reminds me of talking to my brothers.

"How'd weight training go?" Ava asks him.

"It'd go a lot better if you'd join me one of these mornings."

"I told you, I only get up that early for theater."

"But it'd be good for you, babe."

Ava's posture stiffens. "What does that mean?"

"No, I just meant . . ." Drew's cheeks immediately flush. "It's good to stay in shape."

"I *am* in shape. Curves are healthy."

"I know. I didn't—" He looks in my direction, as if I'm going to help him. "Babe, you know how hot I think you are. I didn't mean it like that. I'm sorry."

Ava stares at him, making him sweat for a minute, before reaching for his hand. "Apology accepted."

It's a struggle to keep a neutral expression as they kiss goodbye. Once Drew leaves, Ava points a finger at me. "Don't."

"Don't what?"

"You don't need any more fuel for not liking him."

I've never said I didn't like him. Not out loud, at least.

"He shouldn't have said that to you."

She sits back down next to me. "I'm aware. But he did apologize."

"And that makes it okay?"

"No. But that's not the point. The point is, he realized he was wrong and owned up to it."

"Still. I just—"

Ava puts up her hand. "No one's perfect, Wade. It's okay to forgive someone if they make a mistake."

I keep my mouth shut, even though it seems like she's oversimplifying things. If it were okay to forgive someone that easily, I'd still have a boyfriend.

Later that afternoon at rehearsal, Mr. Z has us blocking what's arguably the most famous part of the show: Higgins and Pickering trying to teach Eliza how to speak like a "proper" lady.

It's a great scene for Reese and Ava. They get to do a lot of bickering and funny bits, like when Higgins places a bunch of marbles in Eliza's mouth, and she accidentally swallows one. My character, as usual, mostly just sits in the background.

It's hard not to be resentful. And as Henry and Eliza quarrel, Ava's words from earlier come back to me: *No one's perfect. It's okay to forgive someone if they make a mistake.* I frown, breaking character. Why can't Reese see that? Why can't he forgive me?

Of course, Ava also said that Drew owned up to being wrong. I never apologized to Reese. Not properly. My feelings were hurt, and if I apologized, it'd be like admitting he was right—that I'll never love anyone more than I love myself.

A lump forms in my throat. The ironic part is, I *don't* always love myself. If I did, I wouldn't compare myself to my brothers, or get so competitive about always wanting to be the best. Still—in that moment, I was a shitty boyfriend. And I haven't owned up to that yet.

After we finish blocking the scene, Gretchen has us clear out early so the crew can have the stage for the rest of the afternoon. Ava practically skips out of the theater, excited to have more time with Drew.

As Reese hangs back to collect his stuff from the auditorium, I take my chance.

"Hey, that was a fun rehearsal."

There's a flicker of surprise in his eyes. "Uh. Yeah, it was."

"I mean, we're not even off-book yet, and you're already killing it as Higgins."

That gets a smile out of him. "I don't know about *killing* it."

"I'm serious. I'm really impressed. And, um—" I run my hand across the back of my neck. "I was wondering if you're doing anything right now. Maybe we could go to Flamin' Joe's?"

That was always our place. Sharing a booth together after rehearsal. But Reese just looks at me and sighs. Which—*fuck*, not a great sign.

"I'm not sure that's a good idea, Wade."

"I just wanted to talk," I say, a little too softly.

"Can't we talk here?"

Crew members are moving onto the stage already, rolling out paint tarps and setting down scene flats. I was hoping for more privacy. But I guess I should be thankful he's at least willing to listen.

I take a breath and go for it. "I wanted to apologize. Because I don't think I've really done that yet."

Reese's eyebrows notch up, waiting for me to go on.

"I got carried away on Valentine's Day," I continue. "I didn't mean to hurt you—but I did. And I'm sorry for that. I know I can't go back and change anything. But, um, I'm trying to do better going forward."

My breathing shallows as I wait for him to say something. *Am I too late? Are we beyond repair?*

"Thanks," he finally says. "That means a lot."

I exhale slowly. One apology can't fix everything, but it did feel good to say it. Especially since I really do care about Reese.

"Do you think we could be friends?" I ask.

Friends who get back together in time for prom?

He bites his lip. "Look, I appreciate the apology. But people don't change overnight. What if we start by being castmates first?"

His tone is gentle, but the message still stings. We're already castmates. Along with forty other people. I don't want to take any of *them* to prom.

"Castmates would be great," I reply. Because what else can I do?

Reese grabs his backpack, giving me a nod. "Cool. See you tomorrow, then."

I sink down into one of the seats as he leaves, slouching until my knees hit the row in front of me. I'm not mad I apologized—it was the right thing to do. I just wish Reese had believed me. I really do want to change. I miss Reese, and I miss all my friends. I'm sick of everyone being upset with me.

Up onstage, there's a commotion. Someone starts yelling.

"What happened?" Gretchen asks.

"He knocked over a paint bucket!"

The "he" in question is that techie. The one I made cry.

"Don't just stand there," Gretchen tells him. "Clean up your mess."

Something knots in my chest as he leaves the stage, red-faced and embarrassed. I told Reese I had changed. But yesterday, when that kid asked for my help, I shot him down. *Am I still an asshole?*

Reese said people can't change overnight. Maybe that's true. But what if I could prove that I'm *capable* of change? That I don't always put myself first?

"Hey, Gretchen," I say. "What's that techie's name?"

"You mean Brady?"

I jump up and hurry to the scene shop. The kid freezes when he sees me, wide-eyed and holding a box of sawdust.

I offer him a friendly smile. "Brady. Hey."

"Um . . ." He blinks. "It's Elijah, actually."

"Oh. Gretchen said—"

"Brady's my last name."

"Right. *Elijah.* I've decided to help you."

He looks around, like maybe he thinks he's being pranked, then offers me the sawdust.

"No, I didn't—" I take the box from him. "Well, yes. I can help with the paint. But I was talking about the other thing."

"You mean . . ." His voice trails off. One corner of his mouth lifts up, wanting to smile.

My chest rises, feeling slightly less asshole-ish already.

"What are you doing this weekend?" I ask.

"I'm, um—nothing."

"Good. We have a movie to watch."

Ten

ELIJAH

"Are we early?" Mom asks as we pull into Wade's driveway. She sounds concerned.

It takes me a second to realize what she's talking about. There aren't any other cars here. I told my parents the entire cast and crew was invited, because I knew how it'd sound if I said I was watching a movie alone with Wade on a Saturday night. It's embarrassing enough when they ask about my friends. I don't want them getting any ideas about me and Wade. I barely even know him, let alone *like* him.

"I'm helping him set up," I say. "Before everyone else gets here."

Mom smiles proudly. "Have fun. And be sure to text me when—"

"Okay," I say, immediately exiting the car.

Making my way to the front door, I take a breath. This doesn't have to be a big deal. Sure, Wade's a senior. And also full of himself. But I only need to use him long enough to teach me how to make some real friends, then we can go back to never talking again.

I ring his bell, my heartbeat echoing in my ears as I wait. A moment later Wade answers in sweatpants and a T-shirt that reads *How do you solve a problem like Maria?* It's always a bit startling to see people out of our school uniform, but Wade especially so. He's usually so put together and perfect-looking.

In fact, maybe I should be offended? Am I really that much of a nobody to him?

"Why didn't you park in our driveway?" he asks, craning his neck.

"Oh, um . . ." If Wade's going to teach me how to win people over, he might as well know the full extent of what he's dealing with. "My mom dropped me off."

He doesn't say anything. But from the way his eyebrows pinch together, it's clear he knows he's in over his head.

"I'm sixteen," I tell him. "I just haven't taken my driver's license test yet."

He nods, and I follow him inside. In the front hallway, there are framed pictures of Wade and two square-jawed guys who are either his brothers or J.Crew models. There's also a piece of inspirational wall décor that says, *In this house we laugh a lot, love a lot, and cheer for the Wolverines until we turn blue.* Whatever that means.

"You want something to drink?" Wade asks.

"Um. No thanks."

"Popcorn?"

I shake my head. I'm way too nervous to eat.

"Well, uh . . ." He scratches the back of his head. The tension in my shoulders loosens a bit. Maybe this is also awkward for him. I mean, he knows absolutely nothing about me. And now I'm in his house. Seeing him in his sweatpants.

"I guess we can head upstairs," he says.

Unsurprisingly, the walls in Wade's bedroom are covered in theater posters. Most of them appear to be from Broadway—*Wicked, Hamilton,* some really cheesy-looking show called *Newsies.* But then there are some above his bed that I recognize as Monroe Academy productions. I can't tell if that's arrogant or funny. Does he fall asleep staring up at them?

On his dresser, there's a framed photo of a younger Wade standing outside a theater where *The Lion King* is playing.

"My thirteenth birthday," he says, smiling when he sees me looking at it. "I begged my parents to take me to New York so I could see my first Broadway show. That's when I knew."

Knew what? That his parents would spoil him?

"I'd seen live theater before," he continues, "but not on that level. As soon as the curtain went up, there was no turning back. I knew I'd do whatever it took to perform on a stage like that someday."

I take a closer look at the photo. Wade's wearing braces, and the smile on his face is so bright it almost matches the lights on the marquee above him. It just seems so . . . wholesome. And not at all what I expected. I guess it's refreshing he doesn't act like he's too cool. But how does this translate into helping me make friends?

"So what's the plan?" I ask. "We watch the movie and then you teach me how I can be more confident?"

"The movie's just to get you caught up to speed," he says, grabbing his laptop. "It'll be hard for you to bond with the cast and crew if you're not familiar with the show."

Maybe. But I could've watched the movie on my own. I came here tonight for Wade's insight and guidance. "I don't think I'm the type of person people want to bond with," I say.

"Okay. Then tell me what type of person you want to be."

"Who I—" I pause, glancing around like I might find the answer in his room. "What do you mean?"

"Eliza Doolittle wanted to become a proper lady who could work

74

in a flower shop. Who do you want to become?"

I shift my weight, thinking back to Connor. How he has two loyal best friends. How everyone in the boys' locker room laughs at his jokes. It'd be nice if I didn't constantly doubt myself. If I felt like I actually belonged.

I inhale slowly, hugging my elbow. "I'd like to be someone who doesn't overthink things. Someone who can walk into a room and easily make friends. I want—" I force myself to look at Wade, so he knows I'm serious about this. "Basically, I want to be the opposite of who I am."

Wade smiles. "The difference between a lady and a flower girl is not how she behaves, but how she is treated."

"Um . . . ?"

"Eliza Doolittle's line. Well, George Bernard Shaw's. He wrote *Pygmalion*, which is the source material for the musical. Shaw took his inspiration from the Greek myth, where a sculptor falls in love with the statue he created."

I frown, unable to keep the skepticism from my voice. "And you think some dude falling in love with an inanimate object is analogous to my problem?"

He rolls his eyes. "Let's just start by watching the movie."

Wade flips off the lights and makes his way over to his bed, and I suddenly realize that *that's* where he intends for us to watch it. The two of us. Next to each other.

My stomach does a somersault. Wade's hot. That's just a fact. It's also a fact that hot guys are intimidating. Usually that's not a problem, because I'm not even on their radar. But right now, Wade's stretched out in front of me, his face illuminated by the soft glow of his screen and a strand of twinkle lights lit up behind him.

I try to think about thirteen-year-old Wade. The one who has braces and geeks out over *The Lion King*.

"You know," Wade says, as I finally start to climb onto his bed, "I'm actually a little jealous of you."

I freeze, one foot still on the floor. "Huh?"

"I've seen this movie at least a dozen times. But this is your first. I'll never be able to experience it like that again."

"Oh." I awkwardly join him on the mattress, sticking as close to the edge as I can. Wade cues up the movie, sighing dreamily as the orchestra starts to play.

The opening title sequence is just a bunch of flowers. And it seems to drag on forever. "I thought they usually saved the credits until the end of the movie," I say, reading the names as they appear in loopy cursive on the screen.

"Not in older movies."

"What year was this made?"

Wade pauses it. "Sorry, I don't mean to be a dick. But if you talk during the movie, it'll ruin the magic."

Ruin the magic? He really just said that with a straight face.

"No one's even on the screen yet," I say. "It's just music."

"*Just music?* It's the overture. Literally one of the best parts of the show."

"What's so great about an overture?"

He shoots me an incredulous look, and I immediately regret asking. "Have you never been to a musical before? With a real live orchestra?"

"Um, my parents took me to *The Nutcracker* once."

"That's a ballet. But yes." He sits up, his body inching closer to mine. "Don't you remember sitting in the audience as you waited for the show to begin? And then the lights start to fade, and everyone goes quiet?"

I remember being annoyed that my mom forced me to wear a tie. But I don't dare tell that to Wade, who seems to be in his element right now.

"It never gets completely quiet," he says. "People are still fussing with their programs or turning off their phones. But then, from inside the pit, the orchestra starts to play." He closes his eyes for a moment, as though he can actually hear it. "An overture's all the highlights from the show—happy songs, romantic songs, songs that make your heart swell. And as you sit back in your chair and let the music wash over you, your body relaxes. Because you know that for the next couple hours, you won't have to worry about your own problems. You get to be transported to somebody else's world."

"You get all that from the music we just heard?" I ask. I don't mean to be judgmental, but come on—*transported?*

"Yes, I do." His tone is dead serious.

As we start the movie over, I try to keep an open mind. I still can't say the overture transports me anywhere, but maybe that's because I'm not able to stop thinking about how I'm lying on Wade's bed right now, with only his laptop to separate us.

After a while, once I get used to the idea of people spontaneously breaking into song, I find myself getting caught up in the movie. Or maybe I'm just caught up in Wade. The way he hugs his pillow tight. The way he keeps breaking into a smile. His excitement is infectious.

When we get to the end of a song called, "I Could Have Danced

All Night," I glance over and see that he's crying. I should look away; this feels too private. But I can't. It's strange to see someone like Wade—someone who's supposed to be laid-back and cool—show his emotions so easily.

"Sorry." He pauses the movie again. "This song gets me every time."

He wipes away his tear with a laugh, not even trying to hide it. "The music's so romantic. And Audrey Hepburn's perfect in it. When she sings about her heart taking flight, you actually wait for her to float away—that's how good she is. Do you know she wasn't even nominated for an Academy Award for this?"

He shakes his head, not waiting for my answer. "It's because Julie Andrews played the role on Broadway, but Audrey got the movie. And even though Audrey took singing lessons, they dubbed over most of her songs."

I thought knowing random, useless facts was sort of my thing. But Wade's like an encyclopedia on this movie.

"Julie Andrews won the Oscar that year for *Mary Poppins*, so everyone thinks Julie got her revenge. But I'm sorry, Julie should've won for *The Sound of Music* the following year. Audrey deserved to win for this."

It's kind of sweet, the way he's so passionate about it. Well, sweet *and* dorky. I can't imagine him talking about any of this stuff at school. *Crying over musicals?* Maybe with other theater nerds, but even then only the hardcore ones. I doubt acting like this is what made him so popular.

"But it doesn't matter that she was dubbed," he continues, lost in his monologue. "During that last song, didn't she make you want to know what it's like to dance around the room and be in love?"

I thought the question was rhetorical. But he's staring at me, waiting for me to answer. With his inquisitive blue eyes burrowing into mine, his bedroom suddenly feels about ten degrees warmer.

"I mean, you can argue Eliza's not in love with Higgins," he says. "But they definitely have a chemistry. You can see it in the way they challenge each other. It's kind of romantic, don't you think?"

"I, um . . ." Heat rushes to my cheeks. Even just *talking* about romance makes me blush. "Sorry, what was your question?"

Wade groans, burying his face in his pillow. "I'm breaking my own rule. No more tangents until after the movie's over, I promise."

As we go back to watching *My Fair Lady*, it's hard not to be charmed by Eliza Doolittle's transformation. I, however, possess none of Audrey Hepburn's grace or sophistication. Maybe I was silly to think Wade could help me. I could never enchant an entire room like she does. My life isn't a Hollywood musical. If anything, it's closer to a horror show.

Near the end of the movie, Eliza and Henry have a falling out. When Henry finally realizes he has feelings for Eliza, he sings a song called, "I've Grown Accustomed to Her Face." Which, I'm sorry— Eliza says she could've danced all night with him, and he just . . . *got used to her face?* She deserves better than him.

In the end, though, she returns. And instead of apologizing, Henry asks her to fetch his slippers. What a dick!

"So?" Wade asks, closing his laptop. "What'd you think?"

"I don't understand. Do they actually get together after that?"

He shrugs. "It's kind of open to interpretation."

"But why would she still want him? He's a jerk."

79

"Well, yes." He frowns. "But this movie was made a long time ago. So if it's sexist, I think that's more because it's a product of its time."

"You're defending it?" I ask, suddenly invested.

"Obviously not the sexist part. But art should be a dialogue. You're allowed to disagree with it." He sits up, pushing his laptop aside. "I'm not saying the ending isn't flawed. But it's not like Eliza ran in there and kissed him. They don't kiss once the whole movie! I like that it's ambiguous. Who's to say what happens next."

I shake my head. "If it were up to me, Eliza would fetch his slippers and slap Higgins upside the head with them."

Wade laughs. "Yeah, he'd deserve that. But maybe Higgins also changes." His face suddenly gets serious, like this is important to him. "Maybe he loves Eliza so much, he decides to become a better person for her."

I think Wade gives him too much credit. But before I can argue the point further, my phone lights up with a text.

"Shit," I say, realizing the time. "I should have my mom come pick me up."

"I can give you a ride," Wade replies.

I stare at my phone, unsure what to do. Wade said he'd help me. But I don't understand why. What's he getting out of this? Most people don't even talk to me, let alone invite me to their house and offer me rides home.

I text Mom back and ask if Wade can drop me off. She responds with a thumbs-up and kissy-face emoji.

"Okay," I say, putting my phone away.

Wade lies back onto his bed, propping his head up with his elbow. His shirt rides up at the waist and I quickly look away. It's a good thing only his twinkle lights are on right now, because I'm sure my face is a million different shades of red. Wade's an attractive guy. That doesn't mean I'm attracted to him, though. I still know how to differentiate between the two.

At least, I think I do.

When I casually glance back over, Wade's staring at me.

"What?" I ask, sure he caught me looking.

"Nothing. I'm just trying to decide what our next step is."

I can still feel his eyes on me. Studying me like I'm the block of marble he's getting ready to sculpt.

Finally, a grin stretches across his face.

"Do you like milkshakes?" he asks.

"Um . . ." I say, somehow knowing this is a trap. "Yes?"

Eleven

If there's one thing I have in common with my brothers, it's my competitive spirit. It's not enough to be good at something. I want to be the *best*. And being the best means never backing down from a challenge. Which is good. Because I'm definitely going to have my work cut out for me with Elijah.

"Just pick one," I tell him.

"I . . . um . . ." He stares up at the menu board, his hands shoved deep into the pockets of his coat. "Which do you suggest?"

"They're all good. Get whatever you like."

He turns to me, his eyes practically blinking out "SOS" in Morse code.

"He'll have a Little Miss Strawberry Shortcake," I tell the person behind the counter, who has a sleeve of tattoos, bright red lipstick, and a button that reads, *Nobody knows I'm a lesbian.* "What's your name, sweetheart?" she asks him.

"Elijah," he mumbles.

Paying for our milkshakes, I lead us out into the seating area, which is more crowded than usual. Thankfully, two guys give us their table when they see me looking.

"Are you sure?" I ask. "We don't want to rush you."

They both smile. "It's cool. We were just getting ready to leave."

My reason for bringing Elijah here tonight was simple. Flamin' Joe's is a queer-run business, which means the majority of its customers are queer. Before I help him become more confident, I want to see how he does in an environment where people are safe to be their true selves. Judging from his behavior so far—hunched shoulders, glancing around like a nervous dog in a room full of toddlers—we need to work on his self-esteem.

"Why don't you take off your jacket," I tell him. "Relax a bit."

He removes his coat, revealing his hoodie, which is a size too large. Confidence comes from within, but outward appearances also matter. This seems to be another problem area for Elijah; he dresses like he's trying to hide himself.

"Have you been here before?" I ask.

He shakes his head.

"Well, what do you think?"

He looks around. "It's . . . um . . ."

Flamin' Joe's is like if a pride parade rolled into a retro diner from the '50s. The booths are crammed with groups of friends who are laughing and taking selfies, while at smaller tables, people sit with dates, flirtatiously sipping their milkshakes.

". . . it's a lot," he says.

"I have a Triple Peach Emoji milkshake for Wade," someone shouts from behind the counter. "And a Little Miss Strawberry Shortcake for . . . Isaiah?"

Elijah winces.

"Don't go anywhere," I say, winking to lighten his mood.

As I head back to get our drinks, a text from Ava pops up on my phone.

Last minute slumber party at Ebony's tonight.

Me, Hannah, Eb, and some cheap wine her mom won't drink.

No Reese.

My mouth drops into a frown. I hate that she has to specify that.

Did he already have plans? I type.

Does it matter?

Only if I'm the backup invite.

Don't be that way. Hannah and Ebony miss you.

I miss them, too. We see each other at rehearsals, but it's not the same, because Reese is also there. And while I acknowledge it's my own actions that are to blame for Reese breaking up with me, part of me still feels hurt that they took his side. They were my friends first.

Tell them I'd love to hang out soon, I type. But I'm busy tonight.

Don't think I won't drive by your house to see if you're lying.

I'm not. I'm hanging out with Elijah.

Who???

I start to type "a charity case," but that feels gross. I'm sure it wasn't easy for Elijah to ask for my help. Especially after the way I first treated him.

New friend, I type. From the tech crew.

Ava sends the eyeball emoji.

Not like that.

If you say so.

It will only fuel her suspicion if I argue. So I let it go. Returning to our table, I set Elijah's milkshake in front of him. As he stares at his luscious mound of whipped cream and edible pink glitter, I lean forward to take a sip of mine.

"Damn." I close my eyes, savoring the sweet, peachy flavor. "That's good."

Laughter erupts at another table. Elijah snaps his head in their direction, as though he's worried he's their target. But he just needs to take a breath and chill. The people at that table are in their own little world.

"How's tech crew going?" I ask.

"Um. Good."

"And this is your first year doing the musical?"

He nods.

"Cool. What made you want to join?"

"Uh . . ." He traces his finger around the base of his milkshake. "It seemed fun."

Okay, so in addition to self-worth and outward appearances, we're going to have to add "making conversation" to the list of things to work on. He can't expect to make friends if he doesn't talk to people.

"You're quiet, huh?"

Something in his posture shifts. He furrows his brow. "Yeah. *And you're tall.*"

"Um, what does that have to do with anything?"

"You were pointing out the obvious, so . . ."

I lean back in my chair, fighting a smile. Okay, there's some personality. I wasn't expecting a comeback from him. "Fair enough," I say. "But you have to admit, you are pretty quiet."

"So? You don't need to point it out."

"Well, I had to say *something*. Otherwise, we'd be sitting here in silence."

To prove my point, I stop talking. It's like a game of chicken. Me staring at Elijah, and him shifting uncomfortably in his chair.

"People always say 'you're quiet' like it's a bad thing," he says, finally accepting defeat. "But quiet people are observant. And just because I don't talk as much doesn't mean I don't have a lot going on in my head."

I lean forward, resting my elbows on the table. "Great. So tell me, what's going on in your head?"

He sits on his hands, like he doesn't know what else to do with them. "Well, when those guys gave us their table earlier, they only smiled at you. Not me. It was like I wasn't even there—not that you noticed. I'm guessing you don't notice a lot of things, though. Like when you came back with our drinks, you dropped a napkin on the floor and left it there. Unless you *did* notice that, and you just assumed someone else would clean it up for you. Oh, and I don't understand why they have a milkshake called Anita Lick. I get that it's supposed to sound like a drag queen. But you don't lick a milkshake. Wouldn't Anita Sip make more sense?"

When he finally stops talking, his eyes go wide. Like he just realized how much he said.

I look under our table. Sure enough, there's a napkin. "Damn," I say, quickly picking it up. "You're good."

His cheeks flush. "I told you. Quiet people notice things."

"Not just quiet people." I point at his milkshake. "I've noticed you haven't touched that. What's that about?"

He stares at it. "Um, I just . . ."

"It's homophobic not to finish one of those. Do you not like strawberry? Because I can get you a different flavor."

He takes a look around, hunching forward to whisper. "Everyone's watching. I'm too nervous to eat."

"What are you talking about? *Nobody's* watching us."

"Oh my god. Can you please not shout?"

"I wasn't—"

I lean in closer, meeting him in the middle of the table. "Why do you think people are watching us?"

"Isn't it obvious? They're wondering what someone like me is doing here with someone like you."

I open my mouth to tell him he's wrong, but the words catch in my throat. It's sad he thinks so little of himself. Especially since it's not even true. Elijah's not unattractive—his hair could have potential if it were styled intentionally, not unkempt. And his freckles are cute.

Besides, he shouldn't compare himself to me. I mean, yes, on a superficial level, I can look in a mirror and recognize that I have some redeeming physical attributes. I'm not clueless as to why those guys who gave us their table were so friendly to me.

But looks are only part of the equation. If I were truly a good catch, I'd be here with Reese. We used to come all the time. Just the two of us, hoping to score one of the booths so we could sit side by side, pressing our knees into each other.

"I'm not hot like you," Elijah says, looking away.

"That's not—" I pause. *Is it weird that he called me hot?* I mean, most people wouldn't say that out loud to me. Unless he meant it objectively, and my ego's just getting carried away again. "I bet there are plenty of guys who would disagree," I tell him.

He laughs, but it's bitter. "Guys don't notice me."

"Why do you assume that?"

"Uh . . . years of experience?"

I give him a look. "Sarcasm is easy. Vulnerability is hard."

"Did you read that in a fortune cookie?"

"No. An acting manual."

He rolls his eyes. "Great."

"Come on. Look at all the guys in here. What do you have to lose by trying to talk to someone? You wanted to be more confident, right? This is how we start. You don't even have to flirt with anyone yet. Just begin with a conversation."

"I can't just *talk* to people," he says, incredulous. "That's not who I am. If you went over to another table, they'd fawn all over you. But if I tried that? Crickets. That's just the way it works. And please don't tell me I'm wrong. It's insulting. Besides, I'd like to be able to give you a little more credit than that."

I'm sorry, but he *is* wrong. I get that people might treat us differently. And yeah, that sucks. But he's not doing himself any favors by putting himself down before anyone else can.

Still, maybe there's a better way to go about this.

"Okay," I say. "Remember what we talked about in my bedroom?"

"That Julie Andrews should've won her Academy Award for *The Sound of Music?*"

I smile, amused he remembered. "Yes. But also, you said you

88

wanted to become someone who's the opposite of who you are now."

He sighs, slouching in his chair. "I don't see how that's possible."

"Easy. It's just like acting."

"Uh, in case you forgot . . . I'm *not* an actor."

"I know. But that's where I come in. I'll teach you."

"I don't think—"

"Acting's not only about memorizing lines," I say, cutting him off. "There's a lot of other work that goes into it. Like finding your character. When it comes to the actual performance, you'll have costumes and makeup to help. But during the rehearsal process, before you even set foot onstage, you start with something else. A name."

Elijah stares blankly at me, as though he's not following.

"When I act, I'm no longer Wade. I'm Colonel Pickering. Or Captain von Trapp. Or whomever it is I'm supposed to be. Now that we know the character you want to play, it would help if we gave him a different name."

"A different name?"

"Yeah. Like a cool nickname."

He shakes his head. "I've never had a nickname before. I'm still getting used to everyone on the crew calling me—"

"Brady," I say. *Why didn't I think of that sooner?* "It's perfect. Whatever Elijah can't do, Brady can."

"I don't think it's that simple," he grumbles.

"Sure it is." I gesture to his milkshake, which he still hasn't touched. "Drink up."

"You don't understand. My stomach's connected to my nervous system. Do you really think slurping down a creamy, glittery milkshake is a smart idea? I might get nauseous and—"

"*Elijah* might get nauseous," I correct him. "Not Brady."

He inhales, still unsure, then leans forward and takes a sip.

"Well?" I ask.

"Oh. Wow." He smiles, oblivious to his strawberry mustache, which is pretty damn cute. "That's fucking delicious."

Twelve

ELIJAH

Trivia fact: the ingredients in a Hostess Twinkie are a protected trade secret. Not because the company's worried about their recipe falling into the hands of their competition. Rather, they're more concerned that if people find out what's actually in Twinkies, they'll stop eating them.

In the three days since Wade took me out for milkshakes, I, too, have felt like I've been carrying around a secret. Sometimes it's exciting, like when Wade says hi to me at rehearsal, and Connor sees us. And sometimes it sends me into a panic, like when Wade texts me to meet him in the auditorium so we can work on Brady.

"We only have forty-five minutes," he says, tossing his backpack into the front row of seats. "Let's not waste them."

I walk up onto the stage, which is currently empty except for the unpainted scene flats that will soon become Henry Higgins's study.

"You can't expect to put up a good show overnight," Wade says, looking up at me. "We still have seven and a half weeks of rehearsal for *My Fair Lady*. I figure it will take us about as much time to transform you into Brady."

"But what if that's not enough?"

He shakes his head. "You could rehearse a show forever and never feel fully prepared. At some point, you have to throw it in front of an audience."

My stomach grumbles. Partly because this is my lunch period, partly because of nerves. I can't believe Wade is ditching his study hall to help me.

"Besides," Wade says, "as soon as the musical's over, we have prom. Then graduation. Our time's limited."

Seven and a half weeks still seems too short, but I nod in agreement. Wade's a senior. I'm lucky he's even helping me.

"Okay, then . . ." Wade lifts himself up onto the stage, forgoing the stairs. "I've broken it down into four separate lessons to get us started. One: Physicality and Vocal Work. Two: Hair and Costumes. Three: Improvisation. Four: Stage Combat."

"Stage Combat?"

He puts up his hand. "Don't jump ahead. We're beginning with the basics today. But first we need to warm up."

I groan, remembering the Name Game. Maybe Wade's taking this a bit too seriously. Do I want to become confident enough to make friends? Yes. Do I want to writhe around the floor and do trust falls? Absolutely not.

"Warm-ups are about getting loose," he tells me. "And I'm sorry, but you could benefit from that."

We start simply enough, shaking out limbs and doing some breathing exercises. I do start to feel a little more relaxed. But then Wade has us sit cross-legged together on the floor until we're so close our knees touch.

"This is a relationship-building exercise," he says. "For the next three minutes, we're going to stare into each other's eyes."

My body immediately tenses back up. I've never stared into any-one's eyes for that long, let alone someone as good-looking as Wade. What if I start thinking about how hot he is, and my facial expression gives me away?

He sets the timer on his phone and begins staring at me. I try to follow his lead, but my gaze keeps traveling upward to the swoop of hair that rests over his forehead. How does he get it to do that? And why does it always look so effortless?

"I'll start the clock over," he warns.

My eyes find his, but as we lock pupils, the absurdity of the situation hits me. *What is someone like Wade doing looking at someone like me? How is this not weird for him?* I only last a second before looking away again.

"Hey." He places a hand on my knee, keeping it there until I look at him again. "It's awkward, I know. But that's the point. You have to keep doing it until you can push past feeling uncomfortable. It'll help with your confidence, I promise."

"I feel like I'm going to laugh," I tell him.

"So laugh. I'm not judging you."

Maybe asking for Wade's help was a mistake. But Dad already bought three sleeping bags for our camping trip, so either I force myself to go through with this, or I tell my parents I'm not inviting anyone.

Telling my parents I have no friends seems worse.

I hold Wade's gaze, trying not to smile. After what has to be the longest few seconds in my life, the muscles in my mouth start to relax. If I shut off my mind and just focus on Wade's steady blue eyes, it becomes a bit more bearable.

The timer on his phone goes off and I let out a tiny sigh of relief.

"Sweet." Wade jumps back up. "Today we're focusing on physicality and vocal work. You can throw a costume and wig on someone, but it won't magically change who they are. That's why we start with what you already have—your body. So let's talk about your posture. The way you carry yourself."

"How do I carry myself?"

"Your shoulders are always hunched. And you keep your chin tucked, like you're trying to cave in on yourself." He bites his lip, shooting me an apologetic look. "Sorry, I'm not trying to be mean."

My face grows warm. I'm not offended, though. If anything, I'm strangely flattered. I never realized anyone even noticed me.

"How do I fix it?" I ask. I should at least try.

He rubs his hands together, like he's excited. "Okay. So when I take on a new role, I start by thinking about which body part the character leads with. If they have a lot of confidence, they lead with their chest. If you want more swagger, it's all about the pelvis."

"I'm sorry. You want me to walk around school *crotch* first?"

"There are other things to consider," he says, ignoring me. "Like gait. Or mannerisms. But I don't want to overwhelm you. Julie Andrews may have won the Oscar for her first film role, but the rest of us have to take baby steps."

Wade has me move around the stage. I try keeping my chin up and my chest out, but while concentrating on that my feet forget how to function normally. "I look like I'm walking through Jell-O," I say.

"It's okay," he tells me. "Just keep going."

I stop. "I look ridiculous."

Wade sighs, running a hand through his hair, messing it. And yet—the swoop still falls back perfectly into place.

"You can't be afraid to look foolish in front of me," he says. "Why do you think actors play all those silly warm-up games? If we're going to trust each other, we have to let our guard down."

"What if I work on this on my own?" I ask. "Like in the privacy of my bedroom."

"Let's move on to vocal work for now." He's trying to sound upbeat, but it feels like I've let him down. "Your voice is a tool," he continues. "One that can be used to command attention. I want you to say something but try projecting it out into the back of the house."

"What should I say?"

"Anything. Literally anything. Pretend you're sitting alone at Flamin' Joe's and some guy comes up to talk to you. What would you say to him?"

I'd say I was dreaming. But I don't want Wade to think I'm not taking this seriously. My mind goes to all the useless facts I've collected over the years, pulling out the first one I think of. "Hey, did you know that a group of chickens is called a peep?"

Wade laughs. "Um, *what*?"

"It's true. There are also more chickens in the world than humans."

"How do you know that? And more importantly, why is *that* the first thing you'd say to someone?"

I shrug. "I like trivia. And I don't know how to make small talk. Which is why I need your help!"

"Okay, okay." He walks up to me. I knew Wade was tall. But this close, he almost towers over me. "It doesn't have the same ring to it that 'the rain in Spain' does, but it'll have to do. Try saying it again."

I take a breath. "A group of chickens is called—"

"Stop. You're talking from the back of your throat. Your voice sounds weaker when you do that. You also tend to swallow your words." He moves in closer. "When Brady talks, I need him to push his words out by using his diaphragm. Which is here."

He places his hand on my stomach; I flinch.

"Sorry." He quickly pulls his hand away. "Is that not okay?"

I wait for my cheeks to stop burning. "Um. It's fine. I just wasn't expecting it."

"Here. Copy me."

Wade puts one hand on his chest, and one on his stomach. I do the same. "When you breathe," he explains, "it should come from down here." He inhales, filling his abdomen with air. We practice this together until he tells me to try my line again.

"A group of chickens is called a peep." This time I hear it. My voice carries out into the auditorium a bit farther.

Wade smiles. I stand a little straighter, proud of myself for getting it right.

"Give me another one," he says.

I breathe like he taught me to. "Teeth are the only part of the human body that can't heal themselves."

He twists his mouth, trying not to laugh.

"I told you," I say, defending myself. "I like trivia."

He nods, amused. "No kidding. You should really go on *Jeopardy!* Or wait—don't we have some kind of trivia club at school?"

"Quiz Bowl."

"Yeah. You should be on that."

"I was," I say, swallowing my words again. "I wasn't very good."

"But you must know all the answers."

I shrug. "Every time I rang the buzzer, I froze. I hated having all those eyes on me, waiting for me to say something."

"Well . . ." He shoots me a wink. "That's what we're here to fix."

Winking is creepy and should be outlawed. But when Wade does it, I get this little nugget of warmth in my chest. It feels special. Another secret between the two of us.

Without waiting for a prompt, I try again: "Cotton candy was invented by a dentist. So was the electric chair."

It doesn't even sound like my voice anymore. Instead of meek and unsure, it's grounded and authoritative. I didn't know I could be those things. Even my posture has shifted: chest out, just like Wade wanted.

His smile is even bigger this time. "That's the confidence I want Brady to have. And now I'm giving you your first homework assignment."

My posture instantly deflates. Being proud of my accomplishments is great. But nobody wants homework.

Thirteen

ELIJAH

When I show up for rehearsal later that afternoon, the crew's laughing and shouting over one another, taking up as much space as we want while the actors work on their musical numbers in the choral room. At least, that's where the actors are supposed to be.

"Sorry . . ." Ava Mehta pops her head into the auditorium. "I think I left my script in here."

"Yes!" Szabo leaps up from his seat, grabbing her binder from the edge of the stage. "I knew it was yours because there was a copy of *Bleak House* in it. I mean, your lines are also highlighted in the script, obviously. But, um, we're in AP English together. *Bleak House* is my favorite Dickens. Well, it's a tie between *Bleak House* and *David Copperfield*, but—"

As if he suddenly realized how much he's talking, Szabo shuts down. He barely even looks at Ava as he hands her the binder.

"Thanks," she says. "And don't tell anyone, but I hardly have time to read the CliffsNotes right now. I'll trust your word that it's good, though."

Szabo just nods, not saying anything as she leaves.

As soon as the door to the auditorium closes again, Rhodes and Yang snicker. "Damn," Yang says. "Whipping out Dickens's greatest hits to impress the ladies. Real smooth."

"Talk about *bleak*," Rhodes adds, cracking himself up.

Szabo grits his teeth. "You guys are such jokers."

I've never seen Szabo so tongue-tied before. I guess it's nice to know that even confident people can be shy. But is that what I look like most of the time? Like I want to disappear? No wonder no one ever talks to me.

If I want to change, I need to continue working on my lesson from today. I get my chance when the crew splits up for the afternoon and I'm paired with Summer again. She leads us up to the catwalks, where she unlocks the security gate.

"I'm surprised they give keys to students," I say, projecting like Wade taught me. Even though, now that we're up here, my confidence is starting to waver. Wade had me practice *on* the stage, not suspended high above it.

"Nah," Summer replies, calm as ever. "Szabo and I borrowed the master set and made a copy for ourselves. We're not supposed to be up here without the technical director. But it's fine, we're not moving any lights today."

Yep. This is officially how I die.

Once Summer has the gate open, she steps out onto the catwalk like it's nothing. The structure is narrow, with grid flooring that lets you see everything below. Since joining the crew, I've dropped a stage light and kicked over a paint bucket. There's no way I'm walking out there and not plummeting to my death.

"Just hold on to the railings and don't look down," she says, reading the fear that's probably plastered across my face.

I follow her instructions, taking my first step. My shoe hits the catwalk and my heart pounds so hard I'm afraid it'll knock me over. But I tighten my grip and force myself to take a second step, followed by my third, and somehow I manage to follow Summer halfway out. She starts explaining things to me, but she may as well be talking underwater.

"Any questions?" she asks.

Forget breathing from my diaphragm. I shake my head, afraid to even speak.

And then, just when I think I'm in the clear, Summer leans against the railing. Like, actually putting her body weight on it.

"You can't fall off and leave me up here all alone!" I shout.

She straightens back up. "Sorry. Didn't mean to scare you."

"I'm not scared. I'm terrified."

Summer walks over and places her hands on top of mine, which are still in a death grip around the railing. "Elijah, when you hang lights, you're going to have to look down. You might as well get the hard part over with now."

My instinct is to slowly back away until I'm off this damn catwalk. But then I remember what Wade said about letting Brady do the things Elijah can't. Maybe I should let Brady take the leap here.

Poor word choice. There will be no leaping.

Before I can talk myself out of it, I look down. My stomach instantly drops to my balls. But it's not actually as high as I thought. I figured everyone would look like ants from up here, when in reality, we're only about three stories up.

Summer takes her hands off mine. "Not so bad, is it?"

"I think I could eventually get the hang of this," I say, breathing again.

My fear hasn't completely gone away. It's just changed. There's kind of a thrill to it now. Like when you step off a roller coaster and immediately want to ride it again.

As Summer continues showing me around, I think about the other things that maybe I've been unnecessarily afraid of. Like speaking to people. After my lesson with Wade today, he told me that in addition to practicing how to walk and talk with confidence, my first homework assignment was to have a conversation with someone—a real one.

Summer's the only person on the crew who calls me Elijah. And she's been really nice so far. It might be easiest to start with her.

"So, um . . ." I pause, already doubting myself. But then I remember what Wade said: push through the awkwardness. "Is it hard working on the show with your sister?"

Her eyes narrow. "Are you friends with Callie?"

"No, I don't think *she'd* say that."

She sighs, nodding. "We have a complicated relationship—her being an actor, and all. But she's family, so I love her."

"Yeah, I'm sorry I didn't know you were related. You seemed kind of upset when I said that last week."

Summer picks at a paint chip that's flaking off the railing. "When people are surprised Callie has an older sister, I never know if it's because they thought she was an only child . . . or if it's because they don't know I came out as trans."

Oh. *Oh.*

"Yeah, I didn't . . ."

"I came out a while ago," she says. "It's not like you would've known me then."

"Still, thank you for telling me."

Below us, people lay out scene flats to paint. I could probably end the conversation here, but I haven't offered up much information about myself. And I can already hear Wade telling me I should.

"I'm gay," I say. "In case you couldn't tell. Or maybe you could? I'm never sure if it's obvious or not."

She shrugs. "I didn't want to assume."

"It's always kind of weird. Figuring out when to tell people."

"Yeah, I get that. Sometimes being trans feels like it's the fifteenth most interesting thing about me."

"What's number fourteen?" I ask, half-joking.

"Getting permanently banned from the Renaissance Faire," she replies matter-of-factly.

"Seriously? What'd you do?"

"Tried to set the jousting horses free."

"Nice."

Her mouth twists into a smile. "Still, other times it feels like being trans *is* something that should define me. I've had to put up with a lot more shit than cis people, and I'm stronger because of it." She pauses, sneaking a glance at me. "No offense to cis people."

"None taken."

"Anyhow, I'll show you the follow-spot booth next."

I like how easily Summer can switch back and forth between talking about those two things. I came out to my parents pretty early. Mostly because they were so annoying about making sure I knew they loved me no matter what I identified as. Which is great. But, like, maybe my sexuality isn't something that needs to be discussed at the dinner table?

Coming out to my classmates has been different. I like to think I'm secure enough in my sexuality. But after I came out to Micah, and he stopped hanging out with me, I learned that maybe it was better to hold certain parts of myself back from people. Which is why I mostly keep to myself now.

As Summer and I leave the catwalks, though, I feel good about opening up to her. Plus, I completed my first assignment. Weirdly enough, knowing that I might've made Wade proud somehow leaves me feeling even better.

Fourteen

WADE

"I can't be expected to be brilliant before noon," Ava moans as we pull into Elijah's driveway.

She's sitting in my passenger seat, wearing oversize sunglasses while gripping a venti coffee with both hands, like she's nursing a killer hangover. Even though she was only hanging out with Drew last night, and Drew never parties the night before a Saturday morning training session.

"You don't have to be brilliant yet," I tell her. "But can you please help me carry in some of these bags?"

With one week down, and seven to go, we're moving on to Elijah's next lesson. I may have gone a little overboard while shopping for him. I couldn't help myself. When he learned to project his voice at our last lesson, there was this look of triumph in his eyes. Like he believed in himself for a moment.

I want to make him feel like that again. Because if I can't be Henry Higgins on the stage, this is the next best thing. And now that I have a purpose again, it stings less to think about the musical.

Of course, my end goal hasn't changed. I still need to show Reese he was wrong about me. But if this also helps Elijah along the way . . . well, that'd be cool, too.

Speaking of Reese, I need photographic evidence of my good deeds.

Grabbing the bakery box from the back seat, I pose and take a selfie with it. After adjusting the filters, I work on coming up with the perfect caption. *POV: You're waking up on Saturday morning and your friend surprises you with cinnamon rolls.*

"Ahem."

I look up. Ava's standing in front of me with shopping bags hanging off each arm.

"Sorry, I'll help."

Carefully balancing a tray of coffees, the box of pastries, and a half dozen shopping bags, we make our way up the driveway.

"Okay, but seriously," Ava grumbles. "What is it about this guy that makes you want to get up early on our last Saturday before weekend rehearsals begin?"

"I told you. He needs my help."

She lowers her chin, shooting me a look over the top of her sunglasses. She probably thinks I have a crush on Elijah, which couldn't be further from the truth. I'm doing this for Reese.

"He's a sophomore, Wade. On the tech crew."

"It's not like you to be so classist," I tease, knocking on their door.

"Oh, you're one to talk. Name three other crew members."

"Gretchen, obviously. And then there's, um . . ."

The front door swings open. A woman in a stylish cardigan smiles politely at us, like maybe she thinks we're here to sell raffle tickets.

"Hi," I say. "We're Elijah's friends."

Her smile widens. "Of course! Please come in. I'll let him know you're here."

She leads us inside and into their kitchen. Standing in front of the stove is a man with reddish brown hair just like Elijah's. Almost as unruly, too. He also looks surprised to see other teenagers in his house.

"Sorry if we're interrupting breakfast," I say.

Mr. Brady wipes his hands on a dishtowel. "Not at all. The more the merrier."

"We brought cinnamon rolls," Ava announces.

Mrs. Brady's face lights up. She cranes her head back toward the hallway. "Elijah, you'd better get down here!"

As his mom takes the pastries from me, Elijah comes down the stairs, rounding the corner in a T-shirt and checkered pajama pants. His feet stop moving as soon as he sees Ava and me, causing the rest of his body to lurch forward.

"What—what are you doing here?"

"We had plans to hang out," I remind him.

He glances at the clock on the microwave. "You're an hour early."

"Am I?" I pretend to look surprised. "I must've gotten mixed up."

Given Elijah's resistance to anything outside his comfort zone, I figured it'd be better to catch him off guard. Besides, if I'm going to help him transform, it's useful to see him in his natural habitat.

"Your friends brought cinnamon rolls," his mom says. "Your favorite."

"I don't have a favorite—" Elijah closes his eyes, looking annoyed. "Never mind."

"He can be so grumpy in the mornings," his mom explains.

I hold up the tray of coffees. "Maybe caffeine will help."

"I can't—I'm not . . ." He pats down the hair that's sticking up at the back of his head. "I haven't even showered yet."

"You can shower while I finish making breakfast," his dad says, pulling another carton of eggs from their fridge. "Does everyone prefer scrambled, or sunny-side up?"

Elijah's eyes go wide with terror. Ava elbows me.

"We ate before we came," I say. It's cute to watch him panic, but I shouldn't torture him. "We have a lot of work to do for our project today. We should get an early start."

"Our project for *school*," Elijah adds, not-so-subtly.

His mom insists on putting some cinnamon rolls on a plate for us first. It's actually sweet, the way they dote on him. I know my parents love me. But after having done everything twice with my brothers already, sometimes it feels like they're coasting.

As the three of us head upstairs, I'm curious to see what Elijah's bedroom looks like. Except for his unmade bed and some rumpled clothes, it's strangely uncluttered. There's a shelf of neatly stacked books behind his headboard, a cozy-looking window nook, and a corkboard above his desk with his class schedule pinned to it. The only thing hanging on the walls are two framed posters—one of the Minnesota Boundary Waters, one of Gooseberry Falls.

"Those people downstairs seem really nice," I say. "But if they're holding you hostage, blink twice and we'll help break you out of here."

Elijah's brow wrinkles. "What?"

"Your bedroom. It looks like an IKEA showroom."

"I think it looks nice," says Ava, ever the peacekeeper.

"It doesn't say anything about your personality," I tell Elijah. "Other than the fact that you like the outdoors, I guess?"

"Actually . . ." he sighs. "My dad picked out the posters."

"See? That just proves my point."

Elijah flops down onto the edge of his bed with the plate of cinnamon rolls. "Is that why you're here?" he asks, biting into one. "To help redesign my bedroom?"

I hand him his coffee. "Not your bedroom."

He looks at me, then the shopping bags, then back at me.

"No. I can't."

"Lesson number two," I announce. "Hair and Costumes."

"That's why I came along," Ava says, setting down her bags. "After spending the last three months obsessing over prom dresses, I have a trained eye for this kind of thing."

"A makeover?" Elijah asks, still catching up.

"You said you wanted people to notice you," I remind him. "We need to make sure it's for the *right* reasons. Because whether it's fair or not, people will judge you based on how you look. And, no offense, but you could use some help in that department."

His jaw tightens. "Prefacing something shitty with *no offense* doesn't give you a free pass on being an asshole."

"I'm not saying there's anything wrong with how you look. I'm just saying you could put in a little more effort. It's okay to care about your appearance."

Elijah shakes his head, still in denial. "This isn't some nineties movie. You can't just take the glasses off the secretly hot nerdy kid and suddenly everyone notices him. For starters, I don't wear glasses. Second, I'm not secretly hot."

Does he think being self-deprecating is cute? Or does he really believe that? Some people may say I'm conceited. But this—not *liking* yourself? Isn't that worse? How can Elijah really think so little of himself?

"You shouldn't put yourself down," I tell him.

"I'm not putting myself down. I'm stating a fact."

"According to *whom*? Did you conduct a survey?"

"If you two are going to bicker," Ava says, "can you at least pass the cinnamon rolls? Some of us haven't had breakfast yet."

As we fuel up on pastries and coffee, Elijah gives in and agrees to let Ava look through his closet. "You have too many neutrals," she says, flipping through his shirts. "And while there's nothing wrong with wanting to dress comfortably, you need to expand your wardrobe beyond hoodies."

Elijah brushes the crumbs off his pajama pants. "What's the point? Everyone at school just sees me in my uniform anyhow."

"What if you had a date?" I ask.

He tilts his head, giving me a look.

"What? It could happen."

"Yeah," he deadpans. "So could the Rapture."

I narrow my eyes. I definitely have my work cut out for me. But at least he's not shy about being sarcastic.

"Can I shower now?" he asks.

"Yes." I empty the contents of one of the shopping bags onto his bed. "But get ready to try these on afterward."

His eyes go wide as he looks at the rest of the bags. "All that's for me? But I—I can't pay you back for everything."

"Don't worry about it," I tell him. "I had a bunch of unused gift cards from my grandma. And we can return whatever you don't like."

I hand him an outfit to change into after his shower. As soon as he's in his bathroom, Ava's head pops out of the closet. "You had *one* gift card from your grandma. It barely covered a pair of jeans."

I shrug. "Can you put a price on style?"

She shakes her head at me. Okay, so I probably shouldn't have spent all that money. But a new outfit really can boost your confidence, which is something Elijah needs. Hopefully he won't mind returning a few things, though. It's hard to hold an after-school job when you have a busy rehearsal schedule. And my parents aren't really into handouts, despite paying for all my brothers' sporting equipment and tournament fees over the years.

After the water from Elijah's shower stops running, he remains in his bathroom a while.

"How's everything going in there?" I ask.

"Um." The door opens a crack. "You bought me the wrong size."

"I bought you the correct size. Your other clothes are too baggy and loose."

"I think I know what size I wear."

"And I think I've been through enough costume fittings to know how clothes are supposed to fit a person's body."

The door opens farther. Elijah comes out in a pair of jeans and a green thermal henley. Now that his hair is wet and not sticking out all over the place, he looks . . . surprisingly good. Objectively speaking, of course. The jeans fit him perfectly, and there's something endearing about the way he's nervously biting his lip.

"Well?" I ask. "What do you think?"

"This shirt's too tight."

"That shirt is supposed to be tight."

"I don't like it."

"Why? Because you're not trying to hide behind clothes that are too big for you? Because if you wear something like this, guys might look at you, and then you'll have to face the fact that someone could actually be interested in you?"

A wounded look flashes across his face. Shit, did I push him too far? Thankfully, Ava steps in to save me.

"We're not going to make you wear anything you're uncomfortable in," she says. "But Wade's right, that shirt looks good on you. You need more earth tones in your wardrobe. This color really complements your red hair."

"I'm *not* a redhead," Elijah says.

"You're auburn," she tells him. "Which, I'm sorry, is closer to red than brown."

"Speaking of hair," I say, "let's take a minute to talk about yours."

Elijah rolls his eyes but doesn't put up a fight as I lead the three of us into his bathroom. "Okay," I say. "Show me how you get ready for school in the morning."

He looks at me through the mirror like I just asked him how he ties his shoes. "I brush my teeth and put on deodorant."

"What about your hair?"

"I let it dry?"

"You mean you don't put anything in it?"

"No."

"And you're *sure* you're not straight?"

"Please," Ava says. "Drew spends more time on his hair than I do on mine."

That only makes Elijah's situation all the more tragic. Even someone who thinks it's acceptable to wear athletic shorts year-round is putting in more of an effort than him.

"You need to start using product," I tell him, studying the wet mop resting on top of his head. "And I'm thinking we reshape some of this volume. Maybe a side part could help."

He leans away from me. "You're not getting near me with clippers."

"Not me. A professional."

"It'll open your face up more," Ava says. "You have great cheekbones."

Elijah leans in closer to the mirror and pushes some of his hair to the side. And for a moment, there's a flicker of a smile, like maybe he can see it. But then he shakes it off and goes back to being impossible.

"I'm not shallow enough to care about any of this."

I frown, trying not to take his choice of words as a judgment against me. "Wanting to look your best isn't shallow," I tell him. "I'm not saying your appearance is the *only* thing you should care about. But if putting on a nice outfit and fixing your hair makes you feel more confident, why not do it?"

Elijah opens his mouth, ready to argue, but I don't let him. "Shallow means having little depth. So if you've already made up your mind about this without giving it a try . . . well then, you, my friend, are being the shallow one."

He crosses his arms. It's hard not to take a little pleasure in winning.

"Fine. Let's just get this over with."

"Get this over with?" I laugh. "Why do you think we came over early? Our day's just beginning."

Fifteen

ELIJAH

"If you don't like it," Wade says, casually sprawled out across my bed, "you have to at least articulate why."

"Uh . . . because this shirt is basically the tiger pistol shrimp of shirts."

He gives me a funny look.

"They can create a sonic boom by shooting jets of water from—" I stop, shaking my head. "It's too loud."

"It's not loud. It's a *print*."

"It looks like a kaleidoscope threw up on me."

While I wouldn't say that I'm a fan of wearing a tie to school every day, there is something comforting about everyone dressing the same. I don't have to worry about standing out or calling attention to myself.

Wade rolls his eyes. "Try tucking it in."

"You know who tucks his shirt into his jeans? My dad. Is that really the style icon I should be aspiring to?"

"Not your entire shirt. Just the front."

I look down, confused. "How does that make it better?"

"It lets people know you're not a shapeless form underneath those clothes. Here . . ." He gets up from my bed. "I'll show you."

Reaching for my waist, Wade suddenly stops himself. He probably remembers when I flinched in the theater. I don't mean to be so jumpy. I'm just . . . not used to guys touching me. Not even in a platonic way.

"Maybe we should take a break," Ava suggests, picking up on our awkwardness.

"Good idea. We can move on to our photoshoot."

"Photoshoot?" My voice cracks as if I'm back in middle school.

"Relax." Wade smiles. "It's an informal shoot. Just a few friends hanging out."

He makes the three of us get on my bed together, sandwiching me in the middle. We're so close, I can smell his soap. It's sweet, but not in a cloying way. More like—*Oh, god. What am I doing?* Don't be a creep.

"Now, there are three rules for taking a good selfie," Wade explains. "Keep your head tilted, your chin down, and don't stick to one pose." He takes out his phone. "And please, no duck lips."

"Technically, that was four—"

"Fourth rule's no talking."

As we pose, Wade breaks his own rule by directing me through the shoot. First I'm not smiling enough. Then my smile's too forced. Then I look annoyed. Which—*fair.* But I'm sorry, who likes having their photo taken?

Wade, apparently. It's amazing how long he can keep his arm suspended above us, like he's developed a special bicep for selfie-taking.

"We got some good ones," he says, swiping through the results before posting. "There. I tagged you on Instagram."

I assume he's talking to Ava. But he looks right at me.

"I—I don't have an Instagram account."

"I know. That's why I made you one. Give me your phone so I can log you in."

I hand it over reluctantly.

"You need to start posting content," he tells me. "Think about what your brand is, the thing that makes you interesting. No pictures of food—unless food is your brand. But it can't be school lunches. The secret to social media is posting photos that make people feel like they're missing out on something."

"That sounds exhausting," I say.

He raises an eyebrow. "It is."

"Then why do it?"

"So people can get to know you. Think of it as your social résumé."

"It's not as fake as he makes it seem," Ava says. "You just have to remember that people are only putting the best version of themselves out there. Whenever I look at someone's feed, I assume they're at least fifteen percent less happy than what their photos show."

Wade hands back my phone. I hate seeing photos of myself, and this one . . . isn't that bad, actually. Despite being in the middle of two very photogenic people, despite wearing the tiger pistol shrimp of shirts, it doesn't make me cringe.

Seven people have liked the photo already. Which seems impossible—he *just* posted it. I read the caption: *Wish I could spend every Saturday morning with these two.*

My heart does a little flip. Does he mean that? Wade and Ava aren't my friends. But once this is all over . . . is there a possibility they could be? Even when I was friendly with Micah, he never came over to my house.

Another "like" pops up. Then two more.

No, that's silly. Wade just told me that social media is fake. He only wrote that to make people feel like they're missing out on something. Besides, this is his account. His followers. None of this is a reflection on me.

"Shoot," Ava says, looking at her phone. "I have to go meet Drew."

"Can't he wait?" Wade whines.

"No. It's our last Saturday before—"

"Before weekend rehearsals begin, I know. But it's only noon."

"Yes, but I also have a paper to write on gender bias in nineteenth-century literature and I've yet to crack open a single book."

"You should talk to Szabo," I say. His face would probably turn bright red if he knew I mentioned his name in front of Ava. But it's true, he's always reading.

Ava looks at me. "Yeah. Okay." She then taps Wade on the chest. "You still need to give me a ride home."

As much as I appreciate their help, I'm relieved Wade and Ava are leaving. Having all that attention on me is exhausting, and I could use some breakfast that isn't covered in icing.

"Decide which outfit you want to wear," Wade says, turning toward me.

"For what?"

"For the rest of our afternoon together."

"But I thought Ava was hanging out with her boyfriend now."

"Yeah. We'll drop her off on our way to Flamin' Joe's."

Playing dress-up for Ava and Wade in the privacy of my home was one thing. Being on display for everyone at Flamin' Joe's is another.

"Why—why are we going back there?"

The corner of his mouth pulls into a smirk. "Because. It's time for your next lesson."

It's almost as if Wade enjoys torturing me. Despite the pool of dread in my stomach, I can't let him win. I change back into the green henley and a pair of chinos. Before this morning, I didn't know what chinos were. Turns out they're just a fancy name for pants.

Back downstairs, my parents are still in the kitchen, trying to act like they haven't been sitting there, waiting for us this entire time.

"You look nice," Mom says, shooting Dad a surprised look.

"Be back later," I reply, hurrying past them. I need to get out of here before they can ask if I need money or a ride home.

"Wait," Wade says. "You didn't tell them the good news."

I look at him, my mind racing as I try to figure out what he's talking about.

I finally have an Instagram account?

I know what chinos are now?

Wade grins at my parents, charming his already captivated audience. "Elijah's decided he's ready to schedule his driver's license test."

Mom's face lights up. Dad actually whoops, holding out his hand to give me a high five. For once I wouldn't mind dying from embarrassment. At least then I'd have a good reason not to take that test.

When we turn into the parking lot of Flamin' Joe's twenty minutes later, I still haven't said anything to Wade since we dropped off Ava. If my eyes could shoot daggers, his dashboard would be slashed to shreds right now.

"I'm sorry," he says, pulling into an empty spot. "But you know I'm right. You can't have your parents chauffeuring you around everywhere forever."

I *do* know he's right, which makes it all the harder to accept. "You didn't have to spring it on me like that."

He gives me a look. "Would you have said yes if I asked nicely first?"

"No."

"Then you're welcome."

He turns off the ignition. And just as I'm about ready to forgive him, he fills me in on the rest of his plan. "Okay, I'll go in first. When you come in a few minutes later, you're not allowed to sit with me. Don't even *look* in my direction. This is your chance to make new friends."

"What—how—" I take a breath. "I didn't agree to this."

"Lesson number three," he says proudly. "Improvisation."

My seat belt suddenly feels like it's choking me, and Wade's infuriating grin isn't helping.

"Don't worry," he says with mock seriousness. "Everyone hates improv."

"Then why am I doing it?"

"Because some moments are better unscripted. Improv is all about letting go of your fear and thinking on your feet."

Wade reaches for the door and leaves. Just like that.

Watching him walk away through the sideview mirror, I remember the last time I tried this: talking to Connor and his friends during gym class. Have I really changed enough since then? I guess there's only one way to find out.

My phone lights up.

Tyler's working the register. You'll like them.

Shoulders back. Chin up.

The café is crowded when I enter. It's a Saturday, and apparently the Iced Coffee Gays have nothing on the Milkshake Gays. Where did all these people come from? The very first thing I do is look for Wade, even though he told me not to. His eyes go wide with annoyance when I find him. He nods toward the register, indicating I should get in line.

I tell myself that if Brady can walk around the catwalks, surely he can handle this. With my shoulders back and my chin up, I join the people waiting to order. My posture might portray confidence, but I still don't know what to do with my hands. So I take out my phone.

A text immediately pops up.

Stop looking at your phone.

Ugh. Fine. I put it away and study the two guys in front of me. One's white, wearing a flannel shirt and a beanie. The other, who looks Asian, has on a jean jacket with a rainbow patch. I must be staring too hard, because the one with the rainbow patch turns to look at me. And it's not just a casual glance. His eyes travel up and down my body.

My heart pounds. Normally when people look at me, I assume they're judging me. But now that I'm wearing the clothes Wade picked out for me . . . I don't know, maybe he's checking me out? It feels conceited to think that. And yet I want it to be true.

I can already hear Wade telling me to smile and say something to him. But as I wait for my pulse to stop racing, Flannel Shirt Boy loops arms with Rainbow Boy, and they walk up to the register together.

My heart sinks. It was too good to be true anyhow. I try distracting myself by looking up at the menu board. The greasy smell of Tater Tots and french fries is already making my stomach grumble, reminding me I haven't had a real meal yet today.

Before I can make up my mind about what to order, I'm interrupted by the person behind me—an elderly white man with bushy eyebrows and a stack of newspapers.

"Sorry," I say. "Were you talking to me?"

"Line's moving. You're up."

"Oh. Thanks."

I move up to the register, a little jostled now that I know people are waiting. The cashier welcomes me with a friendly wave. They have warm brown skin, chipped black nail polish, and a name tag that lets me know this is Tyler and their pronouns are they/them.

"Ready to order?" they ask.

Three words, and Tyler has already managed to turn my brain to mush.

"Um, yes. I'll . . ." I forget to breathe from my diaphragm, and my words get swallowed.

My eyes are still on the board, trying hard to focus. *The Peppermint Patty. The Harvey Milkshake. On Wednesdays We Drink Pink.* It's no use. My tongue's too thick, and everything's blurring together now.

The old man behind me clears his throat, giving me a pointed look.

Tyler rolls their eyes. "Easy, Leonard. No one threw the first brick at Stonewall so you could come in here and harass my customers."

"Sorry," I say, stepping aside. "You should go first."

Leonard pushes past me, placing his order and counting out exact change from the handful of coins in his pocket. I glance over at Wade. He gives me an enthusiastic thumbs-up, unaware of how terribly I'm bombing.

"Don't mind Leonard," Tyler tells me once he's gone. "He's actually very sweet when his blood sugar isn't low."

"Oh," I reply.

I should probably think of something else to say, but it's like I'm back at school again. My shoulders are even starting to sink. Tyler's quick-witted and funny, just like Connor. And I'm still . . . *me*. It doesn't matter what clothes I wear. I'll never be able to think of comebacks or smart one-liners.

"Did you decide which milkshake you'd like?" Tyler asks.

Still frozen with indecision, I pick the first thing my eyes land on. "Yes. I'll try the Shake Your Booty Sha—"

I almost choke, embarrassed by the innuendo. "Wait, I changed my mind." I look up and pick the next thing I see. "Vampires Suck?"

Tyler nods, entering it into the touchscreen. "Name?"

"Elijah. *No*—Brady."

They smile, pretending like I'm not the worst customer they've had all day. "Okay, Brady. Did you want that with teeth or no teeth?"

It takes a second, but their question finally registers with me. *Suck. Teeth or no teeth*. Oh no, I think I just ordered something that's referencing vampiric fellatio. I should have stuck with the Booty Shake.

"I'll surprise you," Tyler says, finalizing my order.

I pay them and get out of there as fast as possible. Scanning the room, there's only one open table. I walk slowly. If someone else grabs it before I can, I'll have a valid excuse to go sit with Wade.

Unfortunately, nobody does. I sit down and take out my phone.

This was a mistake, I text.

You're doing great.

I should just go home.

You should sit up and stop looking at your phone.

I'm not ready for this.

You are. Guys are checking you out.

I don't believe him, but I glance up anyhow. No one's checking me out. No one's even aware that I exist. I may as well—*Shit*. Someone's walking toward me. It's Rainbow Boy, and he's flashing me a smile.

"Hey," he says, radiating a friendly warmth.

I sit up straight like Wade told me to.

"You're not waiting for someone, are you?" he asks.

I shake my head. What's happening? I thought Flannel Shirt Boy was his boyfriend. Why is he talking to *me*? Is this what Wade meant by life not always following a script?

"Would you mind if I . . ." He places his hand on the empty chair across from me.

Fears welds my mouth shut. But it's like when I had to keep eye contact with Wade during our warm-up. I surrender to the awkwardness instead of letting it control me.

"Not at all," I say, finally finding my voice.

"Thanks. You're a peach."

He pulls the chair out and my heart feels like it's going to explode in my chest. But instead of sitting, he picks the chair up and carries it over to another table. Where Flannel Shirt Boy is waiting with their milkshakes.

Heat creeps down my neck. I can't believe I thought—

"Vampires Suck for Brady?" someone yells.

Just when I thought the humiliation was over, my milkshake appears on the pick-up counter. It's blood red, with a mound of whipped cream and a pair of plastic vampire fangs sticking out on top. *With teeth.* I'm too embarrassed to go retrieve it. But the person working behind the counter just calls my order out louder. *"Vampires Suck for Brady?"*

Every set of eyeballs may as well be glued to me as I return to my table with my absurd milkshake. I don't care if Wade's still watching—I slump back in my chair, wanting to disappear completely.

A moment later, a basket of fries lands on my table. I look up, ready to tell whoever put it there that I didn't order any food. But it's Wade. He's brought his chair over with him and sits down to join me.

"I was a failure," I say.

He pushes the basket closer. The greasy aroma hits me, causing my stomach to make noise again. Now that it's just the two of us, and I don't have to worry about impressing anyone, I grab a handful of fries and drag them through a pool of ketchup.

"You tried. That's not failing."

"I'll never be Brady," I reply, talking with my mouth full. "We should give up."

"It's going to take time. We're not even done with your lessons yet."

"What's next? Stage Combat? I have to fight someone?"

Without asking, he pulls my milkshake toward him and takes a sip. "I need you to trust me, okay?"

Trust seems like a big word. I learned my lesson after Micah ghosted me for coming out—better to stay guarded.

Wade flashes me a smile. He slipped in the vampire fangs when I wasn't watching.

I laugh. It's hard not to while looking at that ridiculous face. Shaking my head, the heavy feeling in my body starts to melt away. In this past week, I've spent more time with Wade than anyone else at school. And surprisingly, it hasn't been terrible. Maybe that's reason enough to keep going for now.

Sixteen

WADE

"So, Wade . . ." Dad glances down into his lap, ignoring the forkful of mashed potatoes he's holding. "How are rehearsals going?"

I appreciate being asked. But I'd appreciate it even more if he wasn't also not-so-secretly checking hockey scores right now. I swear, I don't know how my parents survived without smartphones and tablets when they were my age. As adults, they're inseparable from them.

"We haven't heard you talk much about the show," Mom says, eyeing the kitchen counter.

"It's fine," I tell them. "We have to be off-book soon."

Mom nods, getting up to retrieve her iPad. "TJ said he might call early. Becca's cheerleading team is hosting a paintball fundraiser tonight."

Despite having bad-boy college-athlete images to maintain, both my brothers keep weekly FaceTime appointments to call home. I can always tell who's calling based on how my parents are dressed. Dad's the dead giveaway, wearing one of his many Notre Dame sweatshirts. But even Mom has her tell. She puts on a little more makeup when it's TJ's turn, probably because Becca joins his calls now.

"I'm sure you're already memorized," Dad says.

Actually, I haven't even started yet. Memorization comes pretty easily to me. It's the character work I usually spend more time on. But this year, what's the point? No one's coming to our show to see Colonel Pickering. Besides, I've been busy helping Elijah.

"That's him!" Mom announces, accepting the call.

As my parents huddle together in front of the screen, I try to imagine Mom putting on makeup to impress one of my boyfriends. Or Dad wearing an NYU sweatshirt. (Assuming I get into NYU. The thought of him in a Lachlan University sweatshirt is too depressing.)

"Hey," TJ's voice says. "You're not still eating, are you?"

"Just finishing up," Dad replies.

I look down at my half-full plate.

As my parents start talking to TJ and Becca, I get up to excuse myself. Mr. Z gave us the night off from rehearsing, and Elijah's coming over.

"Say hi to your brother," Mom says, flipping her iPad around before I can leave.

TJ and Becca wave hello. When they announced their engagement on Christmas, I was happy for them. Of course, nothing could top my parents' happiness. I could've given my mom a gold-plated iPhone after that, and she hardly would've noticed.

My brothers and I aren't always great at talking. I can't imagine asking them for advice about my breakup with Reese, or texting them juicy theater gossip. It's nice to have Becca now to help keep the uncomfortable silences to a minimum.

"Hey, Wade," she says, flipping back her long, shiny hair. "How's school going? How's the musical? You'll have to be sure to tell your brother when performances are. Maybe we'll make a trip to see it."

It's nice of her to say that, but I doubt they'd drive all the way from

Indiana to see me. During baseball season, no less.

"I hear you're the star," TJ says.

"Um." I look away from the screen, embarrassed to explain the truth. "It's more of a principal role. Not the lead."

"You're a Westmore," TJ tells me. "You'll be the star."

Right. Because *Westmores Always Win.* That's our official family slogan. One that's been painted on banners and chanted at sporting events. My brothers created a family legacy for us at school, and I'm once again proving I don't live up to it.

"How's baseball?" I ask. Even talking about sports is better than this.

"Season starts next week. Go, Irish!"

My brother pumps his fist in the air; I awkwardly try to match it.

"I should run," I say. "I have a friend coming over soon."

"Yeah. Good talk, little bro."

Sadly that *was* one of our better talks.

"Wade," Mom says.

For a moment, I think she's going to remind me to keep my bedroom door open tonight. That was always the rule for TJ and Brett when they had girls over in high school.

"I made lemon bars for dessert," she says. "If you and your friend want some later."

I shouldn't be surprised. Even when Reese was my boyfriend, they didn't really know how to act around him. They were friendly and tried talking to him about soccer, but it was never quite the same as how they were around TJ's and Brett's girlfriends.

Maybe I don't give my parents enough credit. I think my coming out was a bit of a shock for them. To be fair, I did tell them at an

Applebee's. Dad was watching football on one of the monitors, and when he made a sexist comment about a player throwing like a girl, I reminded him that girls play football, too. He then joked that the quarterback's girlfriend would probably be doing a better job, and I said maybe the quarterback had a boyfriend. Dad laughed, as though it was so absurd he couldn't fathom it.

I'd been nervous about telling my parents I was gay. I thought it might change how they felt about me. But in that moment, I was too angry to care. I wanted to burst their narrow little bubble of what being gay looked like.

I can't say I recommend coming out in an Applebee's. Especially thirty seconds before your entrées arrive. Watching your parents cry is unsettling—watching them cry while steam rises up from a skillet of sizzling steak fajitas is worse.

We survived that dinner, and since then, they've always been accepting of me. But I hate that it's something we never discuss. I mean, it's not like they ever talk to my brothers about being straight. It just sucks to feel like this important part of me is something no one wants to acknowledge.

Not that any of this even matters for tonight. Elijah's almost done with his lessons, and now it's time to put what he's learned into practice. At rehearsal, you don't block something once and expect it to be performance ready. You keep running it until it becomes second nature. And usually, along the way, you'll discover new and better ways to play the scene.

Elijah has already shown some improvement. The first time I took him to Flamin' Joe's, he could barely touch his milkshake. I know he thinks he biffed his improv lesson. But when we were there this weekend, not only did he eat my entire basket of fries, we also stayed at our table for an hour, just talking. I could barely get a full sentence out of him the first time. I don't want to congratulate myself yet—there's still a lot of work to be done. But it feels like we're on the right track.

See, I *knew* I'd be a good Higgins.

Heading upstairs, I pick up the clothes that have been crumpled on my bedroom floor all week and make sure my bathroom's not a mess. Checking out my hair in the mirror, I suddenly pause. What am I doing? It's Elijah. He doesn't care about any of this.

At school I spend a lot of time trying to be perfect. Perfect look. Perfect social group. Perfect boyfriend. I still don't think there's anything wrong with wanting to appear your best. But it's also nice when you don't have to try so hard to impress someone.

Studying myself in the mirror, I do, however, spot a pot roast stain on my shirt. Not having to be perfect is one thing. Being an outright slob is another.

I pull off my shirt and head back into my bedroom. Opening my closet, I reach for a button-down. There's an immediate ache in my chest—it's the one Reese got me for my birthday. He always used to smile when he saw me wearing it.

I bring it to my nose and take a whiff.

No Reese. Only laundry detergent.

The ache burrows itself deeper. If Reese were coming over tonight, we'd probably do something low-key, like watch a movie. First, though, we'd argue about it. He'd want something with lots of action; I'd want an old Hollywood musical. I usually let him win, only to have him fall asleep with his head resting on my arm halfway through the movie. I didn't mind too much, though. He had such a cute little snore.

The doorbell rings. I toss the button-down back in my closet and throw on a T-shirt. Hurrying back downstairs, my adrenaline starts pumping. Outside of rehearsals, I haven't been hanging out much with anyone. Ava's always with Drew, and Hannah and Ebony are still being kind of distant. Hopefully, once Reese sees that I've changed, things will go back to how they were before. Until then, it's nice to have Elijah to focus my attention on.

When I let him in and take his coat, I instantly regret not changing into the button-down. Elijah's wearing the striped sweater I picked out for him, and there appears to be product in his hair. My words catch in my throat. I can't believe how good he looks.

"What?" he asks, sounding worried.

Shoot. Am I smiling too much?

"Nothing," I reply. "That sweater was a nice choice."

"Oh." He stretches the sleeves down over his hands. "Thanks."

My cheeks suddenly feel hot. Is it warm in here? Or maybe it's just my sense of pride. Transforming Elijah into Brady these last two weeks has been a lot of work, but it's starting to pay off. And not just the outfit. Something else is different. His eyes aren't bouncing around the room the way they normally do. I've never noticed the tint of hazel in them before.

"So . . ." Elijah says, still standing in our entryway.

I snap out of it. "Right. Sorry."

Now's not the time to get distracted. I have to finish transforming Elijah so Reese can see all the good work I've done. Tonight's our next lesson. And I have a feeling it's going to be our hardest yet.

"Are you going to show me how to punch someone now?" Elijah asks when we get to my room. I have us sit on my bed, noting that his posture still stiffens a bit.

"Not exactly. Stage Combat is a metaphor."

"For what?"

"Getting physical."

His forehead scrunches together, confused. I'm being coy. But I don't want to frighten him too quickly.

"Like . . . with another guy," I add.

Elijah still doesn't say anything. But he doesn't have to. Most of the color has already drained from his face.

"What—what does that have to do with wanting to be more confident?"

"What if someone flirts with you?" I ask. "Or asks you out?"

"That's not going to happen," he replies assuredly.

Seriously? How can he still be thinking that? Yes, I've been helping him change on the outside, but I thought I had also taught him that the right attitude is more important. Elijah's smart, observant, and funny—he has plenty to offer.

"It *could* happen," I say. "Which is why I want you to be prepared. Stage Combat is all about choreographing the moves ahead of time and being in control of what happens. It's also about having a scene partner you can trust."

His eyes pop wide with fear. "I'm not going on a practice date."

"Actually," I tease. "That's not a bad idea."

It takes him a second, but when he realizes I'm joking, he punches me lightly in the knee.

"Hey, I said Stage Combat was a metaphor!"

He shakes his head. "You're such a dork."

I have to bite back a smile. When Elijah and I first started hanging out, I felt like maybe he thought I was too vain or shallow. It'd be one thing if he didn't like Popular Actor Wade. But now that we've been spending more time together, now that I've let him see the parts of me that don't feel like a constant performance . . . well, it'd hurt if he didn't think the real me was worth getting to know either.

"What I meant," I tell him, "is that you can talk to me about it. If there were any questions you had, or anything you're nervous about."

He averts his gaze, smoothing out a square of my bedspread. I know he'll shut down if I push too hard. But I've seen how he acts around other guys, the way he's jumpy about being touched. I just want him to have a safe space to talk about this kind of stuff if he wants.

"Was Reese your first boyfriend?" he asks.

My chest knots as I glance toward my closet. I wasn't expecting *that* name to come up.

"He was the first guy I dated seriously," I offer. "But there were a few guys before him."

"So when you were my age . . ." he pauses, still not able to look at me. "You had already kissed someone?"

"Yes. But actually, I probably would've been better off if I had waited longer. I mean, Jesus was hot. But a mediocre kisser."

This gets the tiniest smile out of him. He looks back up. "Jesus? As in . . . *Christ*?"

"It was a community theater production of *Godspell*." I cringe, remembering how bad this story is. "I didn't find out Jesus had a girlfriend until she showed up with flowers on opening night."

"Wow. Sounds like a mess."

"It was. But at least it was an easy breakup. Unlike . . ." My voice trails off, unable to say the rest out loud. "Well, I'm sure you've heard the rumors."

"Not that many people talk to me," he says. "But it's not my business."

I can't expect Elijah to open up to me if I'm not willing to do the same. I take a breath, unsure where to begin.

"For Valentine's Day, I made Reese promise we wouldn't exchange gifts. No cards, no flowers, not even a box of little candy hearts. I said it was a capitalistic holiday, and that we shouldn't have to prove ourselves. Except I wasn't being honest."

Elijah nods, waiting for me to go on.

"In my head, it played out like a movie. I was going to surprise him with this big romantic gesture, and then everyone would clap, and we'd be the greatest couple at school. So when we were eating lunch in the cafeteria that day, I had flowers delivered to our table."

"And he dumped you for that?" Elijah asks.

"It was six dozen roses," I reply, wincing. "Plus balloons."

Elijah grimaces. Which, coincidently, is the same face my friends made that day.

"Reese said it was manipulative. That I was more concerned about looking like a cool boyfriend in front of everyone than I was about his feelings. And, yeah, in retrospect, I see that now. But at the time, I swear, my intentions were good."

I can still see the hurt look on Reese's face when those flowers arrived. The entire cafeteria witnessed it. I hate that I did that to him. What he said at the time—that I'll never love anyone more than I love myself—was harsh. But that doesn't mean it wasn't true. I *was* more focused on myself in that moment.

"I'm sorry that happened," Elijah says. "For both of you."

I look at him, feeling a sudden lightness in my chest. I'm not saying anyone should've taken my side during the breakup—Reese didn't do anything wrong. But it's nice to have someone be sympathetic about what I went through. Even if it was my own doing.

"It's fine," I tell him. "Reese and I work better as friends."

That's a lie. But I should stop sucking up all the focus again.

"Anyhow, we're supposed to be talking about you right now," I continue. "Not me."

Elijah flops back onto my mattress. "There's nothing to talk about. I've never even kissed anyone before." He stares up at the ceiling and sighs. "No one's ever *wanted* to kiss me."

Ugh. Not this again.

"How do you know?" I ask. "Maybe someone wanted to kiss you, they were just waiting for you to make the first move."

He shakes his head. "I could never make the first move. I'd be too afraid."

"It's just kissing," I say playfully, trying to lighten the mood. "What's there to be afraid of?"

"I don't know . . ." His voice is quieter, more unsure. "Being rejected?"

Elijah turns toward me, his eyes meeting mine. There's something startling about the way he's looking at me. Like he's finally letting his guard down. And for a second, under the soft glow of my twinkle lights, I imagine what it'd be like to lean down and kiss him. Just so he can get it over with and stop worrying. So he can see that his shyness is actually kind of cute, and guys are definitely going to be into him.

His first kiss shouldn't be a pity kiss, though.

And I need to stop trying to play the hero.

"We have plenty of time to work on that," I tell him. "Now that you've learned the basics, we put them into practice. Plus . . ." I reach out and poke his shoulder. Surprisingly, he doesn't flinch. "We still have to complete the final step in your physical transformation."

Elijah looks up at me. His eyes narrow, but there's none of his usual trepidation. "Fine. Just don't make me regret this."

Seventeen

WADE

"Are you ready?" I ask, my voice a little too giddy. "I think you're really going to love it. Wait, close your eyes first."

Ava doesn't close her eyes. She rolls them. "Honestly, does everything have to be such a production with you?"

"First of all, yes. Second, just wait until you see him."

I grab her hand and pull her toward the classroom door. Peering through the window, I spot Elijah at his desk.

No, not Elijah. *Brady*.

"Whoa." Ava leans in closer. "He let you dye his hair?"

"He let the stylist dye it," I reply. It did take a little handholding on my part, but I'm proud of Elijah for trusting me.

"He looks like an entirely new person," Ava says.

It's true. With his new haircut and color, there's no denying he's a redhead. Just like there's no denying that Brady's kind of hot. And not just because of his looks. Yes, it's nice to finally see his face, but he also carries himself differently. He's sitting up straight with his shoulders relaxed. And for once, his tie doesn't look like he slept in it. It's like he actually cares how he presents himself now.

Not to be cocky, but I *knew* he could do it.

"Does this mean your little experiment is over?"

"It's not an experiment," I say, a tad defensively. "We're friends."

Weirdly enough, that's starting to feel true. I thought helping Elijah would feel like work. But I've enjoyed spending time with him. And it's fun to watch him grow more confident. I couldn't wait to get to school this morning and see him as Brady.

Ava raises an eyebrow, still doubtful. "Speaking of friends, you shouldn't keep Ebony and Hannah waiting."

I tap gently on the window. Elijah doesn't hear me, but I wave goodbye anyhow. I can't help myself. I'm just so happy for him.

"You're sure you can't join us?" I ask as we head to the cafeteria. "You're a neutral party."

"Hannah and Ebony aren't mad at you. You just have to talk to them. Besides, Drew wants me to have lunch with him today."

Of course he does. He's going to make Ava sit at a table with all his obnoxious football friends instead of at the theater table, where she belongs, with all our obnoxious thespian friends.

Ava shoots me a look. "What?"

"I didn't say anything."

"You don't have to. I can read it all over your expressive face."

"Okay, fine." The great thing about Ava and me is that we're always honest with each other. Even to a fault, maybe. "I'm jealous Drew gets so much of your time when we're not in rehearsals."

She stops walking. "I'm sorry, have I *not* been eating lunch with you in the prop room every day?"

"What?" I give her an evil grin. "I never said my jealousy was rational."

She shoves my shoulder playfully. "Drew doesn't control me. I make my own decisions."

I know she does. But it still feels like Drew's always taking her away from us. He almost never hangs out with our friend group.

"You should invite Drew to my house this weekend," I say as a peace offering.

She smiles. "Okay."

When we arrive in the cafeteria, Ava wishes me luck before parting ways. I don't know why I'm so nervous. Ebony and Hannah are my friends; I'm sure they'll forgive me. Except forgiveness doesn't erase what happened. I was selfish with Reese and broke our group apart. What if they think less of me now?

After loading up my tray with a veggie burger and two orders of fries to share, I scan the room and spot them sitting at a table near the back. Ebony has her neat little stack of Tupperware containers that she always brings from home, while Hannah has once again chosen chaos: tomato soup, an everything bagel with strawberry cream cheese, and chickpeas from the salad bar.

"Hey," I say, setting down my tray. "Thanks for having lunch with me."

"We're glad you finally asked," Ebony replies, smiling.

Ebony has always been the mature one in our group. This year she's playing Mrs. Higgins in *My Fair Lady*. And while she enjoys doing musicals, straight dramas are where she really excels. I don't think there was a dry eye in the house when she played Emily in *Our Town* last year. She really knows how to get into her characters' psyches, which she hopes will translate into a psychology major at Stanford next year.

Hannah, on the other hand, is a big goof. She has great comedic timing and isn't afraid to ham it up. I doubt there's ever been a funnier Sister Margaretta in *The Sound of Music*. Her top choice for college is Lachlan University, where I might end up if all my New York schools reject me.

"I've missed hanging out," I say.

"Really?" Hannah deadpans. "Because it's not like we changed our phone numbers or entered the Witness Protection Program."

"I know. I'm sorry." I glance over at the table where the rest of our friends are. Reese has his script open, probably working on memorization. A sharp pang stabs at my chest. If we were still together, I'd be sitting next to him, helping him run lines.

"I wanted to apologize for forcing you to take sides between Reese and me," I tell them. "That wasn't fair to either of you."

"We didn't take sides," Ebony says reassuringly.

"Well, you should've. I got carried away. Reese was right to call me out."

Hannah licks a pink glob of cream cheese off her knuckle. "Next time you want to make a grand gesture, try chocolates. At least we could've enjoyed those. The flowers you ordered went home with the lunch staff."

I get that Hannah's trying to defuse the tension, but she turns everything into a joke. And I'm serious about this. If I want any chance of winning Reese back, I have to prove that I've learned from my mistakes.

"I'm sorry if I made things uncomfortable for everyone," I say. "And I'm really glad both of you could be there for Reese. I know I hurt him."

Ebony takes the last carrot stick from one of her containers, snapping the lid shut. "That's big of you, Wade. And for the record, we wanted to be there for you as well. Breakups are hard; nothing's ever black and white."

"Black-and-white cookies," Hannah says excitedly.

Ebony shoots her a look.

"What? Those also would've been better than flowers."

"Anyhow," I say. "I feel bad about ruining the spring musical for everyone."

Hannah laughs. "Okay, that's a bit dramatic—and that's coming from *me*."

"My point was, we haven't been able to hang out like we usually do. Not as a group. I want to change that. I mean, if that's something you'd want, too. My parents will be out of town this weekend for my brother's baseball game, so I'll have the house to myself."

"Your brothers are so hot," Hannah whispers, staring off into the distance.

"Gross."

"I'm sorry! But I like it when athletes wear that black makeup under their eyes. It's masculine, but also kind of feminine. I like blurring the lines, you know?"

"That's grease, not makeup. And yes, we know."

Hannah's our resident bisexual disaster. She's so proud of her title, she once printed it on a sash and wore it around school until the administration caught on and made her take it off for being in violation of dress code.

"We're always down for a party," Hannah says. "Aren't we, Eb?"

Ebony nods. "Definitely."

"Great. But it's more of a gathering. It'll just be the three of us. Plus Ava. And, um . . . hopefully Reese?"

I watch their faces to gauge their reactions. Hannah's looser with her emotions, but even she's not giving anything away.

"You should ask him," Ebony says, sounding cautiously optimistic. "I think he'd like that."

I'm not so sure, but I'm going to try. This get-together is really for Elijah. I figure it'll be like a dress rehearsal—a chance for him to perform, but without a full audience. Still, I can't deny that I might get something out of it, too. If Reese sees all the good work I've been doing with Elijah, he could change his mind about me sooner.

"Oh, and you'll get to meet my new friend," I say, not bothering to hide my smile.

This time their faces are easy to read. The theater table has always been a hotbed of speculation and gossip. Creating drama is in our DNA. Ebony and Hannah are clearly trying to deduce who this mysterious person is, and if this means I've moved on from Reese already.

"New friend?" Ebony asks, slyly making eye contact with Hannah.

"Brady," I say. "He's on the lighting crew. Red hair. Kind of quiet, but also funny . . ."

Hannah squints. "I can't picture him."

"Well, he's only a sophomore. And this is his first show. But I think everyone's really going to like him. There's only one thing . . ."

Ebony and Hannah lean in closer, eager to find out what that is.

"Brady can be a little shy at first," I say. "It's something I've been trying to help him overcome. He's a great guy, he just needs to come out of his shell a bit. So if you two could make sure he feels included at the party, I'd really appreciate it."

"Why are you looking at me when you say that?" Hannah asks. "It's not my fault people find my personality intimidating."

I'm looking at Hannah because she has a big mouth. If I tell Reese that I've changed, that I'm capable of putting other people first, I'm afraid he won't believe me. If Hannah brings it up . . . well, it couldn't hurt.

It's a little manipulative—which I'm not supposed to be anymore. But I want us to have the happy ending we deserve. And prom season will be underway soon. My stomach flutters thinking about us on the dance floor.

"We'll make sure Brady feels welcome," Ebony tells me.

"Totally," Hannah says. "People *love* talking to me."

I look back at our regular lunch table. There's only one more person I have to invite now. Unfortunately, if anyone's going to say no, it will definitely be him.

Later that afternoon, I get my chance to speak to Reese when Mr. Z has us work through "You Did It," our duet at the opening of Act Two. It's supposed to be an energetic, upbeat number. One that draws the audience back in after intermission.

"Hmm." Mr. Z folds his arms over his chest as he stares at Reese and me from the apron of the stage. "We're still missing something."

Behind us, the chorus grows listless. We've spent the past hour running this scene and it's only getting worse. Mr. Z's gaze travels back and forth between the two of us, trying to pinpoint the problem.

"Bromance," he finally says.

There are a few snickers. Either because that's not a word that usually comes out of Mr. Z's mouth, or because everyone knows the history between Reese and me.

"This is a moment of triumph for your characters," he goes on to explain. "They're ignoring poor Eliza because they're too infatuated with themselves. You need to build each other up. Give us more affection."

I get a funny twinge in my chest. Acting like I still have affection for Reese isn't the problem—it's making Reese see that I'm still worthy of his.

We take it again from the top. Reese and I were affectionate as boyfriends, so this shouldn't be hard. We just need to stop acting like we're afraid of each other. As I begin my first verse, I puff out my chest and move to throw my arm around him.

Unfortunately, Reese doesn't see me. He turns at the last second and I almost clothesline him in the neck. We both try to play it off, but I'm thrown for the rest of the scene.

"Okay," Mr. Z says, taking off his bifocals and pinching the bridge of his nose. "We'll work more on this next time."

After dismissing everyone for the day, Gretchen reminds us we need to be off-book when we return from spring break, which starts next week. As if any of us needed a reminder.

"Um, hey," I say, approaching Reese as he uncaps his water bottle. "Sorry if I screwed up that last scene."

He shakes his head. "I'm off my game today."

"Well, I could've warned you before I tried to put my arm around you."

"No. It's what the scene called for. It was a good idea."

A smile tugs at the corner of my lips. Did Reese just give me my first post-breakup compliment? *Not* that I'm gloating about my acting choices. That's something the old Wade would've done.

"We knew this was going to be kind of awkward, right?" Reese says. He takes a gulp of water, and my heart fills with the tiniest bit of hope. He's not trying to avoid me or brush me off. We're having an actual conversation.

"Maybe we just need to give it some more time," I say.

He sighs. "Seems like the show's going to be here before we know it."

I can hear the stress in his voice. I *know* that stress. Having the lead role and feeling like you're going to let the entire cast down if you fail.

"We could try harder," I offer. "I mean, to make it less awkward."

Reese looks at me. There's not going to be a better time to say this, so I just go for it. "I'm having people over this weekend. Ava, Hannah, Eb . . . the usual. It might be good for everyone to hang out again. As castmates, I mean. If you want to join us?"

He bites his lip, thinking it over. If he says no, I don't know what else to do. I'm running out of time.

"Yeah," he finally says. "That might not be a bad idea."

Air fills my lungs. Finally something's going right.

"Cool," I say. "Oh—and my friend Brady will also be there."

"Brady?" He gives me a funny look.

"He's great. I really think you're going to like him."

Reese nods, but I can already see his mind turning. He probably wants to know who Brady is, and why I'm bringing him up. I'm sure Reese doesn't fully trust me yet—which I get. But the last thing I want to do is make him suspicious or jealous. Quite the opposite. I'm doing all this for him. For us.

After saying goodbye to Reese, I practically float out of the theater. Could this be my turning point? If Reese is impressed by Brady, and he finds out I'm the one who's helping him, it could get our relationship—and my senior year—back on track.

Now I just have to make sure Elijah's up to the task.

Eighteen

ELIJAH

The wobble of the traffic cone is so slight, I'm praying my driving instructor chalks it up to a sudden gust of wind. Despite practicing my parallel parking all week, this was sadly one of my more successful attempts.

"Okay," the instructor says. "You can pull ahead and park off to the side."

"We're done?" I ask, my voice cracking.

He takes a sip from his coffee thermos. "We're done."

Shit. How long do you have to wait until you can retake the test? Spring break starts next weekend, and Dad got ahead of himself, already making a reservation for our camper cabin. I knew I'd end up disappointing him.

The instructor sighs as I put the car into park. "Well, Mr. Brady. When you fly a plane, you need to know how to land it."

Sure. But I'm not applying to become a pilot, so I'm not sure what he's getting at.

"You failed the entire parking portion of your test," he tells me.

Oh. He's being a dick. Got it.

He hands me the paperwork. "They'll process everything inside.

Congratulations." Without saying anything else, he reaches for the door handle.

"I'm sorry . . . *WHAT*?"

The instructor already has one foot on the pavement, like he can't wait to leave. But I'm going to need more of an explanation than that. What's there to process inside? Are they handing out participation trophies?

"You passed your test," he says. "By one point."

"But you just said—"

"You failed the parking but did fine on everything else."

It's a good thing we're parked right now; otherwise I'd probably crash straight into the DMV building, setting a record for the quickest turnaround time for a new license being revoked.

"Thank you," I tell the instructor. "You were wonderful."

He gives me a funny look, but I don't care. Now that I have my driver's license, I feel strangely invincible.

"You passed?" There's definitely a question mark at the end of Mom's sentence when I tell her the news, not an exclamation point. Not that I blame her for being shocked. Dad, on the other hand, apparently had faith in me. When Mom and I arrive home from the DMV, he's unpacking groceries in the kitchen.

Parmesan cheese. Heavy cream. A box of fettuccine noodles.

"Well?" he asks, holding a baguette.

I nod.

Dad engulfs me in a hug. Before he can get too excited, I remind him that I have Wade's party tonight. "Is it okay if we save the celebratory dinner for another evening?" I ask.

"Of course. I'll make dinner tomorrow."

"Cool, thanks." I eye the groceries on the counter. Now that I can drive, maybe it's time I learn to leave other parts of the old me behind, too.

"And, uh, as much as I like your fettuccine Alfredo . . . do you think we could do taco night instead?"

Dad doesn't even blink. "Sure thing, kid. This is your celebration. Whatever you want."

Huh. Maybe a little independence is nice.

Putting my newly gained independence to use, it still feels surreal to be behind the wheel on my own as I pull into Wade's driveway later that evening. I don't know that I have more confidence now, but there's definitely less fear. I took my driver's test and didn't fail. Maybe tonight won't be so bad, either.

"Does it hurt?" Wade asks, opening his front door with a grin.

"Does what hurt?"

"Knowing I was right?"

"Calm down," I say, rolling my eyes. "I *barely* passed."

"Still, you can drive now and that's—*Oh*."

I follow his gaze to my car, which I'm realizing is parked at a forty-five-degree angle.

"Can we just go inside?" I ask.

"Wait. I have to give you your present first."

My cheeks flare up. I hate opening presents in front of people. There's too much pressure to act happy, or surprised, or grateful—even when you really are those things. And Wade's already done so much for me. I wasn't expecting this.

"Don't get too excited. It's not much."

He hands me a keychain. One of those fake rabbit's feet.

"I used to bring it to auditions. For good luck." He pauses. And I could be wrong, but his cheeks also seem a bit pink. "Sorry, I should've gotten you something nicer."

I stare at it, rubbing the faux fur with my thumb. This probably means more to him than anything he could've spent money on. It's a small gesture, but I can't think of the last time someone's done anything like it for me.

"Anyway, you don't have to use it. It's more symbolic, really."

"It's perfect," I tell him, which makes him smile again.

When we head inside, Wade takes my coat and I catch my reflection in the mirror that's hanging in the entryway. I'm still not used to seeing myself with my hair like this. Mom and Dad loved the color, which made me want to hate it at first. But I have to admit, even though it calls more attention to me, I kind of like it.

"Checking yourself out?" Wade asks, sneaking up next to me.

I step back, embarrassed. "I wasn't . . . I just . . ."

He leans against the wall, crossing his arms. "C'mon. You know you look good, *Brady*."

Yeah, that's that other part I still haven't gotten used to. I don't feel like Brady yet. But when I look in the mirror, I don't really see Elijah anymore, either. I guess tonight's my first real test to see how much I've changed.

"Remember, this is just a dress rehearsal," Wade tells me. "It's okay to stumble through it."

I look at myself in the mirror again. The hair, my posture, the flannel shirt I picked out . . . *What if his friends see right through them?* I'm glad Wade's here to help me. But *I'm* the one who has to perform. Forget stumbling—I'm afraid I'll choke. And his friends are all actors, so they're going to know.

"Oh, I almost forgot," Wade says. "I'm giving you another homework assignment."

"Seriously?" my voice squeaks. "Don't I have enough to worry about?"

"Brady needs to make a friend," he says, ignoring me. "It can't be Ava, or anyone from the lighting crew. It should be someone you don't know as well yet. And it doesn't have to happen tonight, necessarily—though I want you to at least lay some groundwork."

My skin suddenly itches. It took me a while just to relax around Wade. Do I really have to start over with someone else?

"You said you wanted to be the type of person who could walk into a room and make friends," he reminds me. "Think of this as the first step. *One* new friend. That's it."

I open my mouth to protest, but the front door swings open. Ava and two other girls I recognize from rehearsals come barging in.

"Who ordered strippers?" shouts one of them—a white girl, with an impressive mane of curly brown hair that seems to fly in every direction.

"Do you mind?" Ava gives her a look as she presses her phone to her chest. "I'm talking to Drew."

"Sorry, does Drew have something against women who empower themselves by removing their clothes for monetary compensation?"

Ava rolls her eyes and heads into the other room to finish her conversation.

"Everything okay?" Wade asks, raising an eyebrow.

"Hopefully," says the third girl, who has dark brown skin and wears her braided hair in a bun. When she notices me standing here, she offers a warm smile. "Hey, I'm Ebony. You must be Brady."

I freeze, forgetting for a moment that I am.

"I'm Hannah," says the girl with the curly hair. She opens her bag and pulls out a bottle with brown liquid sloshing around inside. "This here's Jack."

"Whiskey?" Wade asks. "What is this, a Tennessee Williams play?"

"It's not bad if you mix it with Coke."

He takes the bottle from her. "How much have you had already?"

Her mouth drops open, pretending to be shocked. "This is just my boisterous personality. Trust me—when I start drinking, you'll know."

We all head into the kitchen, except for Ava, who seems to have disappeared. Wade sets the whiskey on the counter next to some plastic cups and various bags of chips. "Has anyone heard from Reese?" he asks in a voice that's slightly higher than usual. *Is Wade nervous too?*

"He said he was coming," Ebony replies.

"Yeah. Cool. I'm just trying to figure out how many pizzas to order."

Hannah and Ebony exchange a look. Wade rubs the back of his neck. "Well, um, I'll check on Ava."

He leaves the kitchen. Now that I'm alone with Hannah and Ebony, I feel very much like an underclassman again. They showed up with whiskey. My parents let me have half a glass of champagne

151

at my cousin's wedding last summer, and I spent forty-five minutes hiding in the coat check afterward.

My phone buzzes in my pocket.

Ask questions.

Don't give one-word answers.

Right, I'm supposed to be practicing. "So," I say, straightening my posture as I think of something good to ask. "Do you have any plans for—"

"We've been dying to meet you," Hannah interrupts, latching on to my arm. "Wade says you're funny. But don't worry, I won't put you on the spot. I hate when people expect me to be on all the time, you know?"

She drags me over to the couch, where I suddenly find myself sandwiched between the two of them. "Now tell us something interesting about yourself."

So much for not putting me on the spot. The first thing that pops into my head is that a group of chickens is called a peep. But Wade wouldn't want me to say that, so I keep searching for ideas until I land on something else.

"Um . . . I still have one of my baby teeth?"

Wow. Because that's definitely better.

"Like, in a jar?" Ebony asks.

"No, it's in my mouth."

Fuck. Should've gone with the peep.

"So you and Wade," Hannah says, dropping her voice to a conspiratorial whisper. "He says you've been spending a lot of time together?"

My pulse quickens. How much has he told her? Asking someone

to help you make friends is embarrassing enough. Wade hasn't been telling other people about our deal. Has he?

"Um," I say. "I guess we have."

She smiles. "That's nice."

Her statement feels weighted, though I'm not sure why. Does she think something's going on between us? My makeover was an improvement, sure, but my head hasn't grown big enough to think Wade could ever be into me like that.

"Pizzas are on their way," Wade says, reappearing with Ava.

"Is Drew coming?" Ebony asks.

Ava tucks her hair behind her ears, smiling weakly. "I got our schedules mixed up. But he says hi and he's sorry to have missed out."

Wade puts his arm around her. "Let's head downstairs. Brady, you're in charge of picking the movie."

My stomach flips. It's a small thing, but I don't want the responsibility of making a decision for the group. Which is probably why Wade gave it to me. He shoots me a smile as I get up from the couch. At least one of us seems confident that I can fool everyone tonight.

Nineteen

ELIJAH

Sitting on the couch in Wade's basement—which is covered in Fighting Irish pillows and a Michigan Wolverines blanket—I've somehow escaped having to make a decision. Wade and his friends started listing my choices, and it quickly turned into a debate that's been going on for so long, we probably could've finished a movie by now.

"*Singin' in the Rain*'s too cheesy," Hannah says.

Wade throws up his hands. "Cheesy? It's from the golden age of movie musicals!"

She gives him a glaring look. "Please, I beg you to hear the words coming out of your mouth."

"Maybe we should switch it up and watch a non-musical," Ava suggests.

"A horror movie!" Hannah says.

Ebony shakes her head. "Nothing where the only Black person dies first."

Wade opens a box of pizza, grabbing another slice of pepperoni. "I don't know why we bother fighting it. We're just going to end up watching *High School Musical* like we always do."

Ava tosses a piece of crust at him.

"What? Don't act like you're suddenly above the greatest movie musical franchise of all time."

Ebony turns toward me. "Hey, wasn't Brady supposed to pick? Which movie did you want to watch?"

It's like there's suddenly a spotlight on me. I eye Wade, but he doesn't give me any help. Probably because I have to speak for myself. "I actually haven't seen any of those before," I say. "I'm happy to watch whatever."

"*Any* of them?" Ebony asks, shocked. "Not even at a cast party?"

"*My Fair Lady* is the first play I've worked on."

"Musical," Wade and Hannah say simultaneously.

"Ooh, what about *Mamma Mia!*?" Ebony says. "It's a great introduction to the genre."

Ava frowns. "'Lay All Your Love on Me' will remind me of Drew."

"Ugh!" Hannah jumps up from the couch. "This is going to require more alcohol."

Not everyone is drinking. Which is good—there's no pressure to join them. Not that I would've; I'm not drinking and driving. Plus, playing Brady takes concentration. I need to stay in control.

"Hey," Hannah says, waving an empty two-liter of Coke. "Who wants to be my new best friend and run upstairs?"

"I'll go," I say, a bit too eagerly.

The other thing about playing Brady is that it's kind of exhausting. I could use a break.

In the quietness of Wade's kitchen, I take out my phone and scroll through the Instagram account he set up for me. I have more followers now. Mostly people from the show, including Connor—which is ironic. Maybe he thinks I'll help him get closer to Wade.

Actually . . . I haven't really thought about Connor lately. Like, at all. If Wade hadn't intervened, I'd probably still be trying to get him to notice me. Wade said I shouldn't have let Connor treat me the way he did. Maybe I'm finally starting to agree.

Of course, I have to find *someone* to befriend for my new assignment. Wade's friends seem cool. And so far, even though I'm a sophomore who doesn't share their encyclopedic knowledge of musicals, they've done their best to include me. But I don't think that's the same as them *wanting* to be friends with me. I mean, they hardly know anything about me. I need to work on putting myself out there more.

While I still haven't posted anything on my Instagram, I do like how you can get to know more about people by what pops up in your feed. Szabo, for example, posts reviews of the books he's reading. Rhodes and Yang like to sneak candid shots of each other at the Kowalski's they work at together. They have this ongoing joke where they pose with all the different produce. And Summer takes these really cool black-and-white photos.

I look back at the picture of Wade, Ava, and me on my bed. I know social media can be deceiving, and I only started hanging out with Wade so I could learn how to be more confident. But he set up this party for me tonight, and he gave me his lucky rabbit's foot—those things don't feel fake. Wade wants me to lay the groundwork to become friends with someone. But it feels like I've already done that with him.

Sighing, I put my phone away and grab another bottle of Coke. Before I can head back down, there's a knock on the front door. *Did we order more pizza?* No one comes up from the basement, so I guess it's on me to check.

Since I thought the general consensus was that Reese blew off Wade tonight, I'm a little surprised when I find him standing on the front stoop. "Oh," I say, gripping the door handle tight. "Um . . . hi."

"Hey," he replies, giving me a head nod that just oozes confidence. *How can one person be so effortlessly cool and hot?*

"Everyone's downstairs," I tell him, but of course my voice does this weird wobble thing. "They're still trying to pick out a movie."

"You mean we're not just watching *High School Musical* again?"

"It was brought up. More than once."

He shakes his head, smiling. "I'm Reese, by the way."

"I know who you are," I reply. My face immediately flushes. "Um, I'm Brady."

He squints, giving me a funny look. "Huh, I thought your name was Elijah."

What? My heart slams against my chest. How does he—*Oh*, the Name Game. Elegant Elijah's going to haunt me forever, isn't it?

As much as I want to disintegrate right about now, I can hear Wade telling me to remember my improv lesson: *let go of your fear and think on your feet.*

"Only my parents call me Elijah," I say, rolling my eyes a bit.

Reese smiles again and something lights up inside of me. It wasn't the most brilliant reply—but it worked. Before he can respond, screams of laughter break out from downstairs.

He arches an eyebrow. "Sounds like they're in fine form tonight."

"Hannah brought whiskey."

"Right. Because if there's one thing theater kids need, it's less inhibition." He pauses, rubbing his hand across the back of his neck. "Sorry, that sounded bitchy. I'm obviously in theater, too. I just haven't been at it as long."

"Same," I tell him. "I don't even know what they're talking about half the time."

He laughs. "Yeah, it can seem a bit like a clique. Although I think theater kids are probably more accepting than most people at school."

"What do you mean?" I can't imagine anyone not accepting Reese.

"Well . . . " He thinks about it for a second. "On my soccer team, being gay isn't an issue for most of my teammates. But there are definitely a few guys who seem uncomfortable sharing a locker room with me. When you're doing a show, no one thinks twice about who they're changing in front of. Because it's not a big deal."

I nod. A brief silence falls between us, and it hits me—we're having a conversation. Like, a real one. And I'm not totally freaking out. Maybe it's because I didn't have time to think about it. Or maybe because Reese is surprisingly easy to talk to.

"How are you feeling about this year's show?" I say, remembering to ask questions.

"The honest answer?" He puffs out his cheeks. "Pretty stressed. This is my first time in a lead role. I'm worried I'll fuck it up."

"Did you know they dubbed over Audrey Hepburn's singing in the movie?" I ask. "Her parts were sung by Marni Nixon, who they also used for *West Side Story* and *The King and I*. So, um . . . things could always be worse. At least they're still letting you sing, right?"

Reese tilts his head, slowly breaking into a smile. "Yeah, that's one way of looking at it."

I return his smile. It's a good thing I decided to learn some *My Fair Lady* trivia on my own after the movie night with Wade.

Before I can explain to Reese how it's not meteorologically accurate that the rain in Spain would mainly stay on the plain, the door behind us opens. "Hey, what happened to Hannah's—" Wade stops when he sees Reese standing in his hallway. "Oh. You came."

He shrugs. "I told you I would."

"And you met Brady."

"Yeah, we were just catching up about the show."

Wade shoots me a quick look, like he approves.

"We agreed on a movie," he says. "I could tell you what it was, but then I wouldn't get to see you shiver with antici—"

I wait for him to finish, but he and Reese just stare at each other.

". . . *pation*," Reese finally says, completing Wade's sentence.

Once again, I have no idea what's happening.

"*Rocky Horror Picture Show*," Wade explains, picking up on my cluelessness.

"You've never seen it before?" Reese asks.

I shake my head.

They look at each other. "A virgin!"

I know they're only talking about the movie, but I'm sure my face is bright red again. Thankfully, we head back down to the basement, where Wade huddles everyone together for a quick group photo before we start.

The Rocky Horror Picture Show is pretty much the exact opposite of *My Fair Lady*. There's a time warp, a mad scientist named Dr. Frank-N-Furter, and everyone runs around in their underwear. Also, Wade and his friends keep shouting things at the movie. I don't really get why they're heckling. But that doesn't stop me from laughing along with them.

Halfway through the movie, my phone lights up with notifications from my Instagram. Wade must've logged into my account, because when I open the app, our group selfie is there, along with a caption about watching *Rocky Horror* together. It has a few likes already, and even a comment from Connor, saying he's jealous.

Connor Goldfarb.

Jealous of me.

Looking at the photo, I'm surprised by how genuine my smile is.

A text pops up on my phone: **Having fun?**

I look over at Wade, who's texting me from the other end of the couch. Tonight was only supposed to be a practice run, but it's been pretty fun. If not for me, then for Brady. I like spending time with Wade and his friends.

Yes, I reply.

Good, he responds. **Me too.**

A warm, fuzzy feeling spreads through me. Like taking a sip of hot chocolate on a cold day. Everything good that happened tonight was because of Wade. He did his best to make sure I felt comfortable and prepared. No one's ever looked out for me like that. I know my homework assignment is to befriend someone I don't know yet. But who's to say I couldn't do that and *also* be friends with Wade?

Hey, I text back. Are you doing anything for spring break?

Just memorizing lines. Why?

Everyone shouts at the TV again.

I type out my reply, my heart beating faster as I hit send.

How do you feel about camping?

Twenty

WADE

Last year, I went a bit overboard with my campaign for junior prom king. My competition was stiff; I knew I needed the non–theater kid vote, too. So I hung posters, handed out buttons, and ordered three hundred custom-made chocolate bars that had *Westmores Always Win* printed on the wrapper.

In retrospect, using my brothers' slogan probably wasn't the smartest idea. Especially since I *didn't* win, and then had to live down the embarrassment of being wrong. Part of my motivation for wanting the crown so badly was because TJ and Brett had both won while they were at Monroe. I wanted to prove I was just as good as them.

This year my motivation's a little different.

It's not about beating my brothers anymore. It's about winning back Reese and sharing that kiss on the dance floor after we've both been crowned.

"Greetings, Monroe Academy!" The chipper voice coming over the PA system belongs to Mrs. Lundgren, our dean of students. Anyone who's seen *Fargo* and thought people from Minnesota couldn't actually talk like that hasn't heard Mrs. Lundgren before.

"In just a moment, we'll be revealing the nominees for junior and senior prom court. But first, some important announcements."

People groan and go back to doing unfinished homework and talking among friends.

"Hey," Ebony says to me from one desk over. "Are you nervous?"

"Not really," I lie. "You?"

She shrugs. "I'm not holding my breath."

As Mrs. Lundgren goes on about yearbook orders and an upcoming jazz band concert, the suspense starts getting to me. At least when we're waiting for a cast list to be posted, we know we're competing with a small group of people, not the entire senior class. Plus, for the most part, talent and ability are taken into account.

Prom court's definitely a popularity contest. I was the only non-jock nominated among the junior guys last year, and the crown went to Jeremy Wenninger, who plays varsity baseball and is a total clown. Even if I'm nominated again, I doubt I could get enough votes to beat him.

"Which finally brings us to prom court," Mrs. Lundgren says.

Everyone gets quiet again. She starts with the juniors, and I silently pump my fist when she reads off Reese's name. As someone who does both soccer and the musical, he has a very real chance of winning. Which only adds more pressure on me.

"Before we move on to our seniors," Mrs. Lundgren says, "I'd like to remind everyone that every day, you have the potential to be your own king or queen. True royalty doesn't need a crown."

"What does that even mean," Ebony whispers.

"And now, without further ado, our nominees for senior prom queen are Olivia Campbell, Ashley Kim, Mia Roszkowski, and Ebony Sinclair."

Ebony lets out a shriek, quickly clamping a hand over her mouth.

People start to clap and congratulate her, until Mrs. Lundgren moves on to the candidates for prom king.

"Drew Bauer, Jacob Lombardi, Marcus Paulson, and . . ."

Mrs. Lundgren trails off for a second, like she's lost her place while reading. My heart immediately sinks. There's only one spot left, and she hasn't said Jeremy Wenninger's name yet. There's no way he didn't get nominated.

". . . and Wade Westmore."

Now it's my turn to be shocked. My heart swells as I look around, catching a few smiles directed back at me. I can't believe it. Reese and I are both nominated. We're one step closer to the happy ending I've planned for us.

"That's bullshit," says Evan Connelly, another baseball player. "If we weren't forced to take so many art electives, Jeremy's GPA would still be high enough to be eligible."

Jocks being passionate about prom court. It's so beautiful I could almost cry.

After homeroom gets out, Ebony and I walk to our next class together, linking arms and feeling giddy about our nominations.

"Is it silly that I want to win?" she asks.

"No," I tell her. "Definitely not."

"It's just . . . I've spent the past three years trying to keep my GPA high enough for Stanford. And once college starts, I'll spend the next four years making sure I can get into med school. I want to have some fun now, before it's too late."

If anyone deserves the crown, it's Ebony. She's an exceptional student and a really good person—everything a prom queen should be.

"Hey," Ebony says. "We should celebrate at lunch today."

She's asking me to sit at the theater table again. Where Reese will also be—fresh off his own nomination. And, actually, I can't think of anything I'd rather do more.

At lunch, I grip my tray a little tighter as I approach our table. Everything seemed cool between us when Reese watched *Rocky Horror* at my house this past weekend. But I don't want to push him too far, too fast.

This would be easier if Ava were eating with us today, but since Drew was also nominated, she's at his table. I feel bad campaigning against her boyfriend, and even worse knowing I've probably already lost her vote. Not that I blame Ava for choosing her boyfriend over me. I just wish I had someone who would always put me first.

"Well, if it isn't the Meryl Streep of prom court nominations," Hannah says when she spots me standing in front of their table.

"Okay if I join you?" I ask.

"Sure, if you don't mind sitting in a chair. We have so many nominees at this table, we've run out of thrones."

Hannah's being funny, but there's a hint of bitterness to her tone. I didn't peg her as the type to care about prom court. I think she's a bit like me; we both get jealous when the attention's not on us.

There are two empty chairs at the table. One across from Reese, and one directly beside him. I take a breath and set my tray down next to his.

"Congrats on the nomination," I tell him.

He bites into a chicken nugget, offering me a fist bump. "Likewise."

A fist bump's not very romantic. But it's progress.

"Saturday night was fun," I say. I'm dying to jump right into it and ask if he has a date to prom yet. But I have to be patient. Let him see that I've changed first. "I'm really glad you could come."

He nods. "It was good to get the crew back together."

"And you got to meet Brady."

I watch him closely, waiting for a reaction. But Reese just drags another nugget through the ketchup on his plate. "Yeah. He seemed chill."

"He is. And he's really smart, too. He knows all these trivia facts. Like, did you know a group of chickens is called a peep?" I laugh, remembering Elijah's face when he said that. "Anyhow, it's been fun getting to know him."

Reese raises an eyebrow. "Sounds like you two are spending a lot of time together."

I have to bite back my smile. Maybe Hannah's already talked to him. "Yeah, I guess so. He invited me to go camping over spring break."

"Really?" Reese's voice rises a pitch.

He sounds surprised. Or maybe it's something else? *Does Reese wish I was spending more time with him? Is he jealous of Elijah?* Before I can get too excited, a sour taste hits the back of my throat. *Am I using Elijah to win back Reese?* I mean—I am. But I thought it was okay because we were both getting something out of it.

Now that we're going camping together, though, it feels different. It was really nice of Elijah to invite me; I wasn't expecting that. And I'm actually looking forward to going. My parents are planning to visit TJ for a few days during break, so now I won't be all alone. Plus, I meant what I said about Elijah—I like spending time with him.

"We should hang out again," I tell Reese. "The three of us. I can put us in a group text together."

If I'm going to use Elijah to help me, the least I can do is continue helping him. Spending more time with my friends will be good for him—more practice as Brady.

"Sure," Reese says, oblivious to the dot of ketchup on the corner of his mouth. "And hey, if you still have time over break, maybe we could get together with Ava and run lines. I don't know about you two, but I'm nervous about being off-book."

I could grab him by the face and kiss him right now, ketchup and all.

"That's a great idea," I say, trying to contain my excitement.

Reese wants to hang out with me again, unprompted. Sure, he technically included Ava in that scenario; still, it's a step in the right direction.

While it's definitely too early to start picking out matching boutonnieres, I walk the hallway in a daze after lunch. Strolling down the red carpet with Reese at prom would feel great. But even better than that would be our celebratory dance in front of everyone. My hands on Reese's waist, his eyes locked into mine, the soft touch of our lips finding each other again. That breathless moment that comes with a good kiss.

I have to go all out for my campaign this year. I'm already thinking up better slogans.

Vote for Wade . . . unless you want to seem a tad homophobic.

Much like Simba, I just can't wait to be king!

Wade Westmore: I'm less of a self-centered asshole now, I swear.

Turning the corner, I snap out of my daydreaming long enough to spot Ava. I run up to her, excited to tell her everything that's happened. When I spot the tears on her face, though, my feet stop short.

"Ava, what's wrong?"

She chokes out a sob. "I broke up with Drew."

"What?!"

Her bottom lip quivers. "I don't have a date to prom anymore."

People are starting to stare. I quickly put my arm around her and guide her to the nearest restroom. "What happened?" I ask, checking the stalls to confirm we're alone.

She takes a moment to collect herself. "I was so excited about his nomination today. At lunch I started brainstorming where we could make dinner reservations. You know how we were going to hang out with theater people before the dance, and the wrestling team afterward, right?" She sniffles, taking the piece of toilet paper I offer her. "He tried to change our plans, saying we'd have more fun if we hung out with his friends only, not any of you."

I wish I could take pleasure in being right about Drew. But I'm practically vibrating with anger. And not because he doesn't like me and our theater friends. I'm more pissed that he could do this to Ava. She's been nothing but loyal to him.

"He's an asshole," I say. "You don't need him."

"I know." Fresh tears roll down her cheeks. "But it feels like I might've made a mistake."

The bell rings. I wrap her in the tightest hug possible. "You didn't. I promise."

Ava nods, then mutters into my chest. "Maybe we should just both go stag. Fuck having prom dates, right?"

My vision of kissing Reese on the dance floor flashes before me again. I'm not ready to give up that dream yet. But I can't let Ava down, either. She's my best friend; I'll always be there for her.

"Yeah," I say, trying to reassure both of us. "We'll figure something out."

Twenty-One

ELIJAH

It feels criminal to be standing in my kitchen this early on the first Saturday of spring break. Like, my parents should be in jail right now. Or maybe *I'm* the one who's in jail. I don't know, I've already lost the thread of this metaphor because it's still dark outside and my body knows it should be in bed, deep under the covers.

"You sure you don't want granola bars?" Mom asks.

"We'll get breakfast on the way," Dad replies. "Besides, I made trail mix."

Yeah, enough trail mix that we could get lost in the woods for days and not starve. Which—I really hope that's not Dad's secret plan.

"I wouldn't mind some more coffee," Wade says cheerily, holding up the mug I made in grade school, complete with an unfortunate-looking stick figure family.

Mom smiles. "Of course."

"How about we put it in a thermos," Dad says. "For the road."

It's a three-hour drive to the state park, and Dad's itching to have as much daylight as possible to explore. Once we finally make it out into the driveway, he double-checks everything from his packing list: zero-degree sleeping bags, reusable heat packs, and more wool socks than we could possibly wear in the few days we'll be gone.

"We need a photo," Wade says. "To document the beginning of our trip."

"I can take it," Dad says.

"Selfies are better," Wade explains. "Besides, you're part of this, Mr. Brady."

This gets a big grin out of Dad. "Please, call me Tom."

"Wait . . . *Tom Brady?*" His jaw drops. "Like the quarterback?"

"Yes. But I don't really follow sports."

"He holds the record for having won the most—" Wade stops, shaking his head. "You know what, it's not important."

We take the selfie and Dad finishes loading up the trunk. "Don't put that on Instagram," I tell Wade. "I look like I should be holding up a newspaper with today's date on it."

"It's not for Instagram." He smiles. "But I'm proud of you for showing a little vanity."

"Elijah." Dad holds up his car keys. "Care to do the honors?"

My driving's questionable enough on a full night of sleep. "Maybe on the drive home," I say, opening the door behind the passenger seat.

Wade gives me a look. "You don't want to sit up front with your dad?"

"I want to lie down and not speak to anyone until the sun comes up," I reply, climbing in before he can say anything. It's my birthday trip. The least they can do is give me this.

As tired as I am, once we get on the road, Wade and Dad won't shut up long enough for me to get much sleep.

"I love *Guys and Dolls,*" Wade says. "I bet you made a great Rusty Charlie."

"Well, I don't know about that," Dad replies. "But I had fun."

"The movie's a classic."

"Sinatra and Brando. Can't beat that casting."

"Yes. But Jean Simmons and Vivian Blaine deserve their credit, too."

Dad laughs. "I'm impressed! You really know your stuff."

I should be annoyed with how well Wade and my dad are getting along. But it's kind of nice to see Wade so excitable and dorky. If Connor had come on this trip—which he *never* would have—he'd probably just act like he was above everything.

About halfway into the drive, we pull into a gas station to grab some egg sandwiches that manage to be both disgustingly rubbery and greasily delicious. As Dad uses the restroom before we leave again, Wade wanders the aisles in search of junk food.

I take out my phone while waiting for them and find a text. It's the selfie we took this morning. Except Wade didn't send it only to me. There's another number, one that's not in my phone.

"Hey, I don't know what kind of gummy worm person you are," Wade says, holding up two bags of candy. "Regular or sour?"

"Sour." I hold out my phone. "Who else did you send this to?"

"Reese. I told him about our trip."

"Why?"

He shrugs. "I don't know. Because that's what friends do?"

Sure, but Wade and Reese are friends. I don't factor into that equation. Unless—is Wade trying to give me a head start on my homework assignment? I turn around, hiding a smile. No, that's absurd. Reese and I had one conversation. Besides, choosing someone like him would be like going for extra, *extra* credit.

We still have a lot of driving ahead of us once we're back on the road. But at least the sun is up now. And as we get farther up north, the monotony of the interstate fades away. Billboards and chain restaurants are replaced by farmhouses and long rows of evergreens. Eventually Lake Superior comes into view.

"I forgot how beautiful it is," Wade says.

Dad nods. "It's something else, isn't it?"

Even I can't be cynical about Lake Superior as it zips by my window in an endless blur of glistening blue. It's an impressive body of water. (Trivia fact: Lake Superior holds 10 percent of the world's surface fresh water.)

(Second trivia fact: although Minnesota's known as the "Land of 10,000 Lakes," our actual tally is 11,842.)

(Third trivia fact: Wisconsin tries to claim they have more lakes than us. But Wisconsin is full of cheese-loving liars.)

As Dad and Wade continue taking in the view, my phone lights up with more texts.

Damn. Can't believe you guys woke up that early.

Try not to freeze your asses off.

I look up, waiting to see if Wade will respond. But he's not paying attention to his phone. Great. Reese and I might not be friends, but I don't want him to think I'm ignoring him. I chew my lip, thinking up a response.

Better our asses than our balls.

I'm completely mortified when I hit send. But Reese responds quickly with an LOL.

You're up early yourself, I text.

My five-year-old sister doesn't really get the concept of Saturday mornings.

I stare at my phone, racking my brain for something clever to say. Nothing comes to me, though, so I send back a thumbs-up emoji. When Reese doesn't respond after a minute, it's clear I've killed the conversation—further proof he's too far out of my potential friend orbit.

Finally arriving at the entrance to the state park later that morning, Dad goes into full Boy Scout mode and helps us strap on our backpacks. It's a mile walk just to get to our camper cabin, which is nothing compared to the trails. Hiking still isn't my idea of a fun birthday weekend, but as long as we don't have to survive off wild berries and handfuls of snow, I'll take it as a win.

And actually, now that I've had a chance to wake up and get moving, I'm not hating this. The sun's shining brightly, the air smells crisper, and there's something satisfying about the crunch of snow underneath my brand-new hiking boots.

One aspect I'm still not sold on, however, is the camper cabin. Dad showed me the website ahead of time, so I knew what to expect. But as we arrive at a clearing in the middle of the woods, I'm disappointed to find it looks even smaller in person.

"Sweet," Wade says, walking up the snowy pathway.

The cabin has a picnic table and firepit out front, plus a screened-in porch. None of which seem practical for this time of year. And the inside is sparsely decorated, emphasis on *sparsely*: there's a kitchen table, a futon with a dirty mattress, and a wooden ladder that leads up to a small storage space.

"Well," Dad says. "What do we think?"

My stomach drops as I look around. "Where's the bathroom?"

"You know how to dig a hole, right?"

"Please tell me you're joking," I whisper.

Dad smiles. "There's an outhouse around back. Just don't forget this." He tosses me a roll of toilet paper from his backpack. I'm too shocked to catch it, though, so it hits me in the chest and drops to the floor.

"Wow," Wade says. "We're really roughing it, huh?"

He has a big grin on his face—like he's actually excited about this. I never would've pegged him as an outdoorsman. Wade Westmore contains multitudes, I guess.

"Not fully roughing it," Dad says. "The forecast called for a chance of snow later, and it'll get cold tonight. So we'll be glad to have this baby." He crouches next to an electric heater near the baseboard, letting it hiss to life. "It'll take a while to warm up the place. I figured we could unpack and then go for our first hike."

When Dad stands, he grabs his sleeping bag and tosses it onto the futon. "Heat rises. I'll let you two sleep up in the loft together."

Up in the . . . *what*?

My eyes travel over to the ladder, slowly following the rungs up to the tiny space above. Wade and I are sleeping together? *Next to each other?* I suddenly long for my life a minute ago, when my biggest concern was using an outhouse.

Wade looks at me. "Should we check it out?"

I let Wade climb the ladder first. The space is so cramped he can't even stand upright without his head touching the sloped ceiling. And when we roll out our sleeping bags, they overlap by an inch.

Wade lies down on his side of the loft and pats mine, like he wants me to join him. Since he doesn't seem to think this is awkward, I reluctantly comply.

"Look." He points up. "We'll be sleeping under the stars."

There's a skylight above us. Bare tree branches sway hypnotically in the winter sky.

"Pretty nice, right?" he asks, resting his hands behind his head.

"Yeah. I guess."

He kicks me with his foot.

"Ow. What was that for?"

You guess? He makes a face. "Sorry, didn't realize you were too cool for this."

"I'm not. It's just . . ." I lower my voice, so my dad won't hear. "Camping's more my dad's thing. I didn't ask to go on this trip for my birthday. I usually just let my parents make decisions for me."

Wade turns on to his side, facing me. "Okay. Well, what did you want instead?"

I have to think about it for a second. "Honestly? Most years I just want to stay home and avoid celebrating altogether."

"C'mon. No one hates their birthday."

It's not that I hate my birthday. I just hate most of the things that come with having one. Like the attention. And the parties. It was easy enough in grade school. You didn't have to worry much about whether or not people really liked you then. That was never the point of accepting an invitation to someone's birthday—the point was that you'd get to go bowling or play laser tag, then consume endless amounts of pizza and cupcakes.

It's different in high school. Now that we're old enough to go bowling on our own and order all the pizza we want, the allure of celebrating your birthday is more about the friendship. And so far, being close to people is not something I've excelled at.

So maybe spending the night in the middle of the woods with only my dad and Wade *is* the perfect way to celebrate.

"Fine," I say. "I don't hate this birthday."

Wade gives my shoulder a light shove. "Good."

Being vulnerable makes me want to bury my face in my sleeping bag. But if there's anyone I can open up to, it might be Wade. I mean, in all the time we've spent together, he's never once acted like he's embarrassed to be seen with me.

"I'm really glad you're here," I tell him.

As soon as the words are out of my mouth, I wish I could take them back. Because Wade's just staring at me, blinking his long dark eyelashes as his floppy hair rests perfectly over his forehead like it always does. What if I was wrong about him? What if he's only here because he feels sorry for me?

He smiles. And it's his full Wade Westmore smile—charming, attractive, and bright.

"Yeah. I'm glad too."

I get that warm, fuzzy feeling. The one that makes me feel excited about the possibility of us being friends.

"We should head out soon," Dad calls up from below. "We only have the sun for about seven more hours."

Wade stands up quickly, almost bumping his head. I may not be as excited as he and Dad are, but I'm determined to make the best of it. Seven hours of hiking is better than seven hours of sitting alone in my bedroom, feeling sorry for myself.

After we're properly suited up, we begin our journey. There are a few other hikers out today, but for the most part, the trail seems like it's all ours. Dad points out the different species of trees along the way—aspen, cedar, birch—and Wade looks up at each one with awe, proudly wearing the whistle Dad bought, in case we get lost or run into a bear.

Thankfully, even in the middle of nowhere, there are still occasional pockets of cell service. When I take out my phone, I have a new text from Reese. Except this time . . . *he's only sent it to me?* What the hell? This has to be a mistake.

How's Wade doing? Did you have to call the medevac yet?

I hesitate, but only for a second. Texting Reese is intimidating. But making fun of Wade? That I can do.

Are you kidding me? I type. **He's loving every second of this.**

I don't believe you. Send photographic evidence.

"Hey, Wade," I shout, holding out my phone.

He turns around to look at me. And without me even saying anything, he flashes me a peace sign with his thick winter gloves.

I immediately send it to Reese.

LMAO. What a dork.

Total dork, I reply.

I look at the photo and smile. Dorky Wade is quickly becoming my favorite version of him.

Twenty-Two

WADE

As the shimmery surface of Lake Superior peeks through the breaks in the trees, something wet drops onto my eyelash. I blink it away, thinking it must be sweat—we've been hiking for a while now. But then a thick white flake lands on my jacket. It's just the one at first. Then a few more. Then, quicker than they can dissolve, the flakes begin to multiply.

"It's snowing!"

My voice cracks with excitement. I'm usually well over snow by this time of year. But out here in the middle of nowhere, where I don't have to think about the musical, or prom, or my pending application to NYU . . . it's kind of magical again.

I look to see if Elijah's noticed it yet, but his head's bent over his phone. I scoop up a handful of old snow from the ground and toss it at him.

"Hey! What was that for?"

"You're missing it."

He slides his phone back into his jacket. "Oh. Yeah. Cool."

After we stand there for a minute, taking in the calm silence that comes with snowfall, Mr. Brady pulls out his map. "It's at least another mile to the ice caves. I'm not sure we should continue."

My shoulders sink. Seriously? It's too beautiful to turn back!

He looks up at the graying sky. "The forecast said the heaviest part of the storm would pass by to the south. We'd probably be okay, but I'd hate to get stuck on the trail."

"One mile is nothing," I say. "We could walk faster."

"I don't know. It'll take us a while just to get to the cabin from here . . ."

Elijah looks at me, then at his dad. "C'mon, Dad. You spent forever talking to the guy at the sporting goods store, making sure these were the best boots they sold. We might as well put them to good use. Besides, you said this trip is supposed to be an adventure, right?"

His dad folds up his map. "Okay, but if this weather gets worse, we're turning around."

I've never considered myself much of an outdoor person, so it's surprising that I'm enjoying this as much as I am. I like that there's nothing competitive about hiking. No one's trying to score the most points or be the first to reach the finish line. There's not even an audience to impress. The only person you're doing it for is yourself.

Plus, it's nice to hang out with Mr. Brady and Elijah. Out here Elijah and I don't have to focus on Brady so much, we can just relax and have fun.

Since the trail snakes around, and the uneven terrain is now slick with snow, it takes us another hour to arrive at our destination. Once we get there, though, the view is totally worth it. As we stand on a large rock formation jutting over the water, the lake stretches out before us, eventually blurring with the horizon.

"There are the caves," Mr. Brady says, pointing to the polished sheets of ice that hang over the arches along the rocky shoreline below. "Some years, when it's cold enough for the lake to freeze over, they let you walk around in there and explore."

"Wow," I say, taking it all in. "I bet that's amazing."

"Mmm," Elijah replies.

Except Elijah's eyes are still glued to his phone. If he's not careful, he's going to get a firsthand look at the caves after he walks right off this cliff.

"Do you want me to take a picture of you and your dad?" I ask.

He points his phone toward the sky. "Yeah. Just a second."

"What are you doing?"

"I can't get reception."

"It's a photo. You don't need reception."

"Thanks," he replies dryly. "I'm fully aware of how modern technology works."

"We're in the middle of the woods," I say. "You could just put your phone away for a few hours and, I don't know . . . enjoy your surroundings?"

This cracks him up. Which is *almost* kind of cute. Elijah's definitely starting to let his guard down around me. All the thoughts he would've kept in his head a few weeks ago . . . well, he certainly has no problem saying them now.

"Why's that funny?" I ask.

He gives me a look. "You. Of all people. Telling me to put my phone away."

"I don't spend *that* much time on my phone."

"You posted a photo of your breakfast yesterday."

"Okay, but to be fair, didn't it look like there was a smiley face in my Pop-Tart?"

He shakes his head. "I'm not engaging with that."

"And yet . . ." I cross my arms, smiling. "You're stalking my Instagram page."

He rolls his eyes. "Don't flatter yourself. It was for research purposes."

Elijah can act like he's above it. But I'm proud of him. He's trying—that's good. I just worry about what's going to happen after the show is over, when I'm not around to help. That's why it'll be good for him to start making other friends now.

After I get Elijah and his dad to pose for a photo, Mr. Brady offers to take one of the two of us. I put my arm around Elijah's shoulder as we stand near the edge. To my surprise, he actually leans in toward me without tensing up.

"Smile," Mr. Brady says.

"You have to take more than one, Dad," Elijah explains.

He snaps a few more and hands me back my phone. He didn't take our background composition into account, and the top of my head is cut off in some of them. But when I see our smiles, I feel a little warmer under my layers of hiking gear.

"They're perfect," I say.

The snowfall remains steady as we begin our trek home. "Let's hope I can still get a fire started," Mr. Brady says once we arrive back at the cabin, where the inches have quickly added up on the ground. "Otherwise we'll be dining on hamburger buns and trail mix tonight."

My stomach grumbles. Thankfully, Mr. Brady had the foresight to cover the firepit before we left. While he collects dry logs and kindling from inside the porch, he puts Elijah and me to work prepping the food.

The sky's almost dark now, making the inside of the warm cabin feel even cozier. Sitting at the small wooden table, I cut potatoes into strips while Elijah arranges foil packets for our campfire fries.

"Your dad seems really cool," I say.

Elijah gives me a look. "Nobody thinks their parents are cool."

"Yeah, I guess not." I reach for another potato. "It's nice that he took you on this trip, though. Whether it's cool or not, it's obvious he takes an interest in you."

"He smothers me. Both my parents do."

Still. A little smothering might be nice sometimes.

Elijah places the potato slices and some butter into the packets, sprinkling salt and pepper over them. "Do your parents . . . not do that?" he asks, looking at me.

I pause. Ava's the only person I've really admitted this to. Even when Reese and I were dating, we didn't talk much about this kind of stuff.

"I know they love me," I tell Elijah. "But compared to my older brothers . . . I've always felt like a disappointment to them."

"Why?"

"If there are two things my parents know, it's sports and heteronormative relationships. Unlike my brothers, I don't check either of those boxes."

Elijah doesn't say anything, but I can still feel his eyes on me.

"I'm probably being overly sensitive," I say, grabbing one of the foil packets. "Sorry, we can talk about something else."

"Do you really think that's true?" he asks, ignoring me. "That they love you less because you're gay?"

"No. Probably not." I crimp the foil with my fingers, sealing off the edges. "Sometimes I just think it'd be easier for my family if I were straight."

Elijah's eyebrows knit together. "Do *you* wish you were straight?"

I know I'm supposed to say that I don't. And really, I'm happy being gay. But deep down, I think there's a part of me that believes being straight would be . . . not better, but less complicated. I mean, I doubt anyone was ever worried about coming out as *not* gay.

I feel bad thinking that way, though. And I would never say it out loud. Except, when I look at Elijah . . . I don't know, it feels like maybe he wouldn't judge me.

"I get that adversity is supposed to make us stronger," I say. "But sometimes I wouldn't mind less of it."

He nods, and I could leave it at that. But now it's eating away at me.

"Like in acting. Most leading men are straight. Or straight appearing. And that's because almost all the roles are written for them. As much as I love older musicals, I never see any characters like myself in them. I hate knowing that I might not be considered for a part because I'm gay."

"You're a good actor," Elijah says. "That's all that should matter."

I sigh, letting my shoulders slump. "My application to NYU was deferred, so apparently not that good."

"Oh. I'm sorry." He frowns. "But you could still get in, right?"

"Yeah, I could. I just—" I pause. The pain in my chest—the one I didn't feel while hiking today—is back. "I thought if I could get into one of the most competitive acting schools in the country, it'd give my parents a reason to really be proud of me."

"I'm sure they're proud. It can't be easy to get into NYU."

"Yeah, but it's not easy to get into Notre Dame or the University of Michigan, either. And my brothers managed to do that."

"Maybe you're putting too much pressure on yourself," he offers gently.

It's nice of him to say that. But this is also something I'm passionate about. I don't want to feel like I'm settling.

The door to the cabin opens and Mr. Brady pops his head in, proudly announcing that we have a fire. In addition to our fries, we cook red lentils in a pot to make vegetarian sloppy joes. The food is simple but so good. I can't remember the last time a meal felt this satisfying.

After we take our dishes outside and wash them in the freshly fallen snow, Mr. Brady has me bring Elijah back into the cabin to wait.

"Okay," he calls out a few minutes later. "Tell the birthday boy to close his eyes."

Elijah complies, but only after pretending to look annoyed first.

Mr. Brady enters the cabin carrying a small black pot. He places it on the middle of the table, removing the lid to reveal a chocolate cake inside.

"Can I look now?" Elijah asks.

"Not yet."

Mr. Brady tosses me a packet of birthday candles. Once we have all sixteen lit, we begin singing. Elijah's eyes pop open, looking startled. But then a smile spreads across his face. I grab my phone and snap a picture before he can hide it.

"Did you make a wish?" I ask.

"I'm a little old for wishes. Besides, it's not even my birthday anymore."

"You're never too old for wishes," his dad replies, slicing into the cake.

If I had a wish, it would be that I could take a trip like this for my birthday. Except, when I picture it in my head, I'm with Elijah and his dad, not my own. Which is terrible. But if I were with my dad in this cabin, we'd probably be sitting in awkward silence.

I check out the picture I took of Elijah. His face is illuminated by the candles; it'd be the perfect photo for him to post on Instagram. But selfishly, I want to keep this moment all to myself.

After we manage to polish off the entire cake between the three of us, we get into a game of Scrabble that quickly turns heated.

"You can't use slang," Elijah says.

"You can use any word that's in the dictionary," I tell him.

"*Hussy?* Really? You think that's in the dictionary?"

"Professor Higgins calls Eliza Doolittle a 'brazen hussy' in *My Fair Lady*. If it's good enough for Lerner and Loewe, it's good enough for Merriam-Webster."

Elijah grabs his phone. "If I can get reception again, I'm so challenging you."

"You just don't want me to get the triple word score."

"Yeah, I can't believe my dad left that wide open for you."

Mr. Brady puts up his hands. "Hey, don't blame this on—"

Suddenly, all the lights in the cabin go out. It's kind of eerie. Complete darkness, except for Elijah's face lit up by his phone.

"Uh . . ." Elijah says. "What just happened?"

His dad gets up to inspect the breaker. When that doesn't do any-thing, he concludes that the storm must've taken down a power line. The good news is that he came prepared with an LED lantern for late-night trips to the outhouse. The bad news is that without elec-tricity we don't have heat.

"If conditions weren't so bad right now," Mr. Brady says, "I'd sug-gest we pack up and drive back home."

"We can't leave early," Elijah says.

I smile, remembering how grumpy he was at the beginning of this trip.

Since our disagreement over playable Scrabble words will have to wait until morning, we turn in early for the night. The cabin's pretty warm still, but Mr. Brady gives us each another pair of wool socks and tells us to wear extra layers to bed.

As a steady curtain of snow continues to fall outside, Elijah and I head up to the loft and crawl into our sleeping bags. Although the skylight's covered now, there's still a faint glow of light in the room. Or maybe that's just Elijah's phone.

"You're not going to have any power left for tomorrow," I tell him.

"Shut up. I finally got reception again."

"Tell me you're not looking to see if *hussy* is in the dictionary. Do you really hate losing that badly?"

Elijah's too busy typing to answer.

"Are you texting someone?" I ask, sitting back up.

"No. I'm just . . ."

His eyes are glued to his screen, smiling as he reads.

"Liar!" I try looking over his shoulder, but he turns away from me, using his body to shield his phone.

"Shh," he whispers. "You'll wake my dad."

"Don't think I won't wrestle your phone away from you."

I grab the sleeve of his fleece pullover, only half-joking, but Elijah turns back around. Our faces are suddenly inches away and I'm very aware of my breathing. I should let go. But touching him sends a small jolt of excitement through me.

"It's . . ." He blinks. "It's just a friend."

"Who?" I ask. Did he complete his homework assignment already? That was fast.

"Summer. From the lighting crew."

"Oh." I finally let go. "You should've just said so, then."

"You don't need to know *everything* about me," he replies.

Lying back down, I watch him from the corner of my eye. If he were really talking to Summer, he wouldn't have tried to lie about it. Maybe he *did* complete his assignment. But why all the secrecy? Unless . . . is it a guy? Someone he's interested in?

My chest hitches. I mean, good for him. But couldn't this wait until after our trip was over? I thought we were having fun.

Elijah smiles again, and my heart melts a little. Okay, fine. Whoever this guy is, I just hope he's good enough. Elijah deserves someone who can be patient with him when he's shy. Someone who will appreciate his humor. Someone who—

"Damn." Elijah moves his phone around. "I lost it."

"I'm sure Summer can wait," I say, hiding my smirk.

As we finally settle down, Mr. Brady's muffled snores drift up from below. Despite being worn out from our hike, I'm not really sleepy yet. With Elijah's back to me, I get the sudden urge to wrap my arm around him. Just to see how it feels.

Uh . . . *What?*

Where did that come from?

Maybe I'm just desperate for affection since my breakup with Reese. Ava and I hug all the time, but that's not the same.

"Are you cold?" I ask.

"Not yet."

I wait another minute until Elijah sighs, like he's getting ready to drift off.

"If you do get cold," I say, "we can always snuggle."

He snaps his head back to look at me.

I laugh. "I'm messing with you."

Am I, though? Yes—it's just been a long day.

He turns over again. "Go to sleep, you brazen hussy."

There's less than a foot of space between us, and it may just be my imagination, but I could almost swear he scoots in closer. Closing the gap another inch or two, I lean forward and whisper, "Good night, my squashed cabbage leaf."

I smile, waiting for him to ask me what that means. *My Fair Lady*—act 2, scene 5. But Elijah's already asleep.

Twenty-Three

ELIJAH

It's a bit startling to wake up with ice crystals on your pillow. But to wake up with ice crystals on your pillow and Wade Westmore's arm draped over you? There are no words for that.

We're so close, I can feel his breath softly hitting the back of my neck. My immediate reaction is to throw his arm off me. Except that might wake him up, and then we'd both have to acknowledge that we accidentally spent the night spooning. So instead I just lie here, a little self-conscious, but thankful for the extra warmth.

Eventually Dad starts moving around downstairs and makes a trip to the outhouse. When the cabin door shuts, Wade finally stirs, nuzzling his nose right into the nape of my neck. For a second I can't breathe, but once the initial shock passes, I notice how strong his arm is. The weight of it resting on me. Even though this was an accident, even though it's *Wade*, it's kind of nice to be held like this. It's not real. But still, it makes me feel kind of . . . wanted. And that's not such a bad feeling.

After a while, Wade must realize who he's cuddling, because his body tenses and he slowly slides his arm off me. I wait until Dad returns before I stop pretending to be asleep.

"Hey." Wade's voice is strangely high-pitched. "How'd you sleep?"

"Fine," I reply, a little too quickly. "You?"

He nods. "Uh-huh."

When we make our way down from the loft, Dad informs us that we still don't have electricity. Wade looks disappointed to be ending our trip early. Once we dig the car out of the snow and get back on the road, though, we stop at the first diner along the way, where he quickly distracts himself with the tallest stack of pancakes I've ever seen.

As for me, I'm just relieved to have indoor plumbing and reception again. While charging my phone, I ask Wade to send me the pictures of us by the ice caves. I smile when I see how happy we look.

We survived, I type, sending a photo to Reese.

He responds a minute later.

Aw. You guys look so cute.

Heat blossoms across my face. I turn away from Wade and Dad, not wanting them to see. It's not like Reese is talking about me, specifically, being cute. Or me and Wade being cute together, like, as a couple. I'm sure it was more of a big picture assessment—Wade, the outdoors, our ruddy winter cheeks.

Still, I've never been called cute by someone who wasn't related to me. It's hard not to feel a little good about that.

Hey, he texts. The three of us should hang out when you get back.

My breathing quickens. *Is he for real?* Hanging out with Wade has been great. But he took me on as his project. If Reese wants to spend time with me, he's doing it unprompted. Because he *wants* to. I don't want to get ahead of myself—one invitation does not make us friends. But maybe if I keep acting like Brady . . . well, who knows what could happen?

That'd be great, I text back.

"Hey, buddy," Dad says, refocusing my attention. "Sorry we had to cut your birthday weekend short. I hope you still had a good time."

I look at Wade, sitting next to me and stuffing his face with pancakes. Then I look at my phone, which has a text bubble popping up from Reese. A month ago, no one would even talk to me. So no, it's not a lie to tell my dad I had a good birthday weekend.

If anything, that's downplaying it.

Twenty-Four

If it weren't for the forty-one tracks on the *Les Misérables 10th Anniversary Concert* soundtrack, our drive back to the city would mostly be a silent one.

Elijah's in the back seat again, preoccupied with his phone, and I haven't been talking to Mr. Brady as much because I'm too distracted by what happened with Elijah last night. Or this morning. Or however long it was we ended up spooning.

I wish I could say I woke up thinking he was Reese, and that's why I had my arm around him. But I don't think it registered who was lying next to me. It was a warm body; I was cold. That's all that mattered.

At least that's what I'm telling myself. Because the alternative . . . that I *knew* it was Elijah? I can't make sense of that. I care about Elijah; I think that much is true. But I also care for Ava, Hannah, and Eb. I'm pretty sure I wouldn't have woken up spooning any of them.

I glance over my shoulder and into the back seat.

"What?" Elijah asks, looking up from his phone.

He has that slightly wide-eyed look he always gets. Like he's processing his surroundings, searching for signs of danger.

"Nothing," I reply, shaking my head.

As weird as this feels to admit, spooning with Elijah *was* nice. Even after all our hiking yesterday, the back of his neck smelled clean and sweet, not sweaty. And the way he fit under my arm. It was perfect.

When we get back to their house, Mrs. Brady invites me to stay for lunch. Part of me wants to. I enjoy watching how easily Elijah's parents embarrass him. Plus, it's not like there's anyone waiting for me at home.

But now's not the time to get sidetracked from my plan. I need to focus on Reese.

After Elijah's dad insists that I take the rest of the trail mix home, Elijah walks me to my car. For once, I'm the one who's at a loss for words.

"Thanks for giving up part of your spring break to come camping with us," Elijah says. "To be honest, I didn't know who else to invite."

Is that the only reason he invited me? Because he didn't have anyone else?

"Well, I'm glad you did," I say, brushing aside my doubt. "I had a good time."

He smiles, shoving his hands into his coat pockets. "Yeah, me too. That ended up being one of my better birthdays. So, um . . . thanks. Again."

I match his smile, still not wanting to leave his driveway. Elijah started out as a project for me. And I do feel good about helping him, but more than that—it makes me excited. Like, butterflies-in-my-stomach excited. But not in a romantic way—more like, well, proof that we've done a good job transforming him into someone people want to be around.

When I first met Reese, there was no question I was attracted to him. He was confident, good looking, popular. With Elijah, he was just some underclassman who needed my help. I wouldn't have looked twice at him if we passed each other in the hallway.

Which makes me feel like a gigantic asshole now. Because now that I've gotten to know Elijah, I see all these amazing things about him. His determination. The way he doesn't let me get away with things. All his random facts that make me laugh.

And yeah, I've also come to see that he's pretty cute. But could I *actually* be attracted to him? Or am I just confusing our friendship, the pride I feel in what we're creating together in Brady, with something else?

"Anyhow," Elijah says. "I'll see you back at school next week?"

I open my mouth. I want to tell him that we can hang out before then. Maybe we could do another movie night. Just the two of us. Unlike the rest of my friends, I bet he'd tolerate watching *Singin' in the Rain* with me.

But I'm letting myself get distracted again.

"Be sure to get some rest over break," I tell him. "The last few weeks of rehearsal go fast. And don't forget, you still have an assignment to complete."

"Don't worry . . ." Elijah waves me off as he heads up his driveway. "I'm working on it."

As soon as he's gone, I take out my phone.

Hey, I'm back in town, I text. Still free to run lines this week?

Reese replies almost immediately. **Need all the help I can get.**

It's exactly what I hoped to hear. But for some reason, it doesn't leave me feeling as elated as I thought it would. I look back up at

Elijah's house. Waking up with my arm around him felt like it was part of a dream. And I can't seem to shake it yet.

When we're not busy running lines, I type. Maybe me, you, and Brady can hang out soon?

Yeah, I'd be down for that.

My shoulders loosen. I hadn't realized I'd been hunching them all this time. Reese is willing to spend time with me—that's a good thing. And getting Reese back doesn't mean I can't still be friends with Elijah. I just have to stick to the plan.

When I arrive home that afternoon, there's a Post-it note waiting for me on the kitchen counter. *Hey, camper! There's macaroni casserole in the fridge. Love you.*

I may complain about my parents being more invested in my brothers' sports, but it's not like they don't ever think about me. Besides, noodles and four kinds of cheeses can heal all sorts of wounds. I heat up a bowl for myself.

Sitting on the couch, I inhale my first bite and fan my mouth to cool the molten-hot cheese sauce. My phone lights up with a text. A smile spreads across my face. Maybe Elijah's finally ready to admit *hussy* is a playable Scrabble word.

When I reach for my phone, though, it's Ava. She wants to know when I'm coming home. After I explain about our trip ending early, the gray text bubble appears and then disappears a few times. She's either writing me an entire paragraph or being indecisive about something.

Did you check your mailbox today, she finally asks.

No, I reply, blowing on another forkful of noodles. Why?

More text bubbles appear, followed by more cryptic messages.

Okay, don't panic. It might not mean anything.

Just check.

My chest tightens. I set down my bowl. *Is this about colleges?* No, I would've gotten an email first.

Hurrying outside, I try to figure out what else it could be. *Are people sending out graduation party invites already? Did Hannah pull another prank like the time she pretended to write me a letter from a Broadway casting agency?*

I fling open our mailbox. It's mostly junk mail, plus the latest copy of *Sports Illustrated* for my parents. Nothing addressed to me.

"Was I supposed to find something?" I ask Ava as she accepts my FaceTime call.

She tries to hide it, but her brow creases with worry. "Don't read into this. Because I'm not sure what it means yet."

"Ava . . ." I suddenly feel breathless. Like I just sprinted around the block.

"I got a postcard." She inhales sharply. "From NYU."

My stomach drops. I look down at the pile of mail in my hand. Maybe there's a chance I missed it?

"It was an invitation to attend Accepted Students Weekend," Ava explains. But there's no excitement in her voice, only worry. "Like I said, though, I don't think we should—"

"You're right," I blurt out. "It's nothing to worry about. Sometimes our mail is slow."

I don't think that's true, actually. But it's something I need to believe right now. Because my only other option—well, I can't even think about that.

Trying to play it off like I'm not too concerned, I end my call with Ava and head back inside. I've been so focused on helping Elijah and winning back Reese, it left me with less time to worry about NYU.

Thinking about it now feels too heavy. So I push it away and go back to my casserole, which is finally at a safer temperature. But it's like my taste buds have all died. There's no pleasure in eating it.

I glance at the pile of mail I left on the counter, my stomach squeezing tight. Turns out there are some things noodles and four kinds of cheeses can't fix.

Twenty-Five

When we return to school the week after spring break, rehearsals have a different feel to them. Actors are suddenly tripping over their lines, the crew's anxious to get more time working onstage, and Gretchen has resorted to using a whistle.

"I'm not going to sugarcoat it," she says, once she has our attention. "We're less than two weeks away from tech, and things are only going to get more stressful from here on out. Also, Friday's your last day to turn in an order for a cast T-shirt."

As people start talking and getting ready to leave, I glance around the auditorium, looking for Reese and Wade. The three of us are supposed to go to Flamin' Joe's after rehearsal today. My nerves are a little jumpy, but I'm determined not to screw it up. If someone as popular as Reese wants to hang out with me, I'm obviously doing something right.

"One more thing," Gretchen says, blowing her whistle again. "We need to do a quick light check." She looks over at a group of girls who are sitting together. "Brittany. Would you mind standing center stage?"

Brittany Carmichael, one of the actors, gets back up onstage. Szabo didn't say anything about testing the follow spots today, but they suddenly flick on, zeroing in on Brittany as the rest of the house goes dark.

Up in the sound booth, someone turns on the God microphone.

"Uh . . . hey, Brittany. It's Josh."

Brittany clasps her hands over her mouth as her friends all squeal. This must be another weird theater ritual because I have no idea what's happening.

"There's no denying you're a star," Josh continues, sounding a bit stilted, like he's reading from a script. "And, so, um . . . I was wondering if you'd do me the honor of being my leading lady on prom night?"

Brittany lets out a dramatic scream. "Yes!"

Everyone applauds. And as her friends rush the stage to congratulate her, Summer appears next to me. "It's like throwing lighter fluid on an open flame," she deadpans.

"What?"

"Actors and promposal season."

I laugh. "I take it you won't be attending?"

"I never said that." She tightens the flannel shirt that's tied around her waist. "Hey, Szabo just ordered pizzas. We're staying late to test patches and dimmers."

Pizza sounds amazing. And it'd be fun to have the theater all to ourselves. But I've already committed to milkshakes with Reese and Wade.

"Is that mandatory?" I ask.

Summer blinks. Unlike Brittany, her emotions are subtle; you really have to search for them.

"It's not mandatory. I just thought you might want to hang out and learn."

"I do. It's just . . ." I look for Wade and Reese again. "I already have plans. I'm sorry."

She shrugs. "It's just pizza."

My stomach knots with guilt as Summer leaves. She's been so nice to me. But Wade said I had to make a *new* friend for my assignment. It can't be someone I already know.

"Bad news," Wade announces, coming up behind me. "Ava took that promposal pretty hard. Do you mind if we reschedule?"

I bite my lip, secretly relieved. "Yeah. Don't worry about it."

"Thanks. Oh, and can you let Reese know? I'm going to drive Ava home."

Wade takes off; I look for Reese. He's not in the auditorium, so I check the green room. When I don't find him there, I take out my phone. He's already texted me.

Snuck out early to grab us a table.

Let me know when you're leaving.

Shit. I could text him back and tell him we had to cancel, but he's probably almost there by now. Besides, who cancels on Reese?

Someone who's afraid. Someone like me.

Brady would go. And now that I think about it . . . could Wade have backed out on purpose? Maybe this is a test. To see what I'll do.

On my way, I type, taking a quick breath before hitting send.

Sitting in the Flamin' Joe's parking lot ten minutes later, my heart hasn't stopped pounding since leaving school. Wade was supposed to be my buffer. I don't know if I can do this without him. Sure, Reese and I have been texting. But texting's easier than real-life conversations. You have more time to think before you respond. You don't even have to use words—the right emoji can speak volumes.

Reese is a junior. And Wade's ex-boyfriend. And the star of the show.

I'm just a sophomore techie who can barely drive.

Only—I *did* pass my driver's license test. Even though I didn't think it was possible. Maybe I just have to trust that I've put in enough time practicing as Brady, too.

When I enter the café, a few heads turn in my direction. Including Reese's. He's sitting at a table with his milkshake already. I give him a small wave and get in line, where Tyler is working the front counter again.

"Ready to order?" they ask, flashing me a smile that shows no sign of recognition. Which isn't a surprise. I wouldn't remember me, either.

"Yes." I take a peek at the menu board, forcing myself to make a decision and stick with it. "I'll have the Shake Your Booty Shake."

"An excellent choice. Can I get a name for that?"

"Brady."

Weirdly enough, it feels like less of a lie coming out of my mouth this time. I pay for my order and Tyler hands me my receipt. "Enjoy that Booty Shake, Brady."

This is the moment where Elijah would spontaneously combust, leaving nothing behind but scorch marks on the floor. Luckily, Elijah isn't here. Brady is. And instead of being humiliated, he looks over his shoulder and replies coolly, "Thanks, I always do."

Okay, maybe I'm not that suave.

Maybe I only say "thanks," and my voice cracks a bit.

But the intention is there.

When I join Reese, I try not to think about who might be watching us. I have as much right to be at this table as he does. At least that's what Brady would believe, even if I'm not quite there yet.

Reese leans forward to take a sip of his Cereal Killer Milkshake, complete with Froot Loops, Fruity Pebbles, and Lucky Charms sprinkled on top. "So, looks like Wade decided to ditch us, huh?"

"I think he was just worried about Ava," I say, even though I'm not completely sure that's true. It does seem like Wade has been pushing me toward Reese. He's the one who put us on a text chain and suggested we all hang out.

"You missed a promposal," I tell him. "Josh asked Brittany to be his date."

"How'd he do it?"

"He got on the God mic and . . . asked her."

Reese pops a purple horseshoe marshmallow into his mouth, shaking his head. "Straight boys. So uncreative."

I laugh, but then a silence falls over the table. *Oh no. Have we run out of things to talk about already? Is Reese bored? Does he wish Wade were here?* I look at him and he smiles, which only makes it worse. Because now I'm noticing how cute his dimples are.

Thankfully I'm saved by the person working behind the pickup counter.

"Shake Your Booty Shake for Brady?"

When I return to our table, two bright red maraschino cherries— the "booty"—stare back at me from the top of my milkshake. *Am I really going to let some fruit embarrass me?* I pick one up and bite into it, pulling off the stem.

"All right, Brady," Reese says. "So what's your story?"

I almost choke.

"*My* story?"

"Yeah. How come I never heard about you until a few weeks ago? Why has Wade been hiding you from the rest of us?"

I finish chewing, unsure how to respond. It's absurd that anyone would be possessive of me, like I'm some sort of catch.

"No one was hiding me," I say. "Maybe you just weren't looking hard enough."

Reese cracks another smile. "Okay, wow. Way to keep my ass in check."

Oh god. I don't even know where that came from. I should apologize—I don't want to seem cocky. But then Reese steals the other cherry from my shake. *Without even asking.* He's clearly used to getting what he wants. Maybe he deserves to be put in his place.

"You're right, though," he says, leaning back in his chair. Now that the light's hitting him differently, I notice the bags under his eyes. "For the past month, I haven't been able to focus on anything but the show."

"How's it going?" I ask. "I know you were worried about being off-book."

He sighs. "Don't get me wrong, I'm stoked to have the lead. But I don't know how I'm ever going to be ready in time. I'm not great with memorization."

(Trivia fact: left-handed people are more likely to have a better memory.)

Actually, this could be my in. When Wade asked for help running lines, it was only a ploy to shut Connor up. But it did lead to us working together, which led to us becoming friends. If I helped Reese out . . . maybe we could get to know each other better. And maybe, if I don't fuck it up, I could befriend Reese and complete my next assignment from Wade.

"I could run lines with you," I say. "Not to brag, but I'm pretty good at remembering random stuff. Is it important to know that the Spam capital of the world is Guam? Will that be on the SAT someday? No. But that didn't stop me from learning it."

He raises an eyebrow, then nods. "Okay. But it can't be during lunch tomorrow. I have my first prom court meeting then."

"Mornings are better for me anyhow," I say, since Reese apparently doesn't realize that I'm only a sophomore, and my lunch is the period before his. "Congrats, by the way. On your nomination."

He makes a face. "Thanks. But it's basically a beauty pageant without the swimsuits. It doesn't really mean anything."

I roll my eyes without realizing it—until Reese gives me a funny look.

"You don't think so?" he asks.

"No, it's just . . ." I pause, shifting in my chair. "Of course someone like you wouldn't care about prom court. You're already on it."

"Someone like me?" His eyes narrow. "What does *that* mean?"

"Someone who's popular. Someone who's . . ." I almost say "hot," but thankfully, catch myself in time. "Someone who already has a lot of friends and doesn't have to worry about what other people think of him."

Reese studies me for a moment. *Shit. Is he offended?*

"Yeah, I get that," he finally says. "But it's not like I campaigned for it. People just voted for me. That's not my fault."

"Right." I nod sarcastically. "So now I'm supposed to feel sorry for you."

He smirks, not missing a beat. "Yes."

In some ways, Reese and Wade really are perfect for each other. I've never met two more confident people.

Reese picks up his milkshake and slurps down the rest of it, not noticing when a blob of it lands on his shirt. "I haven't had time to find a date yet," he says. "In case you wanted to feel even sorrier for me."

"You're up for junior prom king and you can't find a date. You know, that might actually be the saddest thing I've ever heard."

He nudges my foot under the table. "Shut up. I haven't been looking very hard. Besides, I sort of like being on my own right now."

I swear my foot is tingling now. I try to ignore it.

"Why don't you go with someone as a friend?" I ask.

"Are you going?"

"Uh . . ." I guess there's no reason to keep hiding the truth. "I'm a sophomore."

He shrugs. "Sophomores can go to prom."

"Only if they're asked by a junior or senior."

"Does that mean you're not going with Wade then?"

My shield of pretending to be Brady slips. "What—" I try swallowing, but my mouth's too dry. "Why would you think that?"

"I don't know. Seems like you two are spending a lot of time together. I thought maybe you were his rebound."

I almost laugh. Should I be flattered? Or mortified?

"I'm nobody's rebound," I say, except it comes out more of a mumble.

Reese gets a sheepish look on his face, which doesn't seem like it happens very often. "I'm not proud of this, but when I first went to meet you at Wade's house for movie night, I was prepared to not like you. I guess I was annoyed that he could replace me so quickly."

My brain literally does not know what to do with that information. How could anyone perceive me as a threat? Especially Reese.

"We're not together," I say.

"That's probably for the best," he replies. "For your sake, I mean."

I open my mouth to agree but something stops me. Wade's never lied to me before. If tonight was supposed to be a test, he would've told me. I'm sure Ava really was upset after seeing that promposal. Wade's being a good friend by being there for her.

"I realize he's not perfect," I say. "But Wade's been really nice to me this past month. More than most people have."

Reese narrows his eyes, giving me a dubious look. "And you're *sure* you don't want to go to prom with him?"

"There's nothing going on between us. I'm serious!" Nothing romantic at least. I do feel like Wade and I have gotten closer, though. Especially after our camping trip. The Wade who wouldn't apologize after running into me onstage isn't the same Wade who spent a night in a heatless camper cabin with me, acting like it was the best spring break ever.

"I know you two have history," I say. "But he's helped me out. He's a good person."

Reese eyes flick back and forth, like he's trying to decide if he should believe me or not. "Yeah, okay. He's a bit misguided at times. But he usually means well."

I take another sip of my milkshake. I can only imagine how big Wade's ego would grow if he knew how much we've been talking about him.

"So how early can you be at school tomorrow?" I ask.

Reese groans. "I'm not a morning person."

"Me either. But you have lines to learn."

"Fine. We're getting coffee and breakfast, too, though."

"Deal," I reply.

When we shake on it, I surprise myself with how firm my grip is.

Twenty-Six

WADE

As an art form, theater is supposed to hold a mirror up to society and reveal something about the human condition. It doesn't matter how light and fluffy the material is. Even a show like *Beauty and the Beast* has a message. (Who you are on the inside is more important than physical appearances—no matter how hot the actor playing Gaston is.)

Sometimes, though, I just like doing theater because it means dressing up. Today's our dress parade. And like most dress parades, it's absolute chaos. People are rushing around, trying to change quickly before heading back upstairs, where Mr. Z and the creative team will see what our costumes look like under the stage lights.

"I hate to break it to you, Westmore. But your reflection can't love you back."

Hannah appears behind me in the mirror, wearing a high-collared dress with puffy sleeves for her role as Higgins's housemaid.

"Shut up. I'm just seeing how everything fits."

"You've been staring at your own ass for ten minutes."

Ten minutes is an exaggeration. But I won't deny the rest. My tweed suit is surprisingly less stuffy than I thought it'd be. Hannah's just jealous because she's not in the ascot race, which has all the best costumes.

In the film version, the white lace dress Audrey Hepburn wore in that scene went on to become one of the most iconic costumes in the history of cinema. While our theater department may not have the same budget as Hollywood, when Ava walks out of the dressing room, everyone stops in their tracks.

"Whoa," Hannah whispers. "Good thing I have a rule about never crushing on straight girls."

Ava's dress isn't an exact replica. Instead of white lace, her fabric is a silky lavender. And she doesn't have a long train, which could be hazardous onstage. But she looks absolutely radiant, just like Audrey Hepburn did.

Of course, the other reason Ava might be glowing is because of the postcard she received from NYU. I check my phone. I asked Mom to text me as soon as the mail arrived today, but I guess she forgot.

"If I can have your attention, please," one of the assistant stage managers yells, pressing her headset against her ear. "Gretchen would like to remind everyone that we still have the Embassy Ball and the entire second act to get through. Can the actors move any slower?"

The assistant stage manager's eyes go wide. "Oops. I wasn't supposed to say that last part out loud."

As everyone starts making their way out of the costume shop, I help escort Ava, who's 90 percent dress at this point.

"You look amazing," I tell her.

She gives my arm a squeeze as we head up the stairwell. "I'm not going to pretend to be modest. I *feel* fucking amazing."

This is the happiest I've seen her since the breakup. And I'm excited for her—truly. But part of me also feels like I can't join in on the celebration yet. Not until I have my answer from NYU. Because I'm holding out hope that I can be excited for *both* of us.

"How are you doing?" Ava asks.

"I'm fine." I clear my throat, trying to hide the strain in my voice.

"Did you hear anything from your mom?"

I shake my head.

Ava pats my arm. "I know it's easy for me to say this, but I don't think you should obsess over it. Maybe they didn't send everyone's postcard at the same time. Your last name does come toward the end of the alphabet . . ."

I appreciate that she's trying to help me, but we were the only two from our group to apply to NYU, and I don't want to be the only one who doesn't get in. Ebony's already been accepted at Stanford, and I tried to get Hannah to apply with us, but she wants to stay close to home. Or so she claims. I think she was just afraid of being rejected.

In retrospect, maybe that's something I should've been more afraid of, too. If I'm not good enough to get into NYU, then I'm probably not getting into Juilliard or Columbia either. Which leaves me with only one other option: Lachlan University.

I should've applied to more schools, I know. I wasn't even going to apply to Lachlan, but my parents said I needed at least one backup. Lachlan was also Hannah's top choice, and they're well known for their performing arts program. But I don't want to be in Wisconsin. I want to be as close to Broadway as possible.

New York was Ava's and my dream. Together.

I can't be the one to let it die.

The stage is packed when we arrive upstairs. Chorus members are wearing large-brimmed hats with extravagant feathers and bows for the ascot race; a giant ostrich plume almost pokes me in the eye.

"We'll start with our leads," Gretchen announces.

Ebony, Ava, and I all step forward. When Reese comes down to join us, the bright stage lights suddenly feel a little hotter. Of course he looks extra handsome in his suit and matching top hat.

"Can you turn profile, please?" Gretchen asks.

While Mr. Z and the head costumer quietly confer, my phone buzzes.

Shit. Normally, I wouldn't dream of bringing it onstage. But if that's Mom texting to say my postcard arrived, this could be one of the biggest moments of my life. My pulse starts racing, imagining what that'd be like.

I'd definitely cry. Fat, sloppy tears of relief and validation. And wouldn't that be a memorable way to find out I got into NYU? Right here onstage, in front of everyone? I'd become a legend; theater kids would talk about it for years—

No. That's something the old Wade would do. I don't have to turn every moment of my life into a spectacle. Besides, this isn't really the time or place for—

Fuck it. I have to know.

Thankfully, the pocket in question is facing upstage. I slowly pull out my phone, just far enough to see my screen.

Nice suit, hussy.

I suck in my cheeks, trying not to laugh as I drop my phone back into my pocket.

"Wade," Gretchen barks. "Chin up, please."

Without turning my head, I glance toward the control booth. It's too dark for me to see, but I'm sure Elijah's in there snickering. Serves me right for checking my texts, I guess.

As Mr. Z moves on to the chorus, the leads are dismissed so we can head downstairs and change into our next costumes.

"I forgot how long these parades take," Reese says, unbuttoning his white dress shirt once we're back in the dressing room. My stomach flutters. The last time I saw him naked, we were still dating.

I face my locker to give him some privacy as I change into my tuxedo for the Embassy Ball. Unfortunately, I'm not very good with cuff links.

"Need some help with those?"

When I turn around, my eyes immediately land on Reese's chest. *Fuck. Don't stare.* If I thought it was hot under the stage lights, now I'm about to break into a sweat. I don't say anything—I'm too afraid of what my voice will sound like if I do.

"These are going to be a real bitch during the show," he says, stepping forward to take the cuff link from me. I hold out my wrist, hoping he can't tell how fast my heart is beating as he lines up the buttonholes on the sleeve of my shirt.

If I don't listen to the muffled footsteps onstage above us, it's easy to pretend that this is our prom night, and Reese is helping me before we pose for all the pictures we'll take. The perfect couple. Together again.

"There." He snaps the cuff link in place. "You're all set."

Neither of us moves for a second. Reese looks me in the eyes, and it's like there's an unspoken question there. *Do you regret what happened? Do you think there's a chance we could make this work again?*

I do regret what happened. I've never doubted that. But the second question—could we be a couple again? I don't know. There's this voice in the back of my head now. And it's asking if I really miss Reese, or if I just miss the way people envied us when we were together.

Where the fuck did *that* come from?

Of course I miss Reese. If I didn't, I wouldn't have spent so much time trying to win him back. I mean, sure . . . I liked walking down the hallway with him and having all eyes on us. Reese is popular and hot. But I'm not so shallow that those were the only things I liked about him. I also liked hanging out together when it was just the two of us. I liked that Reese was curious about theater and would listen to me talk incessantly about it. I liked that he played soccer but didn't make it his entire personality.

"Brady seems like a cool guy," Reese says, crossing back to his locker and snapping me out of my thoughts.

Elijah? What does he have to do with any of this?

"Yeah," I say. "He is."

"He's been helping me run lines before school this week."

"He has?"

My voice wobbles. Elijah mentioned he was helping Reese, but I didn't realize they were meeting so often. I can feel Reese looking at me, like he's waiting for a reaction.

"There's not anything going on between you two, is there?" he asks.

I laugh. It sounds forced, though. *Shit.* What if Reese thinks I'm interested in Elijah instead of him?

"We're just friends," I tell him, which is the truth.

The footsteps above us grow louder. People must be shuffling off the stage. I grab my bow tie and turn back toward my locker, but Reese isn't done yet.

"I think I owe you an apology," he says.

I freeze, because now I'm just confused. Reese didn't do anything wrong.

"Brady told me you've been helping him."

Turning around, I'm afraid to even breathe. Is my plan working? Has Reese changed his opinion of me?

"Anyhow, what I wanted to say was . . ." He pauses, looking down at his feet. "I know actors are supposed to be vulnerable and stuff. But, um, it doesn't always come naturally to me. Which is probably why I was so hard on you after our breakup. Instead of admitting that I was hurt, it was easier to just be mad at you."

"You had a right to be mad," I say. "I was an asshole."

When he looks back up, there's a hint of a smirk curling the corner of his mouth. "You *were* kind of an asshole. But I also know you meant well. We probably could've ended things a lot better than we did. And actually . . . I'm sorry we didn't."

"I'm sorry, too. For everything." The words rush out of my mouth. I've been waiting so long for us to have this conversation. "I swear, Reese. I never meant to—"

The door to the dressing room flies open, and chorus members start pouring in, talking over one another as they begin to change. Reese and I have more to discuss. But not in front of an audience.

Reese smiles at me. "Don't worry about it. We're good now."

I want to believe him so badly. But when he places his hand on my

214

shoulder and gives it a squeeze, I hear that voice again, asking me if this is what I really want.

I pause, still holding my bow tie as Reese leaves to head back upstairs. I've worked so hard to get to this moment. How could my answer be anything other than yes?

Twenty-Seven

ELIJAH

While it's true that actors can be showboating narcissists, one thing I've come to appreciate about them is their commitment. Turning myself into Brady takes time. And now that I'm meeting Reese in the mornings, I have less of it. So I've broken it down into a routine.

One: *Shower. Exfoliate. Brush teeth.*

Two: *Change into school uniform—which I've laid out carefully the night before.*

Three: *Make bed and wait for hair to dry.*

Four: *Style hair.*

Five: *Stare at hair in the mirror.*

Six: *Repeat steps four and five as needed.*

Afterward, I run downstairs to make a piece of toast for breakfast. Technically, it's my *pre*-breakfast breakfast. I also eat with Reese, but I'm so worried about my stomach growling in front of him that I like to have something before I leave for school, too.

I can't say that hanging out with someone like Reese comes naturally to me yet. I may look different on the outside, but on the inside I still worry about saying the wrong thing or doing something uncool. I can't fully relax around him. Not like I can with Wade.

Still, I've yet to majorly embarrass myself. And if that's not a sign that Brady's working . . . I don't know what is.

When I arrive in the kitchen this morning, Dad's at the table, reading the newspaper. "There's a stranger in my house," he says, holding up his hands like I'm about to rob him. "We pay for our son's private school tuition and don't own many valuables."

"Hilarious," I say drily, pulling out the toaster.

Dad smiles, proud of himself. "You've certainly been busy with the show lately."

"We're starting tech this weekend."

"Crunch time." He takes a sip of coffee, nodding knowingly. "I remember it well. Although they never had us rehearsing in the mornings."

"We're not rehearsing. I'm helping one of the actors run his lines."

"Wade?" Dad asks.

There's a slight pit in my stomach. I never thought to ask Wade if he needed help. I could've invited him to join us. Although . . . the whole point of this is to get closer to Reese. So I can complete my assignment and make Wade proud.

"Someone else," I say. "My friend Reese."

Friend doesn't sound right yet. But I'm working on it.

"Well . . ." Dad holds up his mug in salute. "Good luck this morning."

"Thanks," I say, smirking as my toast pops back up. "But in the theater, we say 'break a leg.'"

Sitting together in the hallway later, Reese is too busy laughing at me to remember his next line.

"If you're not going to take this seriously . . ." I say.

"I'm sorry. It's just—"

"I told you. I can't do a Cockney accent."

"No, it's not that." He offers me his napkin. "You have powdered sugar on your nose."

I take it, quickly wiping away any remaining evidence of the donut I just ate.

"Don't worry," he says. "It was cute."

If my cheeks weren't red before, they are now.

"Flatter me all you want," I say, deflecting his compliment. I'm sure he only said it to make me feel less embarrassed. "I'm still not feeding you your next line."

He leans into the locker behind him, sighing. "I'm so entirely fucked."

"Hey." I nudge my elbow into his. "You've improved a lot already. You're going to be fine. I promise."

He frowns. "You're just saying that to make me feel better."

I'm not. Though my reasoning might be a bit unorthodox. It's just . . . people like Reese don't fail. When I'm being Brady, I have to trick myself into being confident about everything I do. But Reese? He could walk out onstage, flub his lines, and still get a standing ovation. He's just effortlessly cool like that.

"Elijah?"

My pulse quickens at the sound of my real name. Two people are walking toward us down the hallway. Levi and Sonya, my old Quiz Bowl teammates. I forgot they practice before school in the mornings.

"Oh. Hey."

My voice is tentative, and my eyes flick back and forth between them. Levi and Sonya are juniors, so I haven't really talked to them

218

since quitting Quiz Bowl last year. And actually, I never told the team I quit. I just stopped showing up. A pang of guilt tugs at my chest.

"We haven't seen you in a while," Sonya says. "Did you do something different with your hair? I don't remember it being so red before."

"Did you know that people with red hair are harder to anesthetize?" Levi asks.

Sonya snaps her fingers. "Right. Because they have a different pain threshold."

"Uh . . ." I side-eye Reese, who's taking all this in. "Yeah, I dyed it."

Sonya smiles. "It looks good."

"Thomas Jefferson was a redhead," Levi adds, a bit too proudly.

Levi was always a know-it-all. But seeing him and Sonya now, I feel a twinge of regret remembering our practice sessions. Even if I was quiet and didn't contribute as much, it was fun to listen to everyone read through old quiz packets and test each other on topics like Norse mythology and the Stuart monarchy. It was nerdy, but no one was there to judge us. And I'm pretty sure the rest of the team didn't care anyhow.

"We should run," Levi says, checking his watch. "Big tournament this weekend."

Sonya gives me a friendly wave. "It was nice seeing you. And, hey, if you ever want to rejoin the Auspicious Kiwis, we could always use another member."

"Yeah," I say, nodding tensely. "Good luck with your match."

I hold my breath as I watch them leave. Quiz Bowl isn't something that would be on Brady's radar. Opening Reese's script, I try to find where we left off before he can ask what that was all about.

"Auspicious Kiwis?" He raises an eyebrow.

"It was our team name. For Quiz Bowl."

He shakes his head. "What's that?"

"An academic competition." I close my eyes, trying not to cringe at how uncool that sounds. "Teams compete to answer questions on different subjects. Like science. And literature. And history."

He smirks. "Please tell me your biggest rival was the Felicitous Flamingoes."

"Kiwi the *fruit*. Not the bird."

This gets an even bigger smile out of him. "Smart. Nothing intimidates competitors more than a piece of fruit."

Yeah, okay. That's equally embarrassing.

"Kiwifruit is rich in folic acid, which can help increase brain function. And since we were participating in a knowledge-based event . . ." I stop myself, a little too late. "You get the idea. It was pretty nerdy."

He laughs. "Yeah. Sounds like it."

My stomach drops—that's exactly what I *didn't* want Reese to think about me. And it's not like he's being an asshole; I'm the one who said it first. I can't slip up like that. Especially in front of him.

"Opening night's almost a week away," I say. "If we stay focused, we can do this."

It's a reminder to Reese, and to myself. I only have Wade's help until the show is over. I need to prove to him—and more importantly, to myself—that I've changed. That all this work has been worth it.

Reese groans. "Okay, fine. Let's start from the top."

I open his script again, ready to give him my best Eliza Doolittle.

Twenty-Eight

WADE

All week long, I've been thankful to have a distraction from thinking about NYU. Instead of worrying about that postcard that still hasn't arrived, I spend my time wondering what to do about Reese.

Maybe part of my hesitation is that I'm nervous about *how* to ask him to prom. It can't be big. Not like the flowers on Valentine's Day were supposed to be. Which rules out any major promposals. It's probably better that I ask him privately anyhow, so he doesn't feel pressured to say yes. Maybe I could take him to Flamin' Joe's—we could sit side by side in a booth, just like we used to.

Of course, there's a chance he'll say no. But Reese *has* been acting friendlier these past few days. We're even sitting next to each other at lunch again. And when I replay our conversation from the dressing room the other day, it makes me wonder if he asked about Elijah and me as a way to confirm that I'm still available?

I should be excited about that. I *am* excited. It's just—what if Elijah thinks I used him to win back Reese? I mean, yes, that's what this started as, though we were both getting something out of the arrangement. Things feel different now—I don't want to hurt him.

"Hey," Ava says, startling me as she plops down next to me on the couch in Henry Higgins's study. "You ready for today?"

Ava—that's another complication. Am I being a bad friend if I ask Reese to prom? It's not like I promised Ava I *wouldn't* ask anyone. But I'm supposed to be less selfish now. And it kind of feels like I'm only thinking about myself here.

"Hello? Wade?" She waves her hand in front of my face. "Where are you right now?"

I shake my head. "Sorry. What?"

"I asked if you're ready for rehearsal."

"Oh. Yeah. I guess."

Today's our last rehearsal before tech week begins. And since Saturday is our cue-to-cue—where we test every single technical cue in the show, a long process that tends to leave people cranky—Mr. Z lets us take this run-through less seriously. We have to stick to the script, but there's no tech, so we're free to overact and crack up our scene partners.

"Have fun this afternoon," Mr. Z announces once we're in places and ready to start. "And don't forget, you have your first audience to impress."

He gestures toward the house, where the crew is seated. The cue-to-cue is going to be hell for them as well, so this is their moment to sit back, enjoy the show, and—well, shit-talk the actors. I can already see the excited glint in Elijah's eyes. He's definitely ready to snicker and make fun of me.

The rehearsal does end up being a lot of fun, though. It's nice not having to worry about hitting a wrong note or flubbing a line. And the scenes between Ava, Reese, and me are on fire. There's a new energy that wasn't there before. It's like Reese and I have finally let our guards down, and our characters can enjoy each other's company now. I think Reese feels it too. After our duet together, he gives me a big grin and a high five.

"Really fantastic," Mr. Z tells us once we're all seated again. "Let's be sure we save that excitement for performances."

Gretchen goes over a few last-minute announcements, then shuts her three-ring binder. "And that leaves one final piece of business." She looks up at the control booth. "Szabo? Are you ready?"

The auditorium suddenly goes dark. The stage is lit in a cool shade of blue. A few people giggle excitedly, others groan. It's another promposal. We've sat through a few of them by now.

This one, though, promises to be a little more entertaining. Because there's music. And I instantly recognize the opening chords.

"You're the One That I Want."

Grease.

A spotlight hits the stage right proscenium. Reese steps out in a black leather jacket, eliciting a few cheers. Before he can sing his opening line about having chills, goose bumps race down my arms.

Holy shit . . . is this what I think it is?

I look at Ava. Her eyes are just as wide as mine. And when I glance over at Hannah and Ebony, they also seem surprised.

I hold my breath as he glides across the stage. If anyone else tried to do this, it'd be beyond embarrassing. But Reese is just charismatic enough. And when he gets to Sandy's lines about needing a man who can "shape up," I sit forward.

Is that why he picked this song?

Is he promposing to me?

My heart starts racing. There's a tingling at the back of my head. A few weeks ago, I couldn't have dreamed up a better outcome than this. But now, as Reese hits every note perfectly, something feels off. Is it possible that I was only in love with the *idea* of me and Reese?

Another spotlight powers on. Reese walks toward the edge of the stage, and Ava grabs my hand. She gives it a squeeze, like she's telling me it's okay. Even though she doesn't have a date anymore, she'll be happy for me if I accept Reese's promposal.

And if Reese really is promposing to me, it's too late to second guess myself and back out. I can't humiliate Reese in front of everyone for the second time this year.

Confident about my decision, I sit up a little taller as Reese belts out his final note and the music starts to fade.

I wait for the warmth of the spotlight to hit me.

I wait for Reese to say the words.

I wait to answer "yes."

After a second, though, I realize everyone's heads are turned in a different direction. Dread pools in my stomach, and when I see who the spotlight has landed on, my breathing stops.

Everything's just gone terribly, horribly off script.

Twenty-Nine

ELIJAH

Everyone's staring at me. And this time it really is true, not just my insecurity talking. Reese has jumped off the stage, walked halfway up the aisle, and is now looking directly at me.

"Brady . . ." His voice is amplified by the wireless microphone he's wearing. "Will you go to prom with me?"

I blink, unable to process what's happening. The auditorium has gone completely silent, except for the pounding of my heart, which I'm pretty sure everyone can hear. If it weren't for the heat of the spotlight on the back of my neck, I wouldn't think this is real.

Next to me, Summer pokes my elbow.

I have to give him an answer.

No one in their right mind would turn down Reese. Except that's the thing: he could ask anyone. But he chose me. And the strangest part is . . . *I made this happen*. Well, Wade and I both did.

I take a full breath, smiling as I answer.

"Yes."

Reese matches my smile, and everyone claps. Maybe I've been hanging out with theater kids too long because, for a brief moment, my chest swells with pride like I've done something worthy of that applause. But then the lights come back up and the spell is quickly broken.

As people start to collect their things and leave, Summer stands up to shuffle past me. "Congrats," she says, in a somber tone that would sound apathetic to anyone who didn't know her well. "I'll see you tomorrow, Elijah."

"Brady," I say, like it's a reflex.

She stops, shooting me a look. "Yeah. Brady."

Summer exits our row, leaving me alone with Reese. In his black leather jacket. And that shiny glow actors get after performing.

"That was . . ." I pause, searching for the right word. "Surprising."

He laughs, taking off his microphone. "For a minute there I thought you were going to leave me hanging."

"No! I was just . . . I didn't . . ."

"It's okay. I sprung that on you."

"Yeah. You could've said something when we were running lines."

Reese leans into the row of seats behind him, another grin sneaking across his face. "Promposals are supposed to be a surprise."

True. But most of the promposals we've been subjected to have been romantic ones. And Reese and I . . . well, that's not what this is. He told me at Flamin' Joe's that he liked being single. Besides, I probably wasn't even his first choice. Everyone else has most likely been asked by now.

"I hope you know I can't dance," I say, which is absolutely true, and something I might as well get out in the open.

Reese crosses his arms, determined. "We have a few weeks to work on that."

Now that I think about it, I'm surprised choreography wasn't one of the lessons Wade gave me. I scan the auditorium. Shit, is it going to be weird that I'm going to prom with his ex? I mean, he did say they work better as friends. And it seemed like he *wanted* me to hang out with Reese. Still . . .

Reese clears his throat. "You know, if you don't want to go with me—"

"What?" I ask, taken aback.

He raises an eyebrow. "You look like you're searching for the nearest emergency exit."

I refocus my attention back on him. Where it should be.

"No. I'm all in."

The next morning is our cue-to-cue. It sucks to be at school this early on a Saturday, but at least there are donuts again. Gretchen's already warned everyone that if they leave any crumbs on the stage, they'll be banned from the theater. Permanently.

Not that the actors seem too worried. They're all sipping their venti Starbucks and lounging around in their pajamas. I guess that's a tradition—the pajamas. And who am I to argue with tradition if it means I get to see Reese in a pair of gray joggers and a faded Monroe Academy soccer T-shirt?

I'm trying not to stare, but I can't help myself. Reese is hot. Yesterday's events still haven't fully sunk in. On my first day of rehearsal, I was afraid to even enter this theater. And now, here I am, going to prom with the star of the show.

"Brady?"

I turn around. Connor's standing behind me. Connor, who wanted nothing to do with me two months ago and barely knew my name when it was Elijah.

"Hey," I say, immediately suspicious.

"Hard to believe it's tech week already, huh?"

"Um, yeah. It's gone by fast."

An awkward silence settles over us. Connor shifts his weight, looking uncertain. "Did you get any donuts yet?" he asks. "I was about to hit up the refreshment table with Callie and Brooke."

God, if there were ever a time to gloat, this would be it. Connor's the reason I joined this show to begin with. And now that I'm friends with Wade and going to prom with Reese, I don't need him anymore. I could brush him off and make him feel as dejected as he used to make me feel.

Instead of feeling good about that, it makes me kind of sad. Not for Connor, necessarily. For myself. Why did I let him treat me like that? Sure, I could be awkward. But that didn't give him the right to be a jerk to me. I wish I could've seen that at the time, instead of thinking *I* was the only problem.

After all, Wade is popular. And he took a chance on me.

"I actually have a lot of cues to get ready for," I tell him—gently, because I don't want to be an asshole like he was. "I'll see you at the potluck, though?"

"Oh. Yeah." His cheeks turn slightly pink. "Well . . . good luck today. I mean, break a leg."

"Thanks. You too."

Having skipped out on donuts, my stomach rumbles as I join the rest of the lighting crew. Thankfully, Szabo followed through with his promise to hook us up with junk food: Twizzlers, Starburst, Peachie-O's, and a two-liter bottle of Dr Pepper for each of us.

Technically, food and drink aren't allowed in the booths. But Szabo says we're good as long as we don't spill or get anything on the equipment. And as it happens, there's plenty of downtime to eat while we wait for the stagehands to work through their set changes.

"This show's going to have a six-hour runtime," Rhodes says from the control booth.

Yang groans into his headset. "Maybe one of the scene flats will fall, putting us out of our misery."

"Let's not joke about any of the actors getting hurt," Szabo replies. "We don't need a repeat of last year."

"What happened last year?" I ask.

From her follow-spot booth on the opposite side of mine, Summer fills me in. "The actor playing Mother Abbess tripped over a stage weight."

Yang snickers. "Ever see a nun in a foot brace sing 'Climb Ev'ry Mountain'?"

"Hello!" Everyone goes quiet as Gretchen's voice comes on over the headsets. "Can we have less chatter on the channel, please? We're trying to work through a very complicated scene change here."

It took us ninety minutes just to get through the first two scenes. There's no way we're not going to be here all day.

Once the stagehands have finished setting up Higgins's study, Gretchen calls our next cue. Szabo does his thing in the booth and the lights come up on Wade and Reese. Wade's wearing the same flannel pajama pants he wore on our camping trip.

Something tugs at my chest as I watch him cross the stage—guilt,

229

maybe? I texted Wade last night, but he never responded. I didn't know if he was just exhausted from the run-through or ignoring me. It's definitely weird that we haven't talked since Reese's promposal yesterday. He's the one who wanted me to put myself out there more.

After we get through a few more cues, Ava makes her entrance. Gretchen instructs us to hold as she turns off her headset to consult with Mr. Z.

"There's a dead spot onstage," Summer says.

"Where?" Rhodes asks. "I don't see one."

"Look at Ava's face. It's only half-lit."

"Oh shit," says Yang. "If there's anyone Szabo was going to give special lighting attention to, I thought for sure it'd be Ava Mehta."

Szabo clears his throat. "There are other people on this channel, Yang."

"I'm just saying . . . I hear she still doesn't have a date to prom."

"Dude, kindly shut the fuck up."

"Maybe you could invite her to Summer's art show next week," Rhodes says.

"It's not an art show," Summer grumbles. "My uncle owns the coffee shop. It's basically nepotism."

Art show?

"But your photos will be on the walls," Rhodes says. "And people can buy them. So that's pretty sweet."

"What are you talking about?" I ask. I thought I was friendly with the crew. Does Summer not like me anymore?

"Okay," Gretchen says, coming back on over the headsets. "We need more light on Ava for her entrance."

"Don't worry," Yang says. "Szabo's all over it."

"Dude," Szabo hisses.

As we continue on to the next cue, my phone lights up.

I told everyone about my show last week.

The night we stayed late to test dimmers.

I frown at Summer's text. That was the night I was at Flamin' Joe's with Reese.

It sounds cool, I reply. I'm excited to go.

She doesn't respond, which makes me feel worse. Have I alienated myself from the crew by spending too much time with the actors?

A minute later, she texts back three black heart emoji. I smile. For Summer, that seems like a big show of emotion.

By the time we finally make it to the end of act one, I have a stomachache from consuming too many Twizzlers, and have chugged more Dr Pepper than is advisable for someone with limited bathroom breaks.

"Okay, we'll break for the potluck," Gretchen announces. "The box office staff was kind enough to set everything up in the hallway."

The potluck is another tradition, apparently. When I told my parents, Dad made a double batch of peanut butter brownies for me to bring. As much as I love Dad's baking, though, I need something more substantial. I grab a plate and head to the non-dessert end of the table. And it's there, over a heaping bowl of tuna-macaroni salad, that I finally run in to Wade.

"Pasta and mayonnaise," he says, frowning. "Who came up with that combo?"

I laugh. He seems more grumpy than amused, though. "I don't know," I reply, loading up my plate. "But I'm starving."

Wade grabs a turkey wrap and some chips. I keep waiting for him to say something about Reese's promposal, but when we sit together in the hallway, he's strangely quiet. Maybe he's just cranky from running cues all morning.

"I completed my assignment," I say.

His eyebrows knit together. Like he doesn't know what I'm talking about.

"Um, in case you missed it . . . Reese and I are going to prom together?"

He nods. "I know."

"Well, you didn't say anything about it." My voice sounds hurt. But I can't help it. I thought this was a pretty big accomplishment. He's acting like he doesn't even care.

"Sorry, I just—" Wade pauses, picking at his wrap instead of eating it. "I'm happy for you guys. You'll have fun."

He doesn't sound happy. He sounds annoyed.

"I didn't know he was going to prompose," I explain. "And when he asked me in front of everyone, I felt like I couldn't say no. Not that I would've wanted to. I mean, you told me to make a friend and I did. This is what we've been working toward, right?"

"Yeah," he replies. "It is."

Except he still sounds unsure.

"So what's my next assignment?" I ask, inhaling a forkful of macaroni noodles.

Wade looks at me. His eyes search my face, but I don't know what he's looking for. After a moment, he smiles. It looks forced, though. Or maybe just bittersweet. "I think we might be finished, actually . . ."

I stop chewing. He can't be serious.

"But we still have a week left," I say, not caring if I'm talking with my mouth full.

"Elijah." His voice is soft. Regretful, almost. "You have a date to prom. I'm not sure what else I can teach you at this point. You should be really proud of yourself."

He has a point, I guess. But this still doesn't feel right. I don't want to be done with Wade yet. I'm not sure I can be Brady without him. And more importantly, I like being his friend.

"I don't have to go to prom with Reese," I say, in case that's what this is about. "I'm sure he'd have no problem finding someone else."

For a moment, I hope Wade will tell me not to go. Which isn't a rational response—*of course I want to go with Reese!* But Wade's my friend. And if he's upset, then that's more important. I don't want to ruin things between us.

He smiles again. There's a little more warmth behind it this time. "You should go with Reese. I mean that—really. I'm sorry I didn't say anything sooner, I've just been distracted with my NYU application."

Oh god. And here I am, thinking this is all about me.

"You still haven't heard anything?" I ask.

"No. And I have a really bad feeling about—" He stops, running a hand through his hair. "You know what, it's better if we don't talk about it."

Wade's shoulders slump, and I feel like I should give him a hug. Except I don't know if we're the kind of friends who do that. He seems comfortable around Ava, Ebony, and Hannah. But maybe it's different for us.

Maybe we're not as close as I thought.

I set down my fork, sad to think that might be true. Everything good that's happened to me is because of Wade. If he hadn't taught me how to be Brady, I never would've been able to *speak* to Reese, let alone accept his invitation to prom.

"I'm sorry," I say.

He shrugs. "It's not your fault."

I know. But that doesn't stop me from feeling like I've done something wrong.

Thirty

WADE

Tech week is always the week from hell. But this year it's not the stress of the show that's getting to me. It's the fact that my entire senior year is falling apart.

"We have to do something *fun*," Hannah whines.

"Café Amore has a private room we could rent out," replies Ebony. "And it's close to the banquet hall, so we wouldn't have to worry about parking twice."

Hannah opens a packet of crushed red pepper flakes, sprinkling them over her mashed potatoes. "Or . . . what if we had food catered to someone's house? That way we could also have alcohol."

"No way." Ebony shakes her head. "I'm not drinking before prom court."

"I thought you wanted to live it up a little before college started."

"I think *your* idea of living it up is probably different from mine."

"Fine. It doesn't have to be alcohol. What if we rented a limo and hit up a bunch of fast-food drive-thrus? We could get an ice cream cake at Dairy Queen!"

"Yeah, maybe," Ebony replies in a voice that says she would hate absolutely every second of that. "Does anyone else have an opinion?"

Reese wipes his mouth with his napkin, clearing his throat before speaking. "Actually, some of my soccer friends already invited me to join them for dinner. But I'll see you all at the dance still. Oh, and we're planning to get a hotel room afterward—if anyone wants to join us?"

"Hotel rooms," Hannah says. "Now that sounds like a party."

Reese's eyes flick toward me, and it's like my body is being hollowed out. He probably thinks he's doing me a favor by going with his soccer friends. But at this point, the night's already ruined for me. I could win prom king and it wouldn't mean a thing.

When Reese first promposed to Elijah, I was too shocked to feel anything but numb. But now that we're back in school, now that people are making plans for before and after the dance, the numbness has worn off and I'm left with this constant ache.

I can't believe he asked Elijah.

I can't believe Elijah said yes.

Not that I blame Elijah. If there's anyone I'm mad at, it's myself. Reese didn't ask Elijah to prom. He asked "Brady." And Brady was my creation. If I hadn't given Elijah that makeover and pushed him to make a friend, none of this would've happened. My own plan backfired on me.

And the worst part is, I'm not jealous that Elijah is going with Reese—I'm jealous Reese is going with *Elijah*.

At first I thought I was just being overly protective. But when Elijah was talking to me at the cue-to-cue, when he basically asked for my permission to go with Reese, he seemed so excited. Elijah's going to be just fine. This is about *me*, and what I want.

I sigh, frowning at the untouched food on my tray. There are less than two months left to senior year. I should be looking forward to my future right now. To college. Except even life past high school is starting to look bleak.

My first official rejection came Monday.

Juilliard.

That wasn't much of a surprise. And Ava didn't get in either, so at least we could be miserable together. But I still haven't received a postcard from NYU. And at this point, it seems unlikely that I ever will.

"I think the drive-thru idea could be fun," Ava says, looking up from the copy of *Persuasion* she's had her face buried in.

Ebony shoots her a look. "You do?"

"Yeah. It could be a good distraction. If we go to a restaurant, I'll probably just spend the entire meal thinking about—"

"Nope." Hannah points a breadstick at her. "You promised you wouldn't speak his name anymore."

Ava pouts. "About *him*."

"Okay, fine," Ebony says. "I'll consider the fast-food idea. But I swear to god, Hannah, if we do this and you end up getting KFC all over my dress . . ."

"Give me a little credit," Hannah replies. "We'd obviously be going to Taco Bell."

Ebony turns to me. "What about you, Wade? What's your vote?"

My vote's that we figure out how to turn back time so I can stop myself from changing Elijah into Brady. No—that's not fair. I should go back and stop myself from causing that scene at our table on Valentine's Day. Then Reese would be discussing getting a hotel room with me, and I wouldn't be having complicated feelings about Elijah.

Although if Reese hadn't broken up with me, I never would've gotten to know Elijah. And that would make me even sadder. We haven't known each other very long, but when I'm with him, I don't spend as much time worrying about trying to be funny or cool. It's like I can just be myself. Maybe that's why I feel so weird about all this.

"Wade?" Ebony asks. "Are you even—"

Out of nowhere, Ava screams.

Everyone in a three-table radius turns to look at us.

"It's here," she whispers, staring at her phone.

The hairs on the back of my neck stand up. I don't need to ask what she's looking at. It's NYU. It has to be.

Ava looks at me with a mixture of fear and excitement in her eyes. I grab my phone. As soon as I open my inbox, my stomach flips. It's a notification that our NYU application status has changed.

"Maybe we shouldn't check these here," Ava says. "In front of everyone?"

The rest of our table is staring at us. Hannah's holding a wedge of her quesadilla, frozen midair, with a string of cheese still connecting to her mouth. "Go," she tells us. "Leave your trays. We'll get them."

Ebony nods. "Text if you need us."

"Good luck," Reese adds.

It kills me that he could be supportive right now. But I don't have time to think about that. Ava and I leave the cafeteria with our phones clutched tightly in our hands.

"Prop room?" she asks.

I shake my head. "Too far."

We duck through the nearest exit, which brings us outside and next to a dumpster. I try not to read into that as a sign.

"How do we do this?" Ava asks.

"We check them at the same time."

"And if one of us doesn't get in?"

Me. She means if *I* don't get in.

"Then we're still happy for the other person," I say. "And no one has to feel guilty."

It's the same etiquette as when you're checking a cast list. No matter how disappointed you are, you don't let it ruin your friend's excitement. Even if everyone knows it's bullshit, you plaster a smile on your face and act like you're happy for them.

My fingers are almost too shaky to log in to the application portal. Once I finally have my letter pulled up, my eyes don't know where to start. I'm too nervous to read full sentences, so I search for words instead. And two sentences in, I find the one I've been dreading: *regret*.

It's with regret that they can't offer me admission into their program.

My throat's so tight that swallowing feels impossible. I wait for the tears to come, but I've never been an angry crier. I'm not even that mad at NYU. I'm more upset with myself. All these years, I told myself I was good enough to get in. And worse, I *acted* like I was. Mr. Z gave me a few good roles and I let them go to my head. I wouldn't shut up about going to NYU someday, as if that were the next logical step. As if it were that easy.

Ava says something to me. But her words are muffled, as though I'm underwater.

I look up at her. Her bottom lip is quivering, as if she didn't get in, either. But then she takes a breath, and her entire body relaxes.

"I'm going to NYU," she says, more to herself than to me.

When I imagined this moment for us—which I've done countless times—we always said that line together. How can I ruin this for her by telling her I didn't get in? It's like the *My Fair Lady* cast list all over again. Except this isn't just one show. It's the next four years of our lives.

The four years we were supposed to spend together.

In New York City.

Ava looks at me, already reading the disappointment on my face. And as if being rejected wasn't bad enough, now I'm about to make Ava feel bad for getting in without me. Unless I don't. Unless . . . I tell her a lie that will temporarily soften the blow.

"I'm waitlisted," I say.

She brings a hand to her mouth. "Oh, Wade. I'm so—"

"Don't you dare say you're sorry. You'll jinx it. There's still a chance I could get in."

I sound so upbeat I almost believe it myself.

Ava nods. "Of course. Not everyone who got accepted is going to enroll. And I bet you're at the top of the waitlist."

Now we're both lying. But it's nice that at least one person believes in me, I guess.

"Come here," I say, wrapping her in a congratulatory hug. "Let's go tell everyone the good news."

Ava gives me a squeeze. "Thank you. For being happy for me."

Of course I'm happy for her. And that's what I'm trying to focus on right now. Because my only other option—the one I can already feel pushing through the cracks like a dam that's about to burst—is being absolutely heartbroken for myself.

The longer the day drags on, the harder it is to keep up the lie. Everyone's rightfully excited for Ava at rehearsal. And around me, they're upbeat and positive, telling me my chances are still good, and that I should feel proud of being waitlisted. As much as I appreciate their enthusiasm, it stings twice as much to know it's nowhere close to being true.

The only person who doesn't sugarcoat it is Elijah. Which I appreciate. Because after Ava, he's the person I hate lying to the most.

"I'm really sorry," he says, as we wait for our run-through to begin. "You must be disappointed."

I give what I'm sure is a very weak smile. "Yeah, it's obviously not the outcome I was hoping for."

"Well, I know we'll probably be exhausted once rehearsal gets out. But if you think a trip to Flamin' Joe's would help, the milkshakes are on me."

It's nice of him to offer. But it wouldn't make me feel any better. Because when I look at Elijah now, the only thing I can think about is him and Reese together at prom.

"Thanks," I say. "I'll let you know."

After our run-through, Mr. Z and Gretchen have a bunch of notes for us. My mind keeps drifting elsewhere, though, and once we're dismissed, I can't get out of the theater fast enough. I don't even bother washing the gray out of my hair. I just want to crawl into bed and wait for this day to finally be over.

When I get home, however, the kitchen table is set with three place settings. Which is strange. Tech rehearsals always go late; Mom and Dad usually eat without me.

"Is that you, Wade?" Mom calls out.

I walk into the living room. There's a college basketball game on the TV, which Dad turns off. Like, immediately. Now I'm positive something's up. *Do they know about NYU? How could they?*

Mom and Dad seem strangely attentive as we sit down to eat. Maybe they just feel sorry for me because of the Juilliard rejection from earlier this week. I keep worrying they're going to ask if I've heard back from any more schools, but they seem more interested in the show.

"Think you'll be ready in time?" Dad asks.

"Um . . . yeah, I guess."

He laughs. "You're usually a lot more nervous during tech week. Remember last year? Mom had to make you smoothies every morning because you claimed your stomach couldn't process solids."

That's right—I'm surprised he remembered.

"I know you're superstitious about us coming to opening night," Mom says. "So I bought tickets for Saturday." She grabs a dinner roll, shaking her head. "Hard to believe this will be our last time seeing you on that stage."

Dad smiles. "Next year, we'll have to get on a plane to watch him perform."

"We don't know that yet," I say, tempering their expectations. "Statistically speaking, I have a better chance of *not* getting into a New York school."

"Well, they'd be foolish not to accept you. That's for damn sure."

Without warning, the tears that I've been waiting for all day suddenly spring to my eyes. Did Mom and Dad really think I was good

242

enough to get in? Or are they just saying that because they're my parents and they have to?

"NYU rejected me," I say. The words just slip right out.

Mom and Dad look at me. And now that I've finally said it out loud, the reality of that statement hits me. Everything I've been dreaming of—living in New York City with Ava, rushing cheap tickets for Broadway shows, training with some of the best acting instructors there are—is dead. At least for the next four years.

I choke out a sob, unable to bear the weight of my disappointment.

"Oh, honey." Mom places her hand on my back, rubbing it.

"Don't be too hard on yourself," Dad says. "It's a very competitive school."

As if I didn't already know. As if that wasn't the point—to prove that I was one of the best. TJ and Brett got into their dream schools. And now that I've been rejected from mine, it's further proof that I'm a disappointment to this family.

"You still haven't heard from Columbia," Mom says, attempting to cheer me up.

"I'm not getting into Columbia," I snap. The anger feels too sharp. I don't know where to direct it. At NYU, for rejecting me. At my parents, for coddling me.

At myself, for being a failure.

"You don't know that," Mom replies. "It's still too early to—"

"You and Dad were right. I should've applied to more schools."

They don't bother arguing with me. Because they know I'm right. I was out of my depth applying for New York schools.

"I fucked up, okay?" My anger subsides as more tears start to well up. I sniffle, trying to hold myself together. "I'm—I'm sorry."

"Wade." Dad gives me a reassuring look. "We'll be proud of you no matter where you go to college. You know that."

"Absolutely," Mom agrees.

I wipe my tears away, not wanting to let my parents see me cry. Onstage, you have to learn how to control your emotions. But here, in our kitchen, my emotions are definitely in control of me.

I want to believe what Mom and Dad are saying. But I can't. Because how can I make them proud if I'm just ordinary?

Maybe it was better when they were downstairs in their sports cave, too busy cheering on TJ and Brett to notice me. Because this— knowing they cared all along? It makes my rejection twice as devastating.

Thirty-One

ELIJAH

On Wednesday we get out of classes early to do a preview performance for a nearby middle school. I didn't think eleven- to thirteen-year-olds would be all that invested in watching a social commentary on the class system in Edwardian London, but they're a surprisingly good audience. Our scene changes are still kind of clunky and I'm late for one of my cues. No one seems too concerned, though.

"We'll have another chance to work out the kinks at tomorrow night's run-through," Mr. Z tells us after the performance is finished. "This evening, I'd like everyone to go home and rest. It's important that we save some energy for opening night."

People haven't cracked open a textbook or seen their non-theater friends since tech rehearsals began. No one's going home to rest. We're all too eager to take advantage of finally having a night off.

"Summer," Szabo says, unlatching the keys from his belt loop and tossing them to her. "You mind locking up?"

While Summer runs up to the control booth, Szabo, Yang, Rhodes, and I all pull a change of clothes from our backpacks. For the show, we have to dress in black. But for Summer's art opening tonight, Szabo thought we should put in more of an effort. We quickly throw on dress shirts and ties. Good ties—not the boring plaid ones we wear for school. Mine has a floral pattern, which I picked out myself. I don't want to get too cocky, but I guess I can pull off prints after all.

When Summer comes back down, there's a slightly panicked look in her eyes. "What—what's happening?"

"This is our first art exhibit," says Rhodes. "We wanted to look nice."

"I already told you, it's not—" She pauses, rolling her eyes. "Fine. You can call it an exhibit. But most people will only be there for coffee and free Wi-Fi."

"Unless we invite more people," Yang says, looking pointedly at Szabo.

Szabo shoots him a look back. "No way."

"I'm just saying, Ava's used to seeing you in your headset. You should talk to her now, while you don't look like you're about to take her order at the drive-thru window."

It's true. It took me a while to accept it, but how you present yourself really does matter. There's nothing wrong with how Szabo normally dresses. But as crew members, it's sort of our job to blend into the background.

Szabo shakes his head. "Ava's out of my league."

If there's another thing I've learned, it's that popularity is kind of bullshit. Forget the class system of Edwardian London, the class system of Monroe Academy is just as absurd. There shouldn't be rules about who you can be seen talking to, or who you can or can't have a crush on. Eight weeks ago, I never thought someone like me could get a prom date. Especially with someone like Reese.

"Ava's really nice," I say. "You should talk to her."

Szabo's cheeks turn pink. "I have. We're buddy reading Jane Austen together."

"Oh damn!" Yang claps his hand on Szabo's back. "Our boy's actually doing it!"

"Soon they'll be sharing Walt Whitman poems," Rhodes teases.

"Hilarious," replies Szabo, shaking his head. "Let's keep tonight about Summer, though."

He has a point. One I already feel guilty about. Popularity may be a social construct, but suddenly finding yourself in two different friend groups, who then invite you to two separate things on the same night, is very much real. Before I knew Summer's exhibit was opening tonight, I had already accepted an invitation to go bowling with Reese and his friends.

His soccer friends. Reese thought it'd be good for me to get to know them since we're all going to prom together. And he's right. But at the same time . . . what if Reese's friends aren't as welcoming as Wade's? What if they don't like hanging out with a sophomore? I don't even know if they like bowling ironically, or as a competitive sport.

The plan is for Reese and me to go to Summer's art opening first, then join his friends over at Lucky Lanes. Only when he comes back up from the dressing rooms after the rest of the lighting crew has already taken off, he tells me there's been a last-minute change.

"How do you feel about mini golf?"

"Um, sure."

The honest answer is that I'm equally ambivalent about both activities. But I don't want Reese to think I'm not interested in hanging out with his friends.

"Sanjay's older brother works over at Putt-Putt Palace, and he's agreed to sneak us wristbands so we can get beers. Which means Ramsey and Coop don't want to drive now. I said we could give them a lift . . . if that's okay with you?"

I doubt many people say no to Reese. Not with that smile. I don't mind if his friends ride with us, I just wish I hadn't already volunteered my car. I was anxious enough about driving one person, let alone three.

"Also . . ." Reese looks me up and down. "I really like that tie on you."

"Thanks," I reply, trying not to be weird. "It's new."

He looks down at his shirt. "Shit. Am I underdressed?"

"No. This is just something the lighting crew was doing. You look fine. Or . . . more than fine. You look great. You always do."

I could be wrong, but Reese seems to blush. Which is strange. Because we're definitely not flirting. Unless . . . *maybe we are?* I bite back a smile; I need to play it cool. I'm starting to feel dangerously invincible as Brady. I mean, if I can make Reese blush, what can't I do? Maybe it's time I stop thinking people are out of my league, too.

When we arrive at the student parking lot, Reese introduces me to Ramsey and Cooper, who are waiting for us.

"Nice tie," Ramsey says, cocking an eyebrow.

It sounds different coming from him. Like he doesn't really mean it.

Although soccer players have leaner builds than most athletes, there's something intimidating about Ramsey and Cooper. Cooper has a permanent scowl on his face, and Ramsey appears to have a five o'clock shadow a whole two hours early.

"So, Brady," Cooper says, pausing to spit, right onto the sidewalk. "Reese told us you're in the play with him?"

I smile, thinking of all the times Wade corrected me for calling it a "play" instead of a "musical."

"Yes. But I'm in the catwalks, not onstage."

"Cool. We had no idea Reese wanted to be an actor."

"Or that he'd be so good at it," Ramsey adds.

"Should've known," Cooper says. "He's a fucking showoff on the field."

"Spoken like a jealous midfielder," Reese replies.

When we arrive at my car, Reese sits up front with me. I can't tell if that makes me less or more nervous. If we're flirting, does that mean I like Reese? Or am I just trying to prove to myself that I can do it—since Wade stopped coaching me.

Buckling my seat belt, I say a prayer that the coffee shop has a nice big parking lot. Or even better: valet service.

"Um . . ." I glance at Ramsey and Cooper through my rearview mirror. "Do you mind putting on your seat belts?"

They comply, but only after giving each other a look.

"So where's this art thing?" Cooper asks.

"Minneapolis," Reese replies.

Ramsey and Cooper share another look. I'm starting to think it's not about the seat belts.

"Would it be cool if you dropped us off at Putt-Putt first?" Cooper asks, catching my eye in the mirror. "I mean, only if it's not an inconvenience. You're already doing us a solid by driving and all."

Reese turns to face his friends. "Putt-Putt's on the other side of town. I told you we had to check out this photography thing first."

"Yeah. I know. It's just . . ." Cooper looks at Ramsey.

"We're not really into photography," Ramsey says. "And you know how Sanjay gets. He's not going to wait for us before they start playing."

Reese's jaw tightens. "Then you guys should've—"

"It's okay," I say. "I don't mind."

Reese looks at me, as if he's trying to see if I'm just saying that because I feel pressured to. *Which I totally do.* But there's no way I'm going to drag his friends to Summer's exhibit if they don't want to be there.

"You're sure?" he asks.

"Yeah. It's cool. I'll just text Summer and tell her we'll be late."

Ramsey and Cooper are suddenly my new best friends. I even get a little shoulder pat from Cooper as we pull out of the student parking lot.

Once we're on the road, I channel my nerves into being an attentive driver. Reese pulls up the GPS on his phone and finds us the quickest route. I'm sure the lighting crew will be at the coffee shop for a while. It's not like we're going to miss much.

"Shit," Ramsey says, looking at his phone. "Can we also swing by Jenna's house?"

Reese's brow furrows. "Doesn't Jenna live in Richfield?"

"Yeah. But that's practically on the way."

"Uh, no. No really."

"Bro." Ramsey leans forward, sticking his head between our seats. "You know I'm already on thin ice with her."

"Jenna has a car. Can't she meet us there?"

"It's her mom's car. And her mom is super strict about that shit.

She still doesn't want Jenna to stay out with us after prom."

"Yeah, that sucks," Reese says. "But now you're making it Brady's problem."

Even with my eyes concentrating on the road, I can feel Ramsey and Cooper staring at the back of my head.

"I don't mind," I say. "Really."

I must sound convincing enough because Reese doesn't push back. Not that he should have to. If I really have a problem with it, I should say so. But as much as I want to be there for Summer, I also don't want Reese's friends to be mad at me.

"You're a gem, Brady," Ramsey says. "Your first beer is on me tonight."

I glance at Reese, wondering if he'll be embarrassed if I tell them the truth. "Thanks. But I don't drink."

Ramsey nods. "That's cool. They also have a kick-ass slushie machine."

It's nice that they're not pressuring me. But what if I had said yes? Were they really going to ply me with alcohol when I'm their ride home?

"Hey," Cooper says to me. "You're getting the hotel room with us after prom, right?"

"Uh . . . yeah. I think."

Reese mentioned it, but I haven't committed yet. I was waiting to see how tonight went first. I like hanging out with Reese. And I want to like Ramsey and Cooper, and whoever else is waiting for us at Putt-Putt Palace. But this feels a little different than movie night at Wade's. I can't see these guys fighting over what musical to watch, or debating which version of Zac Efron has the better hair: *High School*

Musical Zac Efron? Or *The Greatest Showman* Zac Efron?

"Maybe you could drive on prom night, too," Cooper says.

"Coop." Reese shoots him a look.

"What? We'll chip in gas money."

"Dude, he's not your fucking sober cab."

"But he just said he doesn't drink."

"Hey," Ramsey interrupts. "When we pick up Jenna, can we please not mention the hotel room? It's still a sensitive subject."

Cooper punches him in the arm. "Bro. You gotta get Jenna to convince her mom. Prom night's going to be epic."

"You think I don't know that, dumbass?"

As I merge carefully onto the freeway, I wonder what constitutes an "epic" prom night in their eyes. For some reason, my brain skips over the fun parts and goes right to the hotel manager calling our room with noise complaints, and someone holding back their friend's hair as they hunch over the toilet.

By the time we pick up Jenna and arrive at Putt-Putt Palace, it's later than I thought it'd be. I check my phone to see if Summer has texted me back yet, but there's only a message from Szabo, asking if I got lost.

"Sorry," Reese says after his friends all head inside. "I shouldn't have volunteered for us to give them a ride."

"It's fine," I tell him.

And really, none of this is Reese's fault. It's mine. Brady's supposed to have the confidence to stand up for himself, not be a pushover. Maybe I haven't changed as much as I thought I did.

Reese studies his phone, pulling up directions again. "Looks like we'll hit some rush-hour traffic on the way, but we should be at the coffee shop in about . . ." He pauses, wincing. "Forty minutes."

"Are you serious?" I ask.

"Fuck. I'm sorry."

"You don't have to apologize." I reach for my phone and check my messages. "It's not a problem. I'll just text my friends again."

It's only after I send my text that I realize we *do* have a problem. By the time we go to the coffee shop and come back, Reese's friends will be finished playing mini golf. There's no way we can do both anymore.

"If you want to stay here . . ." I say, giving him an easy way out. "I can go to Summer's exhibit by myself. I'll make sure I'm back in time to pick everyone up."

"Brady." He shakes his head, fixing his gaze on me. "I asked you to come along because I wanted to spend time with you. Not to have a personal chauffeur."

"I know. It's just easier this way."

My phone lights up.

My photos will be up all month.

You can come some other time.

It's hard to read someone's tone over a text. Especially Summer's, which is flat and dry to begin with.

I feel bad, I reply. I wanted to be there with the rest of the crew.

It's not a big deal.

Reese looks at me. "We can hang out with my friends later. I don't want to make you miss your thing."

"It's fine," I say, for what feels like the hundredth time. "I'll check out Summer's exhibit once the musical is over."

I can feel his eyes searching my face, trying to determine if I'm full

253

of shit. (Trivia fact: it's easier to fake positive emotions than negative ones.)

"You're absolutely sure?" he asks.

"Yes. It wasn't that big a deal to begin with."

That's a lie. One I'm telling so he won't have to feel guilty.

Which is probably why Summer told it to me.

My stomach sours—I feel rotten for ditching the crew so easily. But then Reese grabs my hand, sending an unexpected jolt of excitement through me.

"I'll just have to make it up to you by making sure we have a lot of fun tonight," he says.

I wait for him to let go. And when he doesn't, it seems like maybe, despite having let my other friends down, I'm still getting one good thing out of this decision.

Thirty-Two

WADE

The final dress rehearsal is always supposed to be a disaster. It means you'll stay on your toes and have a great opening night. At least, that's what actors need to believe, or else we'd never leave the dressing room.

This time last year, I was hovering near the backstage mop bucket, waiting for my nausea to pass. Tonight I'm not nearly as anxious. The success of the show isn't dependent on me. That responsibility falls on Reese and Ava now.

"Oh god," Ava whispers as we wait in the wings for our next entrance. "When did my accent suddenly become Australian?"

I give her shoulder a reassuring squeeze. "You're fine."

Truthfully, her Cockney accent isn't as flawless as it usually is. But this entire run-through has been a mess. In the opening scene, a wheel popped off one of the flower carts, picking up speed as it rolled down the stage and flew into the front row. I could practically hear Gretchen's heart stop beating all the way up in the control booth.

Once we're back out onstage, things seem to run a little more smoothly. We get through the scene where Henry teaches Eliza to speak like a proper lady without any mishaps. But just as Ava, Reese, and I start singing "The Rain in Spain," the stage plunges into darkness.

"Hold," Gretchen barks. "Nobody move."

Normally you wouldn't stop the show during the final dress rehearsal. But not being able to see where you're going is a major problem. The last thing we need is someone falling into the orchestra pit and impaling themselves on a clarinet.

After a moment, the house lights come back on.

"Everything okay?" Mr. Z asks from the back of the auditorium.

Gretchen sticks her head out the window in the control booth. "The light board shut down. Szabo's looking into it."

"Great," Reese mutters. "We're totally fucked."

"No, we're not," Ava says. "Chris will fix it."

"Who's Chris?" I ask.

Ava looks at me. "Szabo."

Oh. I guess I've never heard anyone call him that before.

"I didn't realize you two were on a first-name basis," I say.

"We're working on our AP English papers together. He's nice."

Even without the stage lights, I can see the smile sneaking across her face.

Huh. When did *that* start happening?

Chris Szabo may be a nice guy, but he doesn't seem like Ava's type. Not that there's anything wrong with an actor having a crush on a techie. I mean, look at me and Elijah. *Is it just a crush, though?*

"We have to try rebooting the system," Gretchen announces. "It may take a while."

Mr. Z removes his bifocals, wearily rubbing his eyes. "Okay. Let's do an early intermission."

There's some grumbling as cast members move around backstage and return to the green room. No one thought tech week could possibly get longer than it already was. Reese, however, seems to be okay with it. He jumps off the stage and hurries up the aisle to the back of the theater, disappearing into one of the follow-spot booths. The one Elijah's sitting in.

I shouldn't spy on them. Whatever they're up to is none of my business. My feet, however, don't move.

The booth is barely big enough for the two of them, not that they seem to mind. Elijah holds something out—a Twizzler? Reese leans forward to take a bite, and they both start laughing.

There's an ache at the back of my throat. This is how things began between Reese and me last year. We went from flirty to dating over the course of the show. Is that what's happening with him and Elijah? Or am I just reading into it?

Maybe it's better I don't see them. I duck behind one of the stage flats, trying to erase the image from my mind. I should be happy for Elijah. This is exactly what we wanted—for him to be comfortable around people and make friends. Only I never imagined it'd be with Reese. And I certainly wasn't expecting to feel jealous or hurt. It's just . . . breaking up with Reese was hard. Spending time with Elijah made me happy again. I can't lose him, too.

Eventually we resume our run-through with a fully operational light board. The rest of the show is problem free, except for the beginning of my duet, when Elijah is late shining his spotlight on me. Which—*Come on, has he really forgotten about me so easily?*

"Final dress rehearsals are supposed to be rough," Mr. Z announces once he's finished giving us his notes at the end. "Don't let anything that happened tonight distract you. We're going to have a great opening tomorrow. I'm certain of it."

I wish I could take Mr. Z's advice about tuning out the distractions. But as I sit at one of the makeup tables after changing out of my costume, Elijah appears in the doorway behind me. I stop what I'm doing to watch him. He hardly seems like the same person. He's not the Elijah who always kept his head down anymore. The Elijah who was afraid to talk to people.

He's Brady now. Which is great. But even if he hadn't had his makeover . . . I don't know, I think I'd still like him.

Reese, on the other hand, he only knows Brady. He doesn't know the Elijah who flinches when people touch him. The Elijah who's never been kissed. I know Elijah's not the same person he was before, but I don't want him to feel pressured to rush into anything either, just because he thinks that's what Brady would do.

"Hey," Elijah says, catching my eye in the mirror. "Have you seen Reese?"

"Um . . ." I go back to wiping off my makeup, like he didn't just bust me staring at him. "I think he's in the dressing room."

"Thanks."

My pulse quickens. "Elijah, wait."

When he turns to look at me again, I have no idea what I'm going to say. It's probably not my place to say *anything*, especially since my own feelings are tied up in their relationship. But I feel responsible for Elijah. I don't want him to get hurt.

"Do you have a second?" I ask.

"Sure. What's up?"

"Actually . . ." I look around. There are too many actors lingering about. "Let's go somewhere else."

Elijah and I head to the prop shop, which is already cleared out for the night. Now that it's just the two of us, my insides flutter like I have stage fright.

"Is everything okay?" he asks.

I swallow, trying to steady my nerves.

"You and Reese seem to be getting close," I say.

He shrugs. "I mean, yeah. He's my prom date."

Date. I hate how much that word stings. I know Elijah's not trying to throw it in my face—I told him I didn't care if they went together. But I guess I was secretly hoping he'd be able to tell that I didn't mean it.

"Do you like him?" I ask.

His eyes dart back and forth, not meeting mine. *Is he hiding something?*

"We're going as friends," he says.

"You can be friends with someone and also have feelings for them."

The weight of those words is heavier than I expected. Elijah hugs his elbows, taking his time before speaking again. "Even if I did like Reese," he says softly, "I'm not sure someone like him would—"

"Don't do that." My words come out sharper than I intended. But I'm sorry, were our lessons all for nothing? Can he really not see it yet?

"Don't do what?" he mumbles, still not meeting my eyes.

"Don't act like you're somehow beneath everyone."

"I'm just being realistic. I don't—"

"Elijah." My voice shakes, unable to hide my frustration. "How do you still not know that you're funny? And cute. And infuriatingly modest. Of course someone like Reese could be interested in you. Why do you think he asked you to prom?"

His eyes flick toward mine, and I remember the last time we were in here, when I made him cry. I don't want to push him too far again.

"I just . . ." I take a breath. Am I really doing this to protect Elijah? Or am I being selfish again, trying to steer him away from Reese and back to me? "You should be careful," I say.

His brow furrows. "Of what?"

No, even if Reese and Elijah wind up together, I don't want him to be unprepared. I helped him get this far; it wouldn't be fair to abandon him now.

"I know I told you to let Brady do the things that scare you," I say. "But if you're not ready for something . . . it's okay not to do it."

Elijah's mouth curves into a frown as he catches my meaning. He doesn't say anything for a moment. When he does speak, his tone is more guarded. "Reese is a good person. I don't think he'd pressure me like that."

"No. Of course not. That's not what I—"

"Then there has to be some other reason."

"What do you mean?"

"Some other reason you don't want me to go with Reese," he clarifies.

He's looking at me with the same intensity as when he accused me of making him drop that stage light. I *am* trying to look out for him. But I also can't deny there's something more to it. Only, I don't know how to articulate it yet. So I go for the easier explanation.

"I was hoping Reese would ask me to prom."

I don't know what answer Elijah was expecting, but I don't think that was it. A pained look flashes across his face.

"I should've told you sooner," I say.

He laughs, but it's bitter. "So you're jealous, then."

I open my mouth, but it feels too scary to admit what I'm actually jealous of. Elijah and I created Brady together. Why does it feel like Reese gets the prize at the end?

Elijah shakes his head, trying to process everything. "If you still had feelings for him, why'd you put us on the same text chain when we were camping? Why invite us out for milkshakes? It almost seemed like you were trying to set us up or something."

"Set you up?" Now it's my turn to be confused. "I wanted Reese to know I was helping you, so he'd see that I changed and take me back."

Elijah's face drops. He looks away from me.

Shit. I shouldn't have said that.

"I'm sorry," I say. "I didn't mean it like that. I—I wanted to help you too. I wasn't only doing this for myself, I swear."

"None of this was real," he says, more to himself than to me.

"No. I just told you—"

But he's already made up his mind. "I was supposed to meet Reese after the show," he says, brushing past me. "I shouldn't keep him waiting."

"Elijah, wait. Can we please talk about this?"

He doesn't stop until he reaches the door. "You can try getting back together with Reese if you want," he says, turning to look at me. "That's your choice. But I can make my own decisions, too."

My heart wrenches. If he'd just give me a chance to explain, if he knew how I actually felt . . . But Elijah's already gone. Dramatic exits might be great onstage. But in real life, they fucking suck.

Thirty-Three

ELIJAH

Anger radiates through me as I storm out of the prop room. Maybe it shouldn't have come as a surprise that Wade was only helping me so he could get Reese to like him again. And maybe I don't have a right to feel so hurt about it. After all, I was only using Wade to help me at first, too.

But I *am* hurt.

More than I expected to be.

What Wade and I had—our friendship—I thought that was real. And when he tried to warn me about going to prom with Reese . . . I don't know, I got weirdly excited for a second. Like maybe Wade didn't want me to go for another reason. I mean, he said I was cute. Except he clearly wants Reese back. So I have no clue why he said that.

The only thing I know for sure anymore is that getting involved with Wade was a mistake. He's only been looking out for himself these past couple months. And now it's time I start doing the same for *myself*. Beginning with Reese.

When I return to the hair and makeup room, Reese is nowhere to be found. *Did he leave without me?* I check my phone.

Hey. Looking for you upstairs.

The auditorium is nearly empty by now, and the stage is already reset for the opening of tomorrow's show. Reese is sitting on the steps of the Royal Opera House. He smiles when he sees me, and it's almost enough to make me forget about Wade.

"Hey," I say, sitting next to him.

He knocks his knee into mine. "Hi."

As the few remaining stagehands gather their things and leave, Gretchen comes down the aisle with her three-ring binder and massive set of keys. "You have two minutes," she says, looking at us. "Then I'm locking up."

As she heads backstage, quiet settles over the auditorium. I look at Reese and my heart rate spikes. Although there's been a few signs that he could actually like me—the constant texting, holding my hand in the mini-golf parking lot yesterday—I still find it hard to believe. But maybe it's time I stop listening to that voice. The one that says I'll never be cool enough.

"So, um . . ." I grip the edge of the step we're sitting on. "What are we doing?"

Reese shrugs. "I should probably go home and get some sleep, but I've got too much energy. I'd be down for hitting up Flamin' Joe's. Or maybe getting some pizza?"

"No. I mean *us*. What are we doing?"

His eyebrows push together.

"Are we just friends?" I ask. "Or are we . . . wanting to be more than that?"

If I had time to really think about the words I just said, I'd be freaking out a whole lot more. But I'm mostly focused on Wade, and how I want to prove him wrong for thinking I'm not ready. I worked hard to turn myself into Brady. And, yeah, things are suddenly moving fast. But maybe fast is good, like ripping off a Band-Aid.

"Can I be honest?" Reese asks.

I nod, because after finding out the truth about Wade, a little honesty up front would be nice. But on the other hand, people usually only ask that question when they're trying to let you down gently.

"I really like hanging out with you," Reese says. The look on his face is apologetic, though. "But I'm not ready for anything serious right now. Wade and I were together for almost a year. I think I need time to let that settle, you know?"

"Yeah." My cheeks go warm. "That makes sense."

It's embarrassing. But I'm glad he was honest with me. It's better in the long run.

Reese digs his knee a little harder into mine. "That doesn't mean I'm not open to having some fun, though."

My face must be as red as the stage curtains now. I'm pretty sure I know what he's suggesting.

When Wade gave me my lesson on stage combat, I told him I could never be the one to make the first move. I can think of a few reasons why I'd want to kiss Reese right now. Because he's hot. Because it would make Wade jealous. Because we're sitting in an empty theater, the night before the show opens, and it just feels right.

But the main reason I want to kiss him is to prove to myself that I can. This is my chance to find out if I'm still the same person, or if I've really changed into someone who isn't afraid to put himself out there and try.

I lean forward, my heart pounding in my chest as I close my eyes.

To my surprise, Reese's lips quickly find mine. Before I can over-think it, he slides his hand over the back of my neck, and we start making out. I have no idea how long we're at it, but soon there's a clicking sound above us. We stop and open our eyes. Gretchen must've forgotten we're in here; the stage lights have been shut off.

Reese laughs, then kisses me again.

There's no spotlight. No audience. Only us.

Thirty-Four

WADE

When the majority of your audience is made up of your friends and family members, it's hard to gauge whether your show's actually any good or if everyone's just being polite.

One place the audience never lies, though, is when the curtain first starts to come down at the end. If there's a slight pause before the clapping begins, it means people were so wrapped up in the story, they momentarily forgot they're in a theater.

It means your show doesn't suck.

Tonight, we're playing to a sold-out house. Which is good for the energy levels, but bad if something goes wrong. Thankfully, our set changes run smoothly, no one drops a line, and my duet with Reese is the best it's ever been. There's even applause for our costumes during the ascot race. And when the final curtain starts to come down at the end . . . we get the fucking pause.

I should be ecstatic—and part of me is. But another part of me, the more realistic part, knows that the main reason we got it was because of Ava and Reese. They killed it, earning every last clap that's filling the auditorium right now.

The rest of the cast has to join them for the curtain call, of course.

And when it's my turn to go out there, I still plaster a smile on my face.

"We did it," Ava says, wrapping her arm around my waist as the curtain comes down again after the final bow.

I give her a squeeze back, determined not to spoil opening night.

My biggest test comes later, after we've all changed out of costume and I see the mound of bouquets sitting on Ava's dressing table. The last time I saw that many roses, it was on Valentine's Day. When I tried to surprise Reese and ended up ruining my senior year instead.

"We're going to need more vases," says Ebony.

"Should I give some to other people to bring home?" Ava asks.

Hannah leans against the dressing table with a sigh. "Ava, honey, I love you. But handing out pity flowers is a bigger diva move than just keeping them for yourself."

Ava frowns. "Eb, will you take some home with you? For the cast party."

Ebony gathers a few bouquets and checks her phone. "I should go. I don't want people arriving at my house before me."

"Come on," Hannah whines. "Just stay and do the toast with us. Your parents will be there to let everyone in."

"My parents are busy with the catering," Ebony says. "Being a good host is important to me. We can do a second toast tomorrow night."

Hannah crosses her arms, pouting. "Fine."

"Are you sure you don't need us to pick anything up on our way?" Ava asks. "Some refreshments? More ice?"

Ebony shakes her head. "We've got everything covered. Just don't show up too late."

We usually have two cast parties: one on opening night, and one before our final performance the following weekend. Everyone always wants Ebony to throw at least one of them. Her mom's a successful event planner, and while her parents don't like to flaunt their money, they're certainly not shy about spending it. They go all out for us—cupcake towers, fancy hors d'oeuvres, a root beer float bar.

As people start clearing out for the party, Hannah, Ava, and I head back upstairs for our opening night tradition. First, though, we cram ourselves into the janitor's closet in the scene shop, so we can sneak back into the theater after Gretchen locks up.

Once Gretchen's footsteps taper off into silence, we wait another minute before coming out of hiding. The theater is dark now, except for the red glow of the exit signs and the ghost light—a single bulb that's placed in the middle of the stage when the auditorium is empty. Ghost lights are mainly used for practical reasons, so no one trips over a set piece or stumbles into the orchestra pit. But some people think it's meant to keep the ghosts in the theater company.

I don't know if I believe in ghosts.

But I do believe that this theater has history.

After flipping on a few backstage lights, the three of us make our way up to the fly gallery, where the stagehands help fly in the scenery and backdrops during the show. The platform is narrow, and one story up, which is why I don't like sitting too close to the railing. But we picked this spot for a reason. The ladder we took to get here continues all the way to the catwalks. And about halfway up, you can see where past theater students have spray-painted their names onto the wall.

I think that's an old tradition, because I don't recognize any of the names up there. But freshman year, Ava and I decided that this would be a good place to start our own tradition. Which is why, after every opening night, we come up here to toast the show.

"Since this is our senior year," Hannah says, "I thought we should do it right."

We usually use plastic cups and ginger ale. But when we sit down together now, Hannah goes all Mary Poppins on us and extracts a bottle of sparkling apple cider and three champagne flutes from her bag.

"Where'd you get those?" I ask.

"The prop shop."

Hannah starts unwrapping the foil around the cork, but Ava puts her hand out, stopping her. "Hold on. Before we get started, I have news."

We both look at Ava, but she just blushes, burying her face into her hands.

"Spill it," Hannah says.

Ava picks at the cuff of her jeans, smiling. "I sort of have a date to prom."

Hannah screams, quickly covering her mouth. "Who? Wait— don't tell me you decided to take back Drew. Unless you *did* take him back. In which case, pretend I didn't just say that."

Ava shakes her head. "Not Drew. Chris."

Hannah scrunches her face, confused.

"Szabo," Ava clarifies.

"Ooh." Hannah nods slowly. "I like that. The leading lady and someone from the crew. You can have that whole 'star-crossed lovers' thing going on."

"It's not like we're dating," Ava says. "Though he is kind of cute."

"You're *so* horny for him," Hannah teases.

Ava rolls her eyes, then sneaks a peek at me, as though she's looking for my approval.

"That's really great," I tell her, trying to sound upbeat. "I'm happy for you."

"You don't mind?" she asks.

There's more to that sentence, I think. Do I mind *being the only dateless one in our group now*. Yeah, I'm not exactly thrilled. But that's not Ava's fault. I can't ask her to be miserable at prom just because I'm going to be.

"Of course not," I tell her.

She smiles. "Good. Chris is really sweet. And I want everyone to give him a fair chance."

Ava looks right at me when she says that. I'd be offended, except I was pretty judgmental about her and Drew—even though I ended up being right about him.

"Well, if anything deserves a toast," Hannah says, "it's this."

She pops the cork, letting out a yelp.

"We have to toast the show first," Ava says. "That's the tradition."

As we hold up our flutes, my chest hollows out and the finality of this moment hits me. This is my last opening night, my last time doing a show with all my friends. When I thought about this moment in the past, I had always imagined it'd be bittersweet. That I'd be sad to be saying goodbye to high school but looking forward to everything waiting for me in New York.

Now it only feels bitter.

"To *My Fair Lady*," Ava says.

We clink glasses and take our first sip.

Hannah wants to toast Ava having a date to prom next. Then our senior year. Then her creative writing teacher, Mr. Gerlach, who didn't realize that Hannah just turned in her old *High School Musical* fanfiction as her final project, and still gave her a B-plus.

"Oh," she says, holding up her flute again. "And we definitely have to toast to NYU."

Ava shoots her a look. "Hannah."

"What? You got in. That's fucking amazing. And Wade got wait-listed—which I know isn't ideal. But honestly, in my eyes, it's just as big of an accomplishment. I'm really proud of you both. Why can't we toast to that?"

Ava looks at me.

"To NYU," I say, raising my flute.

After we toast, I'm hoping we can move on. But Hannah's not done yet.

"Plus," she says, topping off her glass, "maybe this will bring Wade good luck."

"Doubtful," I mumble.

"Did you write your letter of interest?" Ava asks. There's a hint of optimism in her voice.

"They don't have an appeal process," I tell her, which is true.

"Okay, but you at least filled out the waiting list form, right?"

"When do they have to let you know by?" asks Hannah.

"Um . . ." I try to remember what the website said. I haven't been able to bring myself to look at it since my rejection came in. "I can't remember."

"You can't remember?" Ava's eyes go wide. "Wade, I know this is tough. But you have to fight for it. You're good enough to get in. I know that. Hannah knows that. *You* know that. You just have to make sure the admissions office knows it, too."

"Yeah," Hannah says. "And even if you still don't get in, at least you'll know you tried."

"I'm not writing a letter," I say, a little too harshly. "It's pointless."

Ava and Hannah glance at each other. "Going to NYU is your dream," Ava replies softly. "You can't give up now."

Hannah and Ava have no idea what they're talking about. I did fight for my spot. I *do* know that I tried. I put all my time and effort into being the best I could be, and I still wasn't good enough.

Just like how I tried fixing my senior year, and it only unraveled more. I don't have a date to prom and Elijah hates me now. Pretty sure the Universe is telling me to stop.

"Not everyone gets to have their dream come true," I say. "The sooner I accept that, the better."

"I'm sorry," Ava says. "I didn't mean to—"

"It's fine," I tell her, except there's still a bite to my voice. "I'll just stay here and be miserable because I'm stuck at Lachlan for the next four years."

Hannah sets down her champagne flute. "Wow. Okay."

Fuck.

"I didn't mean it like that," I say. "Lachlan's a really good school. I'm just upset about not getting into NYU."

Hannah grabs her bag and stands. "You did mean it, though. Because you think being in New York is the only legitimate way of doing things. Like someone who didn't apply to NYU must not take theater seriously. It doesn't even occur to you that people might have dreams that are different than yours, and that maybe you shouldn't shit all over them."

Great. Add this to the list of everything else I've fucked up.

"Hannah, I'm sorry. Please don't go."

She stops, clutching the ladder to head back down. "You can be so fucking elitist, Wade. And the saddest part is, you're the only one who doesn't see it."

I stand, too stung by her words to come up with a response. I mean, is it wrong to want to excel at something? Does that really make me elitist?

Behind me, Ava gets back up with a sigh. "I'll go after her. Maybe you should just meet us at the cast party?"

"I wasn't waitlisted at NYU," I say. Almost in a whisper.

Now's not the best time to bring this up. But I doubt there will ever be one. I should've told her the truth as soon as it happened.

Ava laughs. As if she's not sure if this is some kind of joke.

"What do you mean?" she asks.

"You—" The words are stuck at the back of my throat, like they're glued there. "You were so happy about getting in. I didn't want to ruin it. So I lied."

Her eyebrows knit together. "But then . . ." She stops, still trying to process everything. "When were you planning to tell me?"

"I don't know. I figured I'd wait a few weeks and then tell everyone NYU didn't have room to admit me."

"So you were never going to tell me the truth?" She stares at me, incredulous. "We're supposed to be best friends."

"We are," I reply.

"Best friends don't lie about something like that." She inhales sharply, tears already brimming in her eyes. "If you had told me the truth, I could've been there for you. Instead . . ." She places a hand on her forehead. "Fuck, you let me talk about letters of interest and waitlists. Like I'm a fool."

She's right. I should've told her. But my intentions were good.

Why can't anyone ever see that?

"I was trying to protect you," I say defensively.

"Really? Because it seems like you were only thinking about yourself."

Her words sting, like she just slapped me with them. Ava closes her eyes. "I can't deal with this right now. I have to go check on Hannah."

"Yeah. Okay." I bite my lip, afraid it'll start to tremble. I know I screwed up, but it doesn't seem fair that everyone's mad at me right now. Hannah and Ava are both going to the schools they wanted. I'm the one who had his dream crushed.

Ava takes off, leaving me alone in the fly gallery. I probably shouldn't bother with the cast party anymore. Ebony will take their side, which means I've just managed to alienate all my friends *again*.

Would things have turned out differently if I'd been honest with everyone? If I had told Ava I didn't get into NYU. If I had let Reese know I still wanted to go to prom with him. If I was up front with Elijah about using him to win Reese back.

Maybe it's not too late to fix one thing.

I could try explaining everything to Elijah. He might forgive me.

And even if he doesn't, he deserves to know the truth. Elijah meant something to me. I *need* him to know that.

I hurry back down the ladder and out of the theater. I don't want my last conversation with Elijah to be our fight. I have to go to the cast party and make things right. I won't be able to forgive myself if I don't at least try.

Arriving in the student parking lot, I'm a little out of breath. But then I spot something that stops me altogether: Elijah's car. He's still here. I guess Ava, Hannah, and I weren't the only ones who stayed late.

For a moment relief floods my chest—until I see he's not alone. Forget being out of breath. Suddenly it's as if the wind's been knocked out of me. Elijah is with Reese. And they're not just sitting in his car. Reese is cupping Elijah's face in his hands, and Elijah's letting him— completely oblivious to anyone else who might be in this parking lot right now, watching them make out.

Thirty-Five

ELIJAH

If I had known getting my driver's license would lead to making out with Reese in the front seat of my car, I would've scheduled my test a whole lot sooner.

Reese is a good kisser. At least, I think he is. It's not like I have anything to compare it to. Making out with him definitely leaves me feeling a little breathless and dizzy, though. And my lips—I didn't realize they'd buzz like this.

It's unbelievably hot. Emphasis on the *unbelievable* part. But now that we've been at it for a while, my mind's starting to wander, asking all the questions I shouldn't currently be worrying about. *Does he think I'm a good kisser, too? Is he comparing me to Wade? What if he wants to do more than just make out?*

As if he can read my mind, Reese's hand lands on my knee, giving it a squeeze. It's nice, until he starts inching his way up my leg and we get into inner thigh territory. I laugh. Right into his mouth.

"Sorry," I say.

"Ticklish?"

"Um . . . yeah. I guess."

He kisses my neck. And even though it's exciting, I can feel my body starting to tense up.

"Sorry." He moves his hand away. "Should I slow down?"

I want to say yes, but that doesn't seem like the answer Brady would give. Is it normal to be nervous right now? Reese doesn't seem to be.

"It's okay," I say, trying to convince myself as well as him.

Reese brings me in for another kiss. I try to relax into it, but now I'm thinking about Wade again, and how he said I might not be ready for something like this. I thought he was just being arrogant—but what if Wade was right? What if he knows me better than I know myself?

"Wait," I say, pulling out of our kiss. "I can't believe I didn't say this earlier, but you were amazing tonight."

He smiles. "Thanks."

"I mean, I've obviously seen the show at rehearsals. But tonight felt different. And your song at the beginning . . . the audience ate it up. Did you do something new there?"

"Brady." He bites his bottom lip. "Do you really want to talk about the show right now?"

I laugh, but it comes out sounding fake. "Yeah, I guess not."

We kiss some more. His hand quickly finds my thigh again.

"Aren't we going to be late for the cast party?" I blurt out.

He raises an eyebrow. "Not if we skip it."

I swallow, trying not to let my panic show. Despite how hot Reese looks right now, despite how much I like making out with him, our kiss yesterday was my first. I need more time to warm up to this. Maybe the party will help slow things down a bit.

"You're the star of the show," I say. "You can't skip it."

He nods, sitting back in his seat. "Yeah, you're probably right. We can always pick up where we left off later."

Surprisingly, I *am* a little more comfortable with driving now. Parking, unfortunately, is still not my forte. There's an impossibly long line of cars on either side of Ebony's block. Reese points out an open spot, but I ignore him, driving us all the way to the end.

As we start our trek toward Ebony's house, I can almost hear Wade teasing me about not wanting to parallel park with Reese in my car. *Trying is not failure.* I slide my hand in my coat pocket, running my thumb against his lucky rabbit's foot keychain.

Was it *all* fake? Was Wade really just acting with me the whole time?

"Hey," says Reese, a few steps ahead of me. "You still coming?"

I tune Wade out and catch up.

Based on the rest of the homes in her neighborhood, it's no surprise that Ebony's house looks like a small fortress, complete with a large circular driveway and really nice landscaping. The size is intimidating, but the warm glow of light from inside seems inviting. As does Ebony, who greets us at the front door.

"There you two are," she says, with maybe a hint of suspicion in her voice. "I hope you wore cute socks today, because this is definitely a no-shoes-on-the-carpet kind of household."

I don't know if it's because her house is so fancy, or if it's because I've never been to a real high school party before, but when Ebony escorts us down the stairs and into her basement, I feel like Audrey Hepburn in *My Fair Lady*. Specifically, the scene where Eliza has to walk into the Embassy Ball and try to pass as British royalty.

When I watched that part of the movie with Wade, I didn't think I'd ever be able to pull off that kind of transformation. In eight weeks!

But now, as Rhodes and Yang give me a fist bump at the bottom of the stairs, as people smile at us while we make our way into the room, as no one blinks an eye that I came here with Reese . . . it's like I've already passed the test.

I just feel kind of bad that Wade's not here to witness it.

"Who's ready to party?" Hannah shouts, coming up behind us with her oversize purse and sunglasses, despite it being nighttime.

Ebony sighs. "Look, I don't care if you drink. But can you please keep it on the down-low? Voting for prom court is Monday, and the last thing I need is for some underclassman to get alcohol poisoning at my house." She looks at me. "Sorry, Brady."

No offense taken. I don't even like drinking.

"Why do you assume I was talking about alcohol?" Hannah asks.

Ebony shakes her head, incredulous. "You offered me a drink as soon as I opened my front door."

"Well . . ." Hannah takes her sunglasses off, placing them on top of her head. "It's rude to show up to a party without a gift for the host."

"Just be responsible," Ebony tells her. "No shots."

As Ebony gets pulled away to set up their home theater projector, Hannah, Reese, and I make our way past a large U-shaped couch with about a dozen theater kids sprawled across it, and over to the bar.

"Okay," Hannah says, pulling a bottle of whiskey from her bag. "Shots, then?"

"But Ebony said . . ."

I stop, cringing at how uptight I sound.

Reese smiles. "You're cute when you worry."

I peek at Hannah to see if she's going to react to that, but she's already lining up three plastic cups.

"Do you actually like this shit?" Reese asks, looking at the whiskey label. "Or do you just think drinking it makes you look badass?"

Hannah grabs the bottle from him, shooting him a look. "What is this, International Shit On Hannah Day?"

I didn't notice it before because of the sunglasses, but Hannah's eyes are a little red. Like maybe she's been crying.

Reese puts up his hands. "My bad. Whiskey's cool."

Hannah hands me a cup and I accept it from her. Even if I did like alcohol, I drove here tonight. I can't drink this. But I also don't want to look uncool in front of Reese. As they toss back their shots, I bring mine to my nose. The aroma makes my nostrils sting. It smells like an old boot that's been soaked in kerosene.

"Not a whiskey fan?" Reese asks, reading my face.

"I've just . . . I don't know what it tastes like."

He takes my cup from me and pulls me in for a kiss. With tongue. In front of everyone. The only thing I taste now is panic. *Mine.*

"So that's happening," Hannah says, raising an eyebrow.

My breathing shallows—and not just from the kiss. I can't believe he did that. I mean, I guess I don't care if other people know. But Reese said he wasn't looking for anything serious. If he's that casual about kissing in public, what else isn't a big deal for him?

"I don't think he likes it," Reese says, handing the cup back to Hannah.

She takes the shot for herself, then fishes a key out of a martini shaker on the shelf behind us. "What's your usual poison?" she asks, unlocking one of the cupboards below the bar.

I like staying in control. Which is why the idea of drinking has never really appealed to me before. But tonight, letting go a little might not be the worst idea.

"That one," I say, pointing to a bottle with a palm tree on it.

"Rum," Hannah informs me.

It has a coconutty smell, which doesn't seem like it'd be *too* horrible. But when I take the shot she offers, it's like swallowing suntan lotion. It burns, too. After the initial shock wears off, though, it becomes more of a pleasant warmth.

"You okay?" Reese asks.

I nod, setting my cup back down. Thankfully, we move on to a round of rum and cherry Cokes next. As Reese hands me my drink, I tell myself that I can always get a ride home from someone else later.

After relocking the liquor cabinet, we head over to the couch to watch *Moulin Rouge!* with everyone else. The sweetness of the cherry Coke isn't enough to kill the taste of the alcohol. But if I take baby sips, it's a little more manageable.

I'm not sure how long it takes for someone to become drunk, but soon there's a funny tingling sensation in my head. It's nice, like when you wrap yourself in a soft towel after getting out of the shower.

"Damn," Reese says. "Ewan McGregor could get it." Then he pushes his knee into mine and whispers, "He's not the only one who could get it."

The pleasant buzz is suddenly gone, replaced by an increased throbbing in my ears. Everything seems to be happening so quickly. And as much as I like kissing Reese, I'm worried he'll expect more from me. Like sex. Which I don't think I'm ready for yet.

So I take another sip.

And another.

Until the buzz returns.

About halfway through the movie the booze really starts kicking in—in more ways than one. I ask Reese where the bathroom is, and when I stand up from the couch, my body feels noticeably looser. Like my neck got weaker, or maybe my head is heavier. I walk with concentration, hoping no one can tell how tipsy I am.

After using the bathroom (trivia fact: alcohol works as a diuretic, helping your body rid itself of water), I take a moment to study myself in the mirror. It could just be the combination of soft lighting and rum, but my confidence starts creeping back in. I smile at my reflection. At Brady.

"D'you know who else could get it?" I ask. "Not just Ewan McGregor."

There's a knock on the door. I jump back, startled.

"Just a minute."

(Trivia fact: Romans created the measurement of time with the invention of sundials. No, wait—it was the Egyptians.)

When I open the door, Ava's on the other side. "Sorry," she says. "I was waiting for a while. I wasn't sure if anyone was in here or not."

Heat rushes to my already-flushed cheeks. Maybe I was looking at myself in the mirror longer than I thought.

"I was just . . . I'm done now." I try to get out of her way, clipping my shoulder against the doorframe as I go.

"Are you okay?" she asks.

"I'm not drunk."

She gives me a funny look.

"Have you seen Wade tonight?" I ask, changing the subject before she can ask why my breath reminds her of a trip to the beach.

Her mouth dips into a frown. "I don't think he came."

"Really?"

"Did you . . ." She pauses, gripping her elbows. "Do you know he didn't get into NYU?"

"Yeah. He was waitlisted."

She shakes her head. "No. He just told everybody that."

My limbs go numb again. NYU was his plan, so he could prove to his parents that he's good enough. He must be devastated. I reach for my phone, but then remember that Wade's a liar. He lied about why he was helping me, and now he's lying about NYU. He doesn't deserve my sympathy.

"I have to go," I tell Ava.

(Trivia fact: humans have forty-three facial muscles. It takes seventeen of them to smile, and all forty-three to scowl.)

When I get back to the other room, I head straight for the bar. I need to stop thinking about Wade. Reese may be moving fast, but I'd rather be with someone who's honest about what he wants than with a liar.

Besides, this is what alcohol was designed for: loosened inhibitions and poor choices.

Not that Reese is a poor choice. Hiding under the bar and taking another shot of rum, on the other hand? Probably not my finest moment. It does the trick, though. By the time I get back to the couch, the warm tingling sensation is back.

"There you are," Reese says, pressing his knee into mine again.

This time, I press back.

He leans into my ear. "Should we get out of here?"

My heart races, but I nod. And without saying anything else,

Reese and I get up and leave. I follow him upstairs to the second floor, where we pass portraits of Ebony and two girls I assume are her sisters.

"Is it okay that we're up here?" I ask.

Instead of answering my question, Reese opens a door and pulls me into a room. It's too dark to see anything, and my balance is already questionable, so when Reese starts making out with me, I grab onto him and kiss back.

We bump into a bed, quickly falling back onto it. Having Reese on top of me is hot. But I'm still distracted. Now that my eyes are adjusting to the dark, I can make out framed photos on the nightstand next to us. I recognize one of the girls from the hallway.

"Is this someone's bedroom?" I ask.

"Don't worry. Her sister's away at college."

I close my eyes, willing myself to relax. I'm drunk and making out with one of the hottest guys in school—this shouldn't be that hard.

Oh. Speaking of hard.

Reese is definitely turned on already. He stops to lift his shirt up over his head. I should probably do the same, but my arms refuse to move. The only other person I've been remotely intimate with before was Wade. And that was just spooning. And an accident!

No—Wade's the last person I should be thinking about. I focus my attention back on Reese, but I'm finding that harder to do now that the room is starting to spin. *Am I really that drunk?*

Reese reaches for my belt buckle. My hand shoots out to stop him.

"Is that not okay?" he asks.

"Um . . ."

To his credit, he lets go. I should be able to say something to him, though. The words are right there, stuck at the back of my throat.

No. Let's slow down. I'm not ready yet.

But as Reese continues to grind against me, I can't bring myself to say them out loud. Because I don't want to seem uncool. Because I should be thankful that Reese is even interested in me.

Because this is what Brady would do.

"Just let me know how far you want to go," he tells me.

I'm sure Reese would stop if I told him to. But I continue to make out with him, pushing past my discomfort. I have to prove that I can do this. I can't let Wade be right.

My face starts to feel hot. The alcohol is working. Once I'm drunk enough, I can finally stop being afraid. I can stop thinking about Wade. I can—*Oh no.*

The words finally come to me.

Only, they're not the ones I thought I was going to say.

"Watch out," I say, pushing Reese off me. "I'm gonna be sick."

(Trivia fact: butyric acid can be found in both vomit and Parmesan cheese, making their odors hard to distinguish.)

(Trivia fact: I'm a fucking mess.)

Thirty-Six

WADE

Sitting at my dressing table the week after the cast party, I try not to think about how quiet it is as I apply my eyeliner. Normally, this room would be full of noise. People running vocal scales. Gretchen reminding us to check our props. Ava, Ebony, and Hannah sitting next to me, talking about how sad we are that this is our last show together.

But it's just me in here.

Alone.

After last weekend, I tried apologizing to Ava and Hannah. But they're still too hurt. Even Ebony, who's always willing to talk things through, didn't let me off the hook so easily. She said it'd probably be best if I gave everyone some space.

I thought showing up to the theater early today would be a good way to avoid creating drama and alienating myself further. But now, as I sit here in my costume for the last time, applying my makeup for the last time, it only makes me feel worse. My senior year is going out on the lowest note possible.

"Hard to see a good show come to an end," Mr. Z says, startling me.

He's standing in the doorway. And when I see the stack of envelopes he's holding, my chest tightens. His thank-you cards—for the final performance, he handwrites a note to every cast and crew member, thanking them for being part of the show.

"Ready to bring Pickering to life one last time?" he asks, as he starts distributing the cards to people's dressing tables.

I know his question is meant to be an innocent one. But it twists in my heart like a knife. I still can't bring myself to feel good about playing Colonel Pickering. Not when it's a constant reminder of my failure.

"Um," I say. "Yeah."

I wish I could let it go. But now the question I couldn't bring myself to ask him before is bubbling up inside me. And maybe it's because my friends are mad at me, and Elijah and Reese are hooking up, and it's my very last show and nothing seems to matter anymore . . . I ask it.

"Why didn't I get to play Higgins? Was Reese really better than me?"

I'm being unprofessional. Not to mention shitty. But Mr. Z smiles politely, drumming his fingers against the envelopes he's holding.

"It's not about being better. I know you could've played Higgins just fine."

The knife twists its way in deeper. Then what, he was just fucking with my confidence or something?

"I've seen you play that kind of role before," he continues. "Which isn't to say Reese didn't earn it; you both had strong auditions. But as a teacher, it's my job to challenge my students. That's why I gave you Pickering."

He gave it to me because it was . . . *a better challenge?* That doesn't even make sense. What could be more challenging than playing the lead? They have more stage time. More lines to memorize. More solos to perform.

"You should always want to grow as an artist," Mr. Z says.

I nod, too stunned to say anything else. I'm sorry I asked the question. Not because it was inappropriate—because I got an answer I didn't want. Thinking I was a failure really sucked. But knowing I was good enough and *still* didn't get the part . . . that just seems cruel.

"Well, anyway." He steps forward and hands me my card. "I have a hard time saying goodbye to my seniors. That's why I always write it down."

I take it from him, unable to ignore the sudden pit in my stomach. The one that tells me I'm being ungrateful—Mr. Z has done so much for me these past few years. "Thanks," I say, a little too softly. "For everything."

I can't bring myself to open the card right away. Later, when the rest of the cast starts to arrive, I go hide in the prop shop. And sitting on the velvet tufted sofa, with my heart in my throat, I finally read what it says.

Dear Wade: Every once in a while, I'm blessed with a student whose enthusiasm for theater and performing is greater than any teacher could wish for. It's been an absolute pleasure to have you on our stage these past four years. Your talent is clear, and I can't wait to see where your passion takes you next. Yours, Mr. Zimmerman

I'm blinking back tears before I even get to the end. It was nice of him to say that. But I don't think it's true anymore. I still want to do theater; I'm just not on the same trajectory. At the beginning of this year, I saw myself going to NYU, then Broadway, then the Tony Awards, where I'd be holding my trophy and circling back to this moment by thanking Mr. Z in my acceptance speech.

And now, after alienating all my friends, I won't even be at NYU to sit in the audience for Ava's first performance there.

The intercom speaker crackles, and Gretchen calls places. I head upstairs and join the rest of the cast in the wings. Standing off to the side, in her tattered dress and shawl, is Ava. She's facing the wall and doing her preshow breathing exercises.

If she needs space, I want to respect that. But this is our last show together. I don't want us to regret not speaking to each other—especially because of something I did. Walking over, I gently tap her elbow. When she turns around, her eyes look up at me from under the dark makeup that's smudged across her face to look like soot.

"I just . . ." Colonel Pickering's cravat suddenly feels too tight around my neck. "Um, break a leg today."

She smiles. But it's more sad than happy. "Thanks. You too."

My eyes grow wet again. How'd I fuck this up so badly? Ava and I should be holding hands and acting overly sentimental right now. Not exchanging generic pleasantries like two people who hardly know each other.

I thought I was protecting her feelings so she wouldn't feel guilty about getting into NYU without me. But maybe I was only protecting myself. I was crushed, and instead of turning to Ava for support, I was more worried about how my rejection would make me look.

"Ava, I never should've—"

She grabs my hand, giving it a squeeze. "I'm really sorry you didn't get into NYU."

I nod and give her a squeeze back. "Yeah, me too."

There's a lot more I have to say, but the orchestra pit has stopped warming up. The audience grows quiet while the house lights begin to dim. It's the overture, one of my favorite parts. It doesn't matter that I've heard it countless times by now. I still get goose bumps.

Only my goose bumps feel more chilling this time around. I used to think *My Fair Lady* was a happy show. And that while Higgins was still a flawed character, the ending was ambiguous enough to let you believe he'd eventually change. Now I have no doubt that it's a tragedy. Henry Higgins is a straight-up dick. Instead of admitting his feelings toward Eliza, he asks her to fetch his slippers—like she's still beneath him. Eliza deserves better than him. Just like my friends, Elijah, and Reese all deserved better than me.

I thought I wasn't like Higgins.

I thought I *had* changed.

But I hadn't. Not really. I only befriended Elijah because I thought it would help me win back Reese. It doesn't matter that I genuinely ended up liking him, because that never would've happened if I didn't think there was something in it for me first.

I don't want to be selfish and self-centered anymore. I want to change—*for real this time*. Which means I should let Reese and Elijah make their own decisions, even when they don't benefit me.

The overture comes to an end and the audience applauds. As my castmates make their way out onto the dark stage, I glance up at the follow-spot booth—the one Elijah sits in—and confirm what I've known for a while now:

It's not Reese I'm going to have a hard time letting go of.

It's Elijah.

The lights come up for the opening scene. If I'm late for my entrance and miss the cue for my first line, it'll derail the entire scene. I don't want to be that kind of actor. I may not have the lead, but I'm still part of this show. So I do what I do best: take a deep, full breath and walk into the bright lights, ready to perform.

At the end of our curtain call, we drag Mr. Z on to the stage and make him take a bow with us. Things aren't over, though. Gretchen has the stagehands rush out and present roses to the seniors. This happens every year—but now it's finally my turn. The audience claps a little louder, rising from their seats to give us a standing ovation.

Warmth blossoms in my chest as I look around and make eye contact with Ava. And Ebony. And even Hannah. It's silly, and emotional, and definitely bittersweet. The four of us will probably never share the stage again. Not like this.

When we finally shuffle off into the wings, there are more hugs and congratulations. As happy as I am for everyone, it's hard to be in a celebratory mood. I can still hear Mr. Z's words in my head: *You should always want to grow as an artist.* I didn't grow, though. Not with this show. I could've taken my role as a challenge. Worked on my comedic timing. Learned how to be a good character actor.

Instead most of my rehearsal time was spent feeling sorry for myself. My failure wasn't in not being cast as the lead—it was in not putting in the same effort that I usually would. Mr. Z wasn't to blame for my unhappiness. Neither was Reese. I did this to myself.

Back downstairs, I stop at my dressing table, still holding my rose.

Underneath the cellophane wrapping, one of the petals is already starting to wilt. I set it down, frowning. I'm not sure I did anything to earn it anyhow.

On the counter, my phone lights up with texts.

Hey, little bro.

Sorry I couldn't be in town to see your show with the rest of the fam today.

Mom and Dad said you were great last weekend.

No shit. You always are.

What is Brett talking about? I didn't invite anyone to today's performance. In fact, I told my parents not to bother.

Without changing out of my costume, I head back upstairs. The lobby is packed with people, and I scan the crowd, looking for my parents. *Did they really come again?* When I find them, the bigger surprise is who's next to them: TJ and Becca. I can't believe they drove all this way when I'm not even the lead.

My mouth goes dry as I stand there.

Maybe that doesn't matter to them.

Maybe they'd be proud of me no matter which part I played.

Becca's the first to spot me. She waves excitedly as I squeeze my way through all the bodies. Mom and Dad each give me a hug, telling me what a good job I did. I'm sure they'd say that no matter how my performance was. Still, it's nice to hear.

As someone who loves theater enough to defend shows like *Cats* and *Jesus Christ Superstar*, it's not like I couldn't respect my family's passion for sports. Sometimes it's just hard that my passion doesn't overlap with theirs. That doesn't mean they haven't been here to support me, though. And maybe, since theater's *not* their passion, it makes their support twice as meaningful.

"Hey, you make a really great old dude," TJ says, giving me shit.

I roll my eyes. "Thanks."

"Seriously, though . . ." He pauses, handing me the bouquet of flowers he's holding. "Good job. I could never get up there and do what you do."

My insides immediately turn to jelly. I give TJ a hug, glad to have something sturdy to hang on to. "Thanks for coming," I tell him, my voice a hoarse whisper. "It's really nice to have you here."

Thirty-Seven

ELIJAH

"Let's start with ellipsoidals," Summer says. "Always double-check the gel clip and remember to keep a hand on the C-clamp once the safety cable is off. The last thing we need is to crush someone's skull."

"Right, it's people's skulls you're looking out for," Yang replies. "Not your precious lighting equipment."

Summer shrugs. "Can't it be both?"

Walking out onto the catwalks, it's hard not to think about how much things have changed since my first trip up here. I still get that funny feeling in my groin when I look down. But I'm less afraid now. Or maybe I've just gotten better at not letting my fear control me. It probably helps that I also know what I'm doing. Gel clips and C-clamps—those words aren't a mystery to me anymore as I let my feet hang over the edge, unhanging my first light.

"Hard to believe it's over already," Rhodes says.

"Don't worry," replies Yang. "With the speed some of these actors are moving, I'd say we have a solid three or four hours of strike ahead of us still."

Watching the show come to an end this afternoon was bittersweet. Just as I've finally gotten the hang of everything, we have to take it all down again. I guess no one's a fan of strike, though. Especially the actors, who are forced to stick around and help.

"I can't believe Szabo ditched us to clean the booth with Ava," Rhodes says.

"Please," Yang grumbles. "As if it takes two people to sort gels."

"Better than letting the actors come up into the catwalks," Summer says, unscrewing a bolt like it's nothing.

Rhodes sighs. "You realize he's going to ditch us at prom now, too. He's crossed over to the other side."

"You could join my group," I say. "Reese and his friends are getting a hotel room for after the dance."

The invitation just pops out of my mouth. Maybe it's a sign that I'm becoming more confident. Or maybe it's because I'm still nervous about Reese. We haven't talked much outside of the show—or kissed again—since the opening night cast party. I hope he doesn't regret asking me to prom.

The lighting crew look at each other for a moment, not saying anything.

"Sorry," Summer finally replies. "But I don't think soccer players are really the vibe we're going for either."

"Oh, yeah." I give my crescent wrench another crank, trying to hide my disappointment. "That's cool."

"Besides," Yang says, "we never said we didn't have plans. Summer's boyfriend is breaking us into the planetarium."

"You have a boyfriend?" I ask, jerking my head in her direction.

Her brow furrows. "What, you thought I was taking Yang or Rhodes as my date?"

"No, it's just . . . I've never heard you talk about him."

"We thought Clark was made up, too," says Rhodes. "Until we

met him at Summer's photography exhibit."

"Clark." Yang shrugs. "It just sounds like the name of someone's dad."

"He's not breaking us into the planetarium," Summer explains. "He works there. And he talked his supervisor into letting us design a laser light show for after the dance. You and Reese can come if you want."

A light show does sound fun. And I do want to meet Clark, especially since I wasn't at the photography exhibit—which, *shit*, I still haven't gone to.

"Sure," I say. "I'll talk to Reese."

"Clark's really excited about it." Summer pauses, fighting off a smile, before letting it blossom across her face in a very un-Summer-like manner. "We're both excited."

I look down at the stage, ignoring the pit in my stomach when I spot Reese. He's at the back of the set, holding a scene flat as crew members work to pull the screws out with their power drills. One of the screws must be stripped, though, because it makes an awful screeching noise that echoes across the auditorium.

I should also be excited about prom. But ever since the cast party, ever since I threw up all over the carpet at Ebony's house . . . I don't know, it's like becoming Brady didn't solve my problems in the way I thought it would. I'm glad I did the show. And I'm definitely not the same person I was when I first started this. But am I happier? Or do I just have new problems now?

My hangover after the cast party was enough to set me straight about one thing: no rum for me on prom night. But what about the other part? What happens when we get a hotel room with Reese's friends, and he and I end up sharing a bed?

It seems ridiculous that I'm nervous about hooking up with him. But now the pressure is twice as intense. I already screwed up our first attempt. I can't ruin prom, too. That's something Elijah would do.

To be honest, I'm not sure I would've even tried to kiss Reese if I hadn't gotten in that fight with Wade first. But I made my choice. I have to stick with it.

A few hours into strike, we finish taking down and refocusing all the lights. Most of the other departments have completed their work as well. But we're a crew; no one goes home until everyone's done.

As we wait for the final set pieces to be dismantled, Gretchen recruits a few people to make sure all the posters from the show have been taken down. She pairs Reese and me together, which is a bit awkward.

"I don't know about you," he says as we exit the auditorium, "but I'm ready to go home and take a weeklong nap."

"Yeah," I reply.

"Seems wild that prom's next weekend already. This whole school year will be over before we know it."

"Uh-huh."

I'm reverting to one-word answers again, but I don't know what else to say. *Sorry I tricked you into thinking I'm someone who's marginally cool? Sorry I almost threw up in your mouth while making out?*

"Speaking of prom," Reese says, "Sanjay got his parents to book us an extra room for the night. Everyone will have a little more privacy that way."

"Oh. Great."

I'm sure Reese can see the panic all over my face as we head into the cafeteria. When Wade gave me my lesson on stage combat, he said it's important to have a scene partner you can trust. It's not that I don't trust Reese. I just don't know him very well yet. I'm not even sure how much I like him. I mean, if he's going to be my first, it should be something I want, right? Not just something I'm doing because I think it's what other people would choose.

Reese spots a poster on one of the pillars.

"Have you ever been to a laser light show?" I ask.

He shakes his head. "I don't think so."

"The lighting crew was planning to go to one at the planetarium after the dance. I thought it sounded cool."

"Yeah," he replies, but there's no excitement behind it.

Silence falls between us as he carefully peels the tape off the poster. If I want to go to the light show, I have to say the words out loud, not just leave hints for Reese to pick up. But I still can't bring myself to do it.

"Anyhow," I say. "I'm excited for the hotel room."

He smiles. "Me too. It's going to be epic."

Yeah, an epic disaster.

As we leave the cafeteria, Reese offers me the rolled-up poster he's carrying. "You need one of these still?"

"What for?"

He shrugs. "Most people hang one up in their bedroom."

I take it, and when we return to the auditorium, the stage is finally empty. No set pieces, no backdrops, no spike tape. Crew members are sweeping and mopping up already, getting ready to apply a fresh coat of paint to the floor.

I clutch my poster a little tighter, not sure if I'm ready for it to be over yet. I joined the crew to get closer to Connor. And while that never happened, something a million times better did—I put myself out there and made my own friends. It's going to be weird not to see them in the theater every day. What if we never hang out anymore?

As if the Universe is trying to answer my question, Wade appears onstage, carrying a paint roller. We haven't spoken since our fight in the prop room—when we argued about Reese.

It's hard to believe our eight weeks are over already. I wish I could talk to him now. I'd tell him how I'm nervous about prom night. I'd tell him that I need his guidance, or more lessons on how to handle myself.

I'd tell him how much I miss him.

For a brief moment, as I stand near the edge of the stage, Wade's eyes meet mine. Something inside me shifts, and it no longer matters that he only wanted to help me so he could win back Reese. Our friendship was real. I know that. I *feel* that.

I think I could move past our fight and go back to being friends. But just as I start to smile at him, he turns away and faces upstage. As if he never saw me.

As if I'm not even here.

Suddenly, it's like we're back to the beginning again. There's a bare stage, and Wade Westmore has no idea who I am.

Thirty-Eight

WADE

"Are you sure you want to open this in front of us?" Ava asks.

I look at her, Ebony, and Hannah, all three of whom answered my emergency text and rushed to the prop room. It's been three days since the show ended, and it still feels strange not to be spending every afternoon together.

"Yes," I reply, glancing down at my phone. "I'm sure."

The truth is, I'm *not* sure. If I log in to the application portal for Columbia and it says I've been accepted . . . well, yeah, it's going to be amazing to have my three best friends here.

If I'm *not* accepted—which, statistically speaking, is the more likely outcome—then I'm going to be crushed. Still, if my dream's going to slip away from me while sitting on a stuffy old couch in the basement of the theater, maybe it's better to have a little company to lean on for support.

I take a breath and click the link. My heart pounds faster than should be humanly possible, but the suspense is over within a matter of seconds: *we regret to inform you.*

I close my eyes and shake my head. Before my first tear can slip out, three pairs of arms wrap around me, engulfing me in a fierce group hug. Nobody says anything. They wait for me to speak first.

"Thanks for being here," I say, my voice a choked whisper.

"We're proud of you," Ava replies. "Always."

Knowing that makes me cry harder. I did everything I could to get into these schools. And it wasn't enough. Which sucks—*a lot*. Just thinking about saying goodbye to my dream of going to college in New York creates a hollow pit in my stomach. One that feels like it's trying to swallow me whole.

It's okay to be disappointed. It's okay to be sad. But I don't have to stay in those feelings forever. Going to school in New York was *a* dream. Not *the* dream. People are allowed to have more than one. Which is why I've started to figure out my backup plan.

After wiping my cheeks dry, I grab my backpack. "Here," I say to Hannah, pulling out two Lachlan University T-shirts, one for each of us.

Her face lights up. "When did you—how long have you been carrying these around?"

"About a week."

She grabs my hand, giving it a squeeze. "I know it's not NYU. But their theater program is really strong."

Lachlan wasn't my top choice. But Hannah's right, it's still a good school. And going there doesn't mean that I won't ever get to New York. I'm just taking a detour first. A detour that includes Hannah and some really good cheese curds.

After the bell rings, everyone gives me another hug. Ebony offers to escort me to my next class, linking arms with me as we walk down the hallway together. "Are you sure you won't go to prom this weekend?" she asks. "It's not too late to change your mind."

There's an ache at the back of my throat. It's the same one I used to get when I thought about Reese after he dumped me. Except now it's Elijah I'm thinking about. When he came up to me at the end of strike, it killed me to pretend like I didn't see him standing there. But if Elijah and Reese want to be together, the right thing for me to do is not get in the way.

Which is why I can't go. I don't trust myself not to say something.

"What if you just joined us for dinner," Ebony says. "You know my mom's going totally overboard. She even rented out a selfie station."

Ebony and Hannah finally came to a compromise on their pre-prom plans. They're still doing fast-food drive-thrus like Hannah wants. But instead of eating in the limo, Ebony's taking advantage of her mom's catering know-how and orchestrating a fancy outdoor picnic for them.

"I appreciate it," I tell her. "But I'm actually looking forward to a quiet night at home."

"And you really don't care about prom court?"

I stop for a moment, imagining everyone cheering as my name is called. I can't pretend like I wouldn't enjoy the attention still. But is that really what's going to make me happy? I thought wearing the crown and sharing a kiss with Reese in front of everyone would somehow save senior year. But looking back now, it wasn't a total bust. Not when I was eating lunch in the prop room with Ava. Or having movie night with my friends again. Or getting milkshakes with Elijah.

I clear my throat. If I sound upset, hopefully Ebony thinks it's related to my rejection from Columbia still.

"The only thing I'm going to regret missing," I say, "is if you win prom queen and I'm not there to cheer you on."

She smiles. "Part of me knows it doesn't really mean anything. But I don't want to look back at high school and only remember doing homework and busting my ass to get into Stanford. Besides, I've had to work twice as hard as most students just to prove myself at this school. So, yeah, I feel like I deserve a tiara for that."

I really hope she wins. And I do feel guilty about not being there with my friends. But I have to do what's right. No matter how hard that is.

When Saturday rolls around, doing the right thing is harder than I expected it to be. I made Ava, Hannah, and Ebony promise they'd let me chauffeur them around to their various pre-prom appointments. I want to be there for them, like they've been here for me this past week. But now that I see them with their prom nails and prom hair, getting caffeine boosts from their pre-prom Starbucks, the little itch of jealousy I feel is getting harder to ignore.

After dropping Ebony and Hannah off at their homes, I pull into Ava's driveway and purposefully leave the engine running.

"You're really not going to come upstairs?" she asks, pouting. "Don't you want to see me in my dress?"

Of course I want to see her in her dress. But if I go up to her bedroom, it'll be twice as painful when I have to come back down.

"You've tried that dress on for me at least five times already," I say.

"But you haven't witnessed the full effect. Besides, what if there's a loose string in the back, or my makeup's smudged? You know my parents are going to tell me I look beautiful no matter what."

Even though she's wearing a loose-fitting top and no makeup, she looks just as radiant as she did when she wore Eliza's dress for the ascot race. "You should listen to your parents for once," I tell her. "They're right."

She groans. "I just want everything to be perfect."

"Perfection's overrated."

She arches an eyebrow at me, which—*fair*.

"You must really like Chris," I say.

She blushes, pursing her lips. "I'm not looking for another relationship right now. But this was a nice surprise. I'm rolling with it."

Szabo seems like a decent guy. And I'm glad Ava has him. I never would've pictured them as prom dates, but if there's one thing I'm coming to understand, it's that life doesn't follow a script—even when you try to force it to.

"You'd better text me pictures," I tell her. "And I'm expecting a full rundown tomorrow."

"Are you sure you're going to be okay tonight?" she asks, frowning.

"Yes. I'm actually looking forward to a quiet—"

"Wade." She gives me a look, having already heard me feed that line to everyone else. "I wish you'd tell me the real reason you're not going to prom."

"I did tell you. I didn't want to go if I couldn't find a date."

Her face softens. "No offense, but did you even try?"

"Yes!"

"It's just, guys are usually throwing themselves at you. I find it hard to believe no one said yes."

"Well . . . everyone was booked."

"Who did you ask, though? Because I can think of at least two guys from the chorus who aren't—"

"Okay, *fine*." It's no use trying to lie. She'll list every guy we've ever done a show with who isn't straight. "I'm not going because I don't want to ruin the night for Elijah and Reese."

Her forehead creases. "Why would you ruin their night?"

I lean back into the headrest, sighing. I'm still not proud of what I did. But if there's one person who's going to forgive my flaws, it's Ava. "The reason I gave Elijah a makeover in the first place was because I wanted Reese to see that I wasn't a jerk anymore. Except I am a jerk. I hurt both of them. And now that they're in a relationship, it's better if I just remove myself from the equation altogether."

She bites her lip, processing this new information. "And you're *sure* they're in a relationship?"

"Yes." I close my eyes, just wanting this conversation to be over. "I saw them making out before the cast party."

It's practically burned into my memory. Reese cupping Elijah's face. Elijah kissing him. I flick my eyes back open, shaking them from my thoughts.

"Okay, so they made out," Ava says. She squeezes the armrest, like she's trying to make up her mind about something. Szabo's going to be here soon if she doesn't hurry. "But did you *ask* him if they're actually dating?"

"Why would I do that? He's taking Elijah to prom. Reese clearly doesn't have feelings for me anymore."

"I didn't mean Reese."

Suddenly it's like all the air has been sucked out of my car. I can't turn to look at Ava, because if I do, my face is going to confirm what she's hinting at.

"Why—why would I ask Elijah that?" My voice comes out all wrong. It's too strained.

"Sorry," she replies quickly. "Maybe I was mistaken."

I don't respond to her. I *can't*. Ava undoes her seat belt, careful not to mess her hair. "I should get going," she says. "Thanks for driving us today."

I nod, my hands gripped tightly around the steering wheel. Admitting to myself that I have feelings for Elijah was hard enough. If I say it out loud to someone else, it will become too real.

When I try to speak again, my voice is still off. "Have fun tonight."

Ava gets out of my car, but she doesn't close the door right away. After waiting a moment, she takes a breath and leans back in. "Reese told Hannah he wasn't looking for anything serious. I just thought maybe you'd like to know."

I look at her, my heart leaping into my throat.

"What am I supposed to do with that?"

"I don't know. Maybe you should figure it out." She gives me a pointed look. One that says, as my best friend, she knows exactly what I should do but she can't solve this problem for me.

Ava closes the door. With the engine still running, I sit in her driveway and watch as she hurries up to her house to finish getting ready for prom. Suddenly, I'm in no condition to drive.

Thirty-Nine

ELIJAH

"Are you having a good time so far?" Reese asks, his arms wrapped around my waist as we pose for a group shot for the photographer.

I try not to blink as the flash goes off. "Yeah. I am."

My answer is as fake as the smile that's stretched across my face. But I don't want Reese to feel bad. It's not his fault I can't relax around his friends—it's mine. I'm still too anxious about what's going to happen later tonight. And without the show—*without Wade*—it's like I'm forgetting how to be Brady.

"How about we try a few fun ones?" the photographer asks.

Reese's soccer buddies and their dates, it turns out, aren't too cool for silly photos. While they make peace signs and duck lips, I just stand there, sticking to the same rigid pose because I can't think of anything better to do.

After photos, we decide to walk around a bit. The venue our school rented for the night is an old train depot that's been converted into an upscale party space. There are swaths of white fabric cascading from the ceiling, twinkle lights wrapped around the columns, and a large archway of gold and silver balloons that leads to the dance floor, which is empty for now.

"We should claim a table," says Jenna, Ramsey's date.

Ramsey glances at Sanjay and Cooper. "Cool. I think we're going to head outside for a minute."

"Outside?" Jenna's perfectly made-up eyes pop with disbelief. "But we just got here."

"Babe, I wanna sneak in a quick vape. So I can spend the rest of my evening with you."

She sighs. "Just don't smoke that watermelon shit. I'm not dancing with a can of tropical fruit punch all night."

Ramsey pulls her in for a kiss, and the other two girls we're with—Amber and Nadia—swoon like they're witnessing major relationship goals.

"Do you want to join us?" Reese asks, looking at me.

"Uh . . ." I'm a little nervous about what they might actually be vaping. Even if it's a legal substance, my stomach's been queasy all day. And Reese clearly noticed, since he asked if I was feeling okay at our dinner earlier.

"I'm good," I tell him.

If he's disappointed, it doesn't show. Reese and his soccer buddies head off toward the outdoor patio area, leaving me alone with their dates, who feel less like my friends and more like a group of disinterested babysitters.

"They'd better not be drinking already," Jenna says.

"Yeah," replies Nadia. "Not without us."

Jenna gives her a disapproving look. "It won't kill us to hold off a few hours until we get to the hotel."

"Speaking of the hotel . . ." Amber holds out her clutch, waving it. "I brought extra condoms. In case anyone needs them later."

"Amber." Jenna shakes her head. "We only have two rooms for the night. It's not like there's going to be a massive orgy."

Amber shrugs. "You never know. Especially once everyone starts drinking. Besides, I'm tired of having sex with Coop on that nasty old couch in his basement. It'd be nice to know what it's like to get penetrated in a bed for once."

Jenna's mouth falls open. *"Penetrated? Seriously?"*

"I can call it whatever I want. Don't slut shame me."

Jenna rolls her eyes and leads us over to a table, which has a bottle of water and a disposable camera at every place setting. Everyone also gets a commemorative picture frame, with inspirational quotes like, "Friendships like this will last a lifetime." And "Tomorrow's memories are being made tonight."

As the four of us sit down together, it reminds me just how weird prom themes are.

"Fire and Ice," for example, shares its name with a Robert Frost poem we studied in my American Lit class this year. It's about how human emotions like desire and hate are destructive enough to bring about societal collapse and the end of the world. *That's* what people want to be thinking about on prom night?

Or how about "Around the World"? There's no way that doesn't quickly veer into cultural appropriation. And because this is prom, there'd be enough photographic evidence to haunt people for years.

When our prom committee decided to go with "These Are the Days" as our theme, it seemed a bit vague, but innocent enough. But now, as I sit here with three girls I barely know, waiting for Reese and his soccer buddies to finish vaping, it feels more like a threat.

These are the days. Is this what I'm destined to remember about high school? Awkward social interactions? Pretending to be someone

I'm not? Feeling sad about not being friends with Wade anymore? Maybe things were better back before I tried to change.

"What about you, Brady?" Nadia asks, turning toward me.

My stomach goes queasy again. Oh god, I hope they're not still talking about the hotel room and who plans to get penetrated.

(Trivia fact: female penguins will have transactional sex with males who are not their partner, in exchange for pebbles to build their nests.)

"Sorry," I say. "I was thinking about something else for a second."

Jenna laughs. "You're kind of quiet, aren't you?"

I inhale sharply, trying not to let my annoyance show. It's not like she's wrong. I have been quiet tonight. And even if Wade and I aren't friends anymore, I can still hear him telling me I need to put myself out there and let people in.

"I was thinking about prom themes," I say. "And how a lot of them are actually morbid. Like, 'Starry Night.' Sure, everyone knows the Van Gogh painting. But did you know it was inspired by the view from his room at a psychiatric asylum?"

The three of them share a look.

"Yeah," Jenna says. "I guess that *is* weird."

Except the way she says it, it's obvious she thinks *I'm* the weird one for bringing it up.

I smile politely as they go back to more socially acceptable topics, like whose dress looks expensive and whose looks like it was bought off the clearance rack. While glancing around to see if Reese is back yet, I spot Yang and Rhodes over by the deejay booth.

"I need to use the restroom," I say, excusing myself.

Walking over to the booth, my steps feel lighter. I don't know if

Yang and Rhodes would consider me their friend, but when you're hanging out in the theater way too late on a school night, having a heated debate over the headsets about the merits of Lagoon Blue light gels verses Scuba Blue light gels, it can make you feel strangely connected to someone.

Currently, Yang and Rhodes seem to be in a bit of a debate with the deejay.

"No offense," Rhodes says. "But we've worked on shows *way* more complex than this."

"Seriously, dude," Yang tells him. "We could do this in our sleep. With flashlights."

The deejay shakes his head. "Whatever. Just don't miss your cue."

This gets a chuckle out of Yang. "Yeah, like we'd ever be able to live that down."

When the two of them turn around and see me, their faces light up. "Brady," Yang says, giving me a fist bump. "Looking sharp."

"What was that about?" I ask.

"Yang and I are pulling double duty tonight," Rhodes explains. "The prom committee hired us to run the spotlights during prom court nominations. It's not much, but it helped pay for the upgrade on our suits."

Their tuxedo jackets are made from velvet—maroon for Yang, emerald for Rhodes. It's a nice change from seeing them dressed all in black for the show.

"You guys look great," I tell them.

Yang smiles, grabbing his lapels. "Obviously."

"Hey," Rhodes says. "There's Summer."

I turn around. She's all glammed up too, but without losing her typical Summer style. Her dress is long and black, leaving only her shoulders exposed. And her hair's pinned to the side in wavy curls that cover part of her face, kind of like a vintage movie star.

"Wow," I say.

She blushes. "Wow yourself."

"Where's Clark?"

She points to a tall, lanky guy with a handsome face and glasses who's over by the candy table. "I told him to stock up. Free snacks for our light show. Speaking of which, are you and Reese coming?"

The heaviness I felt earlier returns. I really want to go. And not just because a laser light show sounds like it'd be a lot more fun than sitting in a hotel room, watching Reese's friends get drunk. I also just really want to be Summer's friend. Once the musical was over, I finally went to see her photography exhibit. It was really cool. I told her how much I loved it, but I was still embarrassed about having ditched her the first time. Just like all the other times I've ditched the lighting crew so I could hang out with Reese, or Wade and his friends.

"We're going straight to the hotel after this," I tell her.

Her smile doesn't waver, but I feel like I've let her down again.

"Hey," Yang says. "Has anyone seen Szabo yet?"

"They just got here," Summer replies. "I think they're having their group photo taken."

Rhodes cuts in: "Speaking of groups, maybe we should go hang with our dates before they think we've abandoned them."

Summer looks at me again. "Come find us later, okay?"

After they leave, I continue walking around instead of heading back to my table. I don't know if it's a conscious decision or not, but I end up back toward the entrance again, where the photographer's station is set up.

Maybe it's silly, but I feel like if I could just see Wade for a minute, then everything would be okay. I don't know what it is, but it's like I'm the best, most confident version of myself around him.

When I find Szabo and Ava's group, however, Wade's not posing for pictures with them. In fact, I don't see him anywhere. He wouldn't ditch prom, would he?

There's a tap on my shoulder. Relief washes over me, but only for a second. It's Reese, not Wade, who's standing behind me.

"Thinking of leaving already?" he asks.

"Oh, no. I was just . . ."

"I'm kidding." He smiles. "Sorry to ditch you back there. I was just trying to keep an eye on my friends. I don't want things getting too wild before prom court's announced."

I swallow, trying not to think about what happens *after* prom court.

"Yeah," I tell him. "Don't worry about it."

Reese runs his hand along the back of his neck, as though he's suddenly shy about something. When he speaks, his voice is softer, more hesitant. "Hey, we've kept things real between us, right?"

"I think so," I say, even though I feel like I've been the opposite of real with him.

"And you're sure you're doing okay tonight?"

"Yes. Of course."

My answer comes too quickly. Reese seems to buy it, but I know why he's asking me that. My insecurities have started to get in the way again. And I don't know if it's because I'm forgetting how to be Brady, or if I'm just tired of pretending to be him.

The truth is . . . it takes me a while to warm up to things. And, unfortunately, time's not something I have a lot of right now. To quote the commemorative picture frame that's waiting for me back at the table: *Tomorrow's memories are being made tonight.*

"We should get back to your friends," I say.

As we walk away, I take a quick glance over my shoulder to be sure Wade's not here. My disappointment feels irrational. I'm here with Reese. He's the one I should be worried about. He's the one I should be searching for whenever we're not in the same room together. He's the one who actually asked me to prom.

Forty

WADE

Old Hollywood musicals have always been my go-to comfort movies. I love the spectacle, the big emotions, their willingness to be over-the-top and cheesy. Which is why tonight, after I made some popcorn and changed into my pajamas, I put on *South Pacific*. I was hoping it would help me forget about everything else for a while.

Only now, as I lie in my bed with my laptop, I'm finding it impossible to watch Nellie Forbush wash a man right out of her hair. My mind keeps drifting to what Ava said—*that Reese wasn't looking for anything serious.*

I don't know why that should matter to me. That's Reese and Elijah's business. Not mine.

Only, I can't ignore the tug at my heart—the one that says I should be with Elijah. And that maybe, if I'm lucky, Elijah might want to be with me? I mean, we've gotten to know each other pretty well. And if he was looking for something more serious, I could give that to him.

Pausing the movie, I grab my phone and open our texts. We haven't talked since the show ended. What would I even say to him? *Hey, hope you're having fun at prom. Oh, and just in case you don't like Reese . . . I also have feelings for you?*

No. I'm being selfish again. Elijah chose Reese. If I really like him, I have to respect his decision.

I close out my texts and switch over to Elijah's Instagram. Besides the group selfie from our *Rocky Horror* movie night, which I posted, the only other photo is the two of us standing in front of the ice caves. He added that one himself. Like it meant something to him.

The tug in my heart becomes a full-on ache. I wish we could hang out again. Just to see him smile. Hell, I'd even take him rolling his eyes at something I said.

A text comes in and my heart leaps in my chest.

But it's from Ava. A group selfie from the dance floor.

Elijah's probably not even thinking about me right now. Which hurts way more than I knew it could. I don't know why it took me so long to realize how I felt about him. I guess I was too afraid to admit it to myself. Though not because I was ashamed to have feelings for Elijah.

Because I was scared those feelings might be real.

It's not like my feelings for Reese *weren't* real. But Reese was different. Everyone knew who he was, and I think part of my liking him was just wanting to have what everyone else wanted. Best acting roles. Best colleges. Best boyfriend.

Elijah wasn't on most people's radar. So if I fell for him, it wasn't because of what other people thought of him. It was because of what *I* thought of him. And if my feelings for him were real, and he didn't like me back . . . well, then it might hurt a whole lot more.

I did fall for him, though.

Which is why this hurts so much now.

I close Instagram, not wanting to torture myself. Reese isn't looking for anything serious. Maybe Elijah isn't, either. And even if he is,

I doubt he'd be looking for it with me. Not after the way I've treated him.

I reach for my laptop, wanting to get lost in someone else's problems for a while. But first, there's a knock on my door.

Dad pops his head into my room. "Hey, just thought I'd check on you."

My parents were more than a little concerned about my decision not to attend prom tonight. They offered to take me out to dinner, which was nice, but I politely declined. I'm feeling sorry enough for myself as it is. I don't need them giving me sad looks over a basket of spicy buffalo wings on top of that.

"Watching anything good?" Dad asks.

"*South Pacific.*"

"A classic," he replies. And while I can bet my dad's never seen this movie before, I appreciate his effort.

I wait for him to leave. But he just stands in my doorway, looking at me. "You sure you're okay up here?"

"Yeah. I'm fine. You don't have to—"

I pause. I always thought my parents paid more attention to my brothers and their girlfriends, and that talking about boys with me made them uncomfortable. But maybe it's possible I also shut them out because it's not always easy for me to talk about, either. I like to think I'm secure in my sexuality. But I guess sometimes I'm still too caught up in comparing myself to my brothers and hating myself for not being more like them.

I shouldn't be afraid to open up to Dad. It just feels so weird. I mean, even the fact that he's standing in my room right now, surrounded by all my theater posters, is a little odd. But this is who I am.

And I know that Dad loves me. *All* parts of me.

"There's this boy, Elijah," I tell him. My pulse races just saying his name. "And I like him. More than I've liked anyone else before."

I search for any panic in Dad's face. But he just nods, waiting for me to go on.

"I'm afraid to tell him," I say. "Because I'm worried he won't feel the same way, and I'll make a fool of myself."

"Well . . ." Dad grabs the doorknob. Maybe this is awkward for him as well. Or maybe he's just thinking it over, taking his time to give me his best fatherly advice. "I've never known you to not go after what you want, Wade."

He's right. Which is exactly what I was afraid of.

"And if he doesn't feel the same way about you," Dad adds, "he's the fool. Not you."

Okay, now he's just being a dad. It's kind of nice.

I shut my laptop as Dad leaves, my adrenaline already pumping. It's like when I'm standing in the wings, waiting to make my first entrance. Only for this show, I don't know any of my lines or blocking. So I have to do what every actor dreads: improvise.

Forty minutes later, I'm slamming on my brakes to stop myself from running a red light. This has to be the absolute worst time to tell Elijah I have feelings for him; I'm supposed to be *less* self-centered now. But I couldn't sit at home any longer. Not when Elijah might think I've been ignoring him on purpose. Not when he could fall for Reese and end up getting hurt or do something else tonight that he may later regret.

Elijah can make his own decisions. I know that. But wouldn't it be better if he could make a decision that's fully informed—like knowing he has options?

I glance at my phone. The dance has been going on for a few hours already. I can't waste any more time. Finding a parking spot in downtown on a Saturday night, however, is proving impossible.

The second the light flicks to green, I hit the gas. I've been down this block three times already and I still don't see any spots. There's a pay lot to my left, but I left my house in such a hurry, I forgot my wallet.

Fuck it. I pull into the lot anyhow. I don't care if my car gets towed. Losing Elijah would be way more devastating.

I probably should've waited and parked closer to the venue. My lungs start to burn after a few blocks, and the slip-on tennis shoes I grabbed before leaving aren't helping. But I don't let that slow me down. The words I have to say to Elijah burn more.

I like you. It's such a simple thing. But my chest swells with happiness just thinking about it. I only hope I'm not too late.

When I finally arrive, I take the front steps two at a time. Inside, the lobby is filled with balloons and leftover specks of confetti. There's a check-in table, and a girl sitting behind it, scrolling through her phone.

"I have to talk to my friend," I say, the words rushing out of me as I run up to her.

Her eyes go wide. She seems young, probably an underclassman. "Do you have a ticket?" she asks, taking in the jeans and T-shirt I'm wearing.

There's a set of doors behind her, but they're closed. A heavy bass pulsates from the other side of them, causing a slight vibration on the floor.

"Have you ever been wrong about something?" I ask, my chest rising and falling as I try to catch my breath. "I don't mean like on a test. This is more important than that. It's like—" I stop, smiling as I picture Elijah's face. "It like the perfect person was right there in front of you the entire time. But you couldn't see it. Because you were stuck on this other idea of what your life should look like."

"Um . . ." She blinks. "I'm not supposed to let people in unless they paid for a ticket."

"I like Elijah Brady," I tell her. Now that I've admitted it to myself, now that I've said it to my dad, I want everyone to know.

The girl looks nervously over her shoulder. "One of the chaperones just stepped out. They should be back in—"

"I hate to do this," I say, stopping her. "But is there any chance *you* could help me?"

She shifts in her chair. I'm not supposed to be a shameless flirt anymore, charming people to get what I want. But occasionally, I may still have to use my powers for good.

"Please," I say, giving her my most winning smile.

She blushes. "Maybe someone will let you in by the back patio?"

I mouth "thank you" and run back outside. Taking out my phone, I hurry around to the other side of the building. Ava has better things to be doing than checking her texts during prom. But she's my best friend. If anyone's going to be thinking about me tonight, it's her.

The patio's empty when I arrive. Through the arched windows of the old train depot, my classmates are crowded together on the dance floor, moving in sync with the music. I look for Elijah, then Ava, before hanging back by some shrubs so I don't get caught.

The longest two minutes of my life later, Ava appears. She props the door open with her clutch and rushes over, looking absolutely stunning in her strapless yellow gown.

"Wade. What are you doing here?" She looks me up and down. "And why are you dressed like that?"

"You were right." I take a breath, steadying myself. "I have feelings for Elijah."

She doesn't bother trying to hide her smile. "I fucking knew it."

"Gloat later," I tell her. "Right now I need your help."

"What are you planning to do, exactly?"

A cheer rises up from inside. People have cleared a space on the dance floor, directing their attention toward a red carpet that leads up to a raised platform.

"Prom court," Ava says. "I have to be there for Ebony."

"I'm coming with you," I say.

As Ava sneaks me inside, I search for Elijah again. But it's too crowded. The music suddenly fades, and the doors to the lobby are lit up with two spotlights.

"Students of Monroe Academy," the deejay's voice comes on over the speakers. "Let's hear it for your junior and senior prom court!"

The doors open and everyone starts making noise again. The nominees walk out in pairs, with Reese in the lead couple, grinning like the star he is. While I can't deny he looks good in his tux, I don't feel the same spark I get when I think about Elijah now.

Drew brings up the rear, which also seems appropriate. He has two girls, one on each arm, picking up the slack after I dropped out. I glance at Ava. She keeps her chin up, not acknowledging him.

Once the nominees all make it to the stage, our dean of students, Mrs. Lundgren, joins them. "My goodness," she says, holding the microphone a little too close to her mouth. "Should we get this party started?"

The crowd roars back. And as the chaperones get ready to hand out sashes and consolation flowers, Mrs. Lundgren starts with the junior king and queen.

"Reese Erikson-Ortiz and Madison McCormick."

When Reese steps forward, the crowd whoops even louder. My heart twists a little. Reese and I dated for almost a year. Even if we didn't work out together, he still meant something to me. So I'm glad he won. He's a gracious winner, probably because he doesn't get obsessed with status and other superficial things like I sometimes do.

My eyes are quickly back on the dance floor, though. Where's Elijah? Did something happen to make him leave early?

"Now for our senior prom king," Mrs. Lundgren says. She opens the envelope slowly, adding a dramatic pause. "Drew Bauer."

As people cheer for Drew, Ava smiles politely and gives him a more enthusiastic clap than he deserves, proving once again why she belongs in one of the country's top acting schools.

"And finally, our senior prom queen." Mrs. Lundgren smiles as she reads the name, like she's pleased with the result. "Ebony Sinclair."

I should probably be keeping a low profile, but I can't help myself. I grab Ava's hand and we scream as we bounce up and down.

Once the winners are officially sashed and crowned, they move onto the dance floor as the deejay puts on a slow song. Both couples have a spotlight on them as they sway back and forth. And even though I'm glad I dropped out of the race, it still feels like this would've been a perfect moment to end senior year.

Except I don't want to be dancing with Reese anymore. I scan

322

the crowd again, desperate to tell Elijah how I feel. How I've *always* felt—even when I didn't know it. When I finally find him, my breath catches in my throat.

I know Elijah thinks Brady is this persona we created. But Brady was always part of him. He was just buried under the lack of confidence and self-doubt. And when I look at Elijah now—standing directly across from me on the dance floor—I want to run over there and tell him everything.

I want to tell him he's perfect as he is.

I want to tell him I'm sorry it took me so long to realize I liked him.

I want to tell him he looks unbelievably cute in a tux.

Every feeling I had while running here tonight surges through me again and I give him a wave, trying to get his attention. But Elijah doesn't see me. And when the winning couples break apart, the deejay puts on another slow song and their dates for the evening walk out to join them.

I keep waiting for Elijah to notice me. But he's already in the middle of the floor, wrapping his arms around Reese's neck. It's like I'm watching it in slow motion. My heart doesn't just ache. It cracks, splitting in two. Everything I wanted to tell him, everything I had to say—it's too late. I've missed my chance.

Forty-One

ELIJAH

There's a reason I liked being on the tech crew. It let me feel like I was an important part of the show—keeping the stage well lit, making sure actors never got lost in a shadow—while still standing in the back of the theater, where no one could see me.

Out here on the dance floor, there are too many eyes on me. I'm slow dancing with the junior prom king. Who's incredibly popular and well-liked. Even if I'm not the main attraction, people are definitely paying attention to me.

This is what I worked for.

It's everything I'm supposed to want.

"Congratulations," I say, smiling at Reese. "It's really cool that you won."

He laughs, his hands on my waist as we sway back and forth. "I'm not going to lie; it's a bit strange to be wearing a crown on my head."

As we continue to dance, more couples come out to join us. Some of them talk to each other, and some just stare longingly into each other's eyes. Summer rests her head on Clark's shoulder, looking like there's nowhere else she'd rather be.

Reese and I don't do any of those things. Which makes me feel kind of guilty. Shouldn't I be enjoying this moment more? When

Wade and I watched *My Fair Lady* together, I remember how he cried during "I Could Have Danced All Night." He said it made him want to know what it felt like to float around the room and be in love.

Maybe I'm putting too much pressure on myself, but my feet aren't exactly lifting off the dance floor. In fact, if I had a choice between dancing all night with Reese or watching a movie with Wade again . . . I'd pick Wade.

Spending time with Wade made me happy. When I first asked him to help me, I said I wanted to be more confident. But along the way, I think I confused confidence with popularity. What I really wanted was friends. People who would accept me for who I already was, not for who I was trying to be.

I still needed Wade's help for that. Without him, I never would've put myself out there, or let people get to know me.

The person I got to know the best, though, was Wade.

The person I wish I was here with tonight is Wade.

"I haven't kept things real between us," I suddenly say.

One of Reese's eyebrows notches up—he waits for me to go on. When I felt shy or nervous in the past, I let Brady do the talking for me. But if I want to leave Brady behind for good and tell Reese the truth, I have to speak for myself.

"This isn't who I really am," I explain. "Nobody called me Brady until I started doing the musical. Nobody even knew who I was. I wanted to change that, so I asked Wade to help turn me into someone different."

Reese nods, but his face doesn't give away his emotions.

"So what exactly is the problem?" he asks.

"I think—I think I like Wade."

As soon as the words are out of my mouth, I know they're true. That's why it hurt so much when he said he was hoping to get back together with Reese. I wanted him to want *me*. Only, from the very beginning, I didn't think something like that would ever be possible. So I took my feelings for him and buried them deep, not wanting to embarrass myself. I guess what I didn't realize is that those feelings never went away. They're still here.

Wade still may not like me like that. But I like myself now. And I can't keep lying to Reese. I just hope I haven't ruined prom for him.

"Yeah," he says. "I could tell something was off between us."

He sounds annoyed—which is fair. But then his brow smooths back out, like maybe he's also kind of relieved. Because the truth is, if I had gone to the hotel with everyone, I probably would've ruined prom for him anyhow. Maybe we're both better off this way.

"If we're being totally transparent," Reese continues, "I think part of the reason I asked you to prom in the first place was because I knew it'd make Wade jealous."

"What—" I shake my head, confused. "Why would he be jealous?"

He drops his chin, looking at me like the answer should be obvious. "I saw the way he always looked at you."

I stop moving. There's a sudden throbbing in my ears. I can't tell if it's my heartbeat, or the music—the deejay has transitioned into an upbeat tune, and more people are coming out on the dance floor to join us.

"So, um, now what?" Reese asks.

"I feel bad," I say. But then something inside me shifts. Neither of us were perfect. The apology doesn't need to be *all* on me.

I drop my hands to my side. "I guess we should stop trying to force this."

"Yeah." Reese lets go of my waist. "That's probably a good idea."

"You should go have fun with your friends. I'll be fine."

And it's true. I think I will.

Reese doesn't need much convincing. With the crown still on his head, he says goodbye and disappears into the crowd.

Before tonight, I might've felt self-conscious about being on the dance floor alone. But if people want to think I'm a weird loner, that's on them. I know I did what was right. I also know that I'm not actually alone. I look for Summer and Clark.

"Mind if I join you?" I ask, making my way to them.

Summer smiles, swaying her shoulders to the beat. "Of course not."

Dancing to a fast song still makes me a bit self-conscious. But Yang and Rhodes are moving their spotlights over the crowd and everyone else seems to be into it. So I close my eyes and try. I might've made a mistake with Reese, alienating Wade in the process. But at the beginning of the year, I never would've believed that I'd be at prom—let alone on the dance floor. Maybe I won't dance *all* night, like Eliza wanted to in *My Fair Lady*. But right now, in this moment, I choose to enjoy it.

When I open my eyes again, I catch sight of something that makes my feet stop moving. My heart squeezes in my chest, and I can't breathe. *Wade's here.* Except he's dressed in his regular clothes and talking to Ava. He gives her a hug, then turns to leave.

We haven't talked since our fight, but every cell in my body is telling me to run over there and find out what he's doing here. What would I say to him, though? I still don't understand why Reese thought taking me to prom would make him jealous. I mean, I *do* understand it. But I can't bring myself to believe it yet.

What I'm sure of, though, are my feelings for Wade.

They're big, and real, and yeah—a little terrifying.

As people continue bopping up and down on the dance floor, Wade passes under the archway of balloons. I start trying to push my way through the crowd, but someone bumps into me, causing me to lose sight of him. When I find him again, he's headed toward the exit.

"Wade!" I shout.

The music swallows up the sound of my voice. I have to stop him, but as the spotlights continue sweeping over us, the circle of bodies around me grows tighter.

"Wade!" I try again.

The throbbing in my ears is back—this time, it's definitely my heartbeat. All the feelings I tried to bury are ready to burst out of me. If I don't tell him how I feel right this minute, I might explode.

I take out my phone—there's no way I'll reach him in time. But instead of calling him, I come up with a better idea. One that feels strangely appropriate.

"Summer," I shout.

She looks at me. I toss her my phone.

"Call Rhodes and Yang. I need their help."

Forty-Two

WADE

Arriving at the doors that lead out into the lobby, the lump in my throat grows bigger, making it impossible to swallow my emotions back down. Doing the right thing should feel *good*. Not like you're making the biggest mistake of your life.

This isn't a mistake, though. Elijah and Reese looked happy together. And if that's what Elijah wants, I shouldn't spoil it. I just need to hold everything together long enough to make it back outside. Then I can fall apart.

As I reach for the door, however, something stops me. An important skill you learn as an actor is how to find your light. It takes some practice; you can't just stare directly into whatever's shining on you. Instead, you train yourself to feel the heat from the beam on your face.

Currently, it's not my face that's feeling the heat. It's the back of my neck. A pool of light surrounds me, making the hairs on my arms stand up.

I have no idea what's happening right now. Is it some kind of prank? Does it have something to do with dropping out of prom court?

And then it hits me: I *do* know who ran one of the spotlights for *My Fair Lady*.

I can't bring myself to look where the light is coming from yet, because I want to believe this has something to do with him. Just for a moment. Just so I can feel that happiness again. Even if I'm wrong—which I really hope I'm not.

When I finally turn back around, there's a second beam of light pointing down at the edge of the dance floor. My heart rips wide open.

Elijah.

He's standing in the middle of it.

I take a step forward, then pause. A couple of people have stopped dancing to watch us. I look down at my tennis shoes. The jeans I threw on before leaving my bedroom. My *How do you solve a problem like Maria?* cast T-shirt.

Elijah's staring at me. I have no idea what he's thinking right now, or what happened between him and Reese. But I do know my cue when I see it. And so, with my follow spot still on me, I walk over to him until our two circles of light combine into one.

"You must be an official theater kid now," I say.

His eyes search mine, worried. "Why?"

"Because that was really fucking dramatic."

He gives me a crooked smile. "How else was I supposed to get your attention?"

I try to smile back, but I'm too nervous. In all the time we've spent together, Elijah's never given any indication that he has feelings for me. If anything, he was usually too busy rolling his eyes at something I said. What if he's only interested in being friends?

"Elijah, I'm sorry I—"

"I'm so glad you—"

We both stop, not wanting to talk over each other.

"Sorry." He laughs, shyly rubbing his hands against the sides of his tuxedo pants. "You go first."

"No, what were you going to—"

Someone clips my shoulder as they try to move around us.

"This is kind of awkward," I say.

"Do you want to dance with me?" Elijah replies, speaking up as the music grows louder.

I nod. "Okay."

He slides his hands around my neck, causing my pulse to race in sync with the booming bass. I place my hands on his hips, hoping to steady myself, but touching him only makes me more light-headed.

"This isn't really a slow dance song," I say.

He shrugs. "Does it matter?"

I glance around the dance floor. Although most of our classmates are busy having their own fun, we're definitely getting a few looks. I'm sure people think we're being weird, or cheesy, or too over-the-top. But so what, maybe I am those things.

One thing I don't feel right now is brave. The words I was aching to tell him earlier suddenly feel too scary to speak. I've never been one to suffer from stage fright, though. So I tell myself to pretend that this is another show, and these are my lines. They just happen to be some of the most important ones I've ever said.

"Elijah," I start.

The music is hard to talk over. But I can't let myself chicken out.

"There's something I have to tell you."

"Huh?" he says.

"I have something important to tell you," I yell.

He shakes his head, pointing to his ear. *"It's too loud. I can't hear you."*

I lean in close, trying to speak into it.

"I said—"

Elijah turns his head, bringing his lips to mine. My whole world stops. I freeze, too shocked to respond.

"Sorry," he says, taking a step back. "Was that not okay? I thought . . ."

Maybe I don't have to say it. Maybe I just have to show it. I grab his face and pull him into me, kissing him the way he's always deserved to be kissed.

Soft, and slow, and sweet.

The music swells and people start cheering. Because of the song—not because of us. Elijah and I may as well be in our own little world right now. And that's just fine. This definitely wasn't how I imagined my senior year ending. It's a total surprise. Which is maybe even better.

Forty-Three

ELIJAH

Kissing Wade at prom is better than a dream. Because this is real life. And when our lips part, I get to stare up at his face. The swoop of hair that hangs over his forehead. His eyes, which are looking at me as if he thinks *he's* the lucky one right now.

The song finally ends, transitioning into something mellower. Wade and I continue to slow dance, oblivious to everyone around us.

"So," he says, his eyes crinkling as he smiles. "That was pretty cool."

I laugh. It *was* cool. Only now my definition of that word has changed. Cool shouldn't be about doing what's popular by everyone else's standards. It should be about having enough confidence to be who you are, and not caring if that makes you stand out.

It's okay to be quiet.

It's okay to say the wrong things.

It's okay if it takes you a while to warm up and feel comfortable.

Which isn't to say that you should never push yourself outside your comfort zone. If I hadn't joined the musical, I never would've gotten to know Wade. Maybe we weren't perfect in getting to this moment. But now that we're here . . . I don't want it to end.

"Do you want to go to the planetarium after this?" I ask, our bodies pressed close as we sway back and forth. "Summer's putting on a light show."

"Can I invite my friends?"

"Yeah. If they don't mind hanging out with techies."

He cracks another smile. I don't think I'll ever get tired of making him do that.

"Can we take a short detour first?"

"Detour?" My stomach flips, more excited than anxious.

He raises an eyebrow. "Does Szabo still have keys to the theater?"

I scan the dance floor. Szabo has a stunned but happy look on his face as he slow dances with Ava.

"Summer has an extra set," I say. "But why are we breaking into the theater?"

"I thought maybe we'd want a quiet place to talk first."

On the way to my car, I text my parents about my change of plans for the evening. Dad sends back a photo of my bedroom, showing off the *My Fair Lady* poster I wanted to hang on my wall. As much fun as our camping trip was, I told my parents the nature theme they had originally picked for my room wasn't really my style.

Looks perfect, I text back.

When Wade and I arrive at the theater, he tells me to wait while he runs to turn on some lights in the scene shop. The auditorium is eerily silent. I walk a few steps out onto the stage, which is shiny from its recent coat of fresh black paint. It still feels strange to see it so empty. It took us two months to get the show up and running. And now all our work is gone. Like it never even happened.

It won't stay empty for long, though. There's the fall play. And the winter one-act. And the next spring musical. I think I'd like to be a part of those shows, too. I just wish so many of my friends weren't seniors now.

"Boo!"

Wade sneaks up on me, causing me to jump.

"You scared me!"

He laughs, wrapping his arms around me from behind. "Don't worry. It's just us in here. Well, if you don't count all the ghosts."

"Ghosts?" I can't hide my skepticism. "You don't really believe in that, do you?"

"It's cheesy, but . . ." He takes a breath, his chest rising and falling against my back. "I like to think every show leaves a piece of itself behind."

I look out into the dark auditorium. There have been a lot of stories told on this stage. I guess all that energy has to go somewhere.

"I wish you weren't graduating already," I tell him.

He kisses the back of my neck. "I'm not leaving until the fall. And Lachlan's only a two-hour drive away."

I lean into him, wanting to stay like this forever. I know I can make new friends if I do more shows next year. I was even thinking of giving Quiz Bowl another try. But Wade—I don't want to have to say goodbye to him.

He drops his arms and I instantly miss the weight of him. But then he grabs my hand, lacing his fingers through mine. "Come on. Let's go to the fly gallery."

Sitting on the narrow platform up there, we face each other with our knees touching. It's like when he made us warm up by staring into each other's eyes for three minutes. Only this time, it's not awkward. I already trust Wade.

"Why'd you want to come up here?" I ask.

Even without all the backstage lights on, I catch the color flushing his cheeks. "It feels kind of silly now," he says, looking away.

I poke his knee. "Actors aren't supposed to feel silly, remember?"

"It's—the thing I was trying to tell you earlier, when we were on the dance floor . . ."

He takes a breath before letting his eyes meet mine again. My heart flutters—nervous, but in a good way, I think.

"I like you, Elijah. And I'm sorry it took me so long to realize it."

I almost laugh. How could that be silly? And *why* is he apologizing? Wade likes me! I realize I'm supposed to be more confident now. But if I'm being honest, there's still a part of me that doesn't believe any of this is real.

"Say it again," I tell him.

He gives me a funny look. "What?"

"Tell me you like me. I want to hear it again."

"Okay." He leans forward. "I like you, Elijah Brady. *A lot.*"

My heart feels too big for my chest. I know I should say it back. But first, I pull his face toward me, giving him another kiss. Wade kisses back, and it's not as innocent as what we shared on the dance floor. Soon I'm on top of him, which—considering where we are—is probably a safety hazard. It's also really hot. But after a minute, I get the giggles.

"What's so funny?" he asks, pulling back.

"Gretchen," I reply. "She's probably at some after-party right now, wondering why she's suddenly breaking out into a cold sweat."

Wade laughs, running his thumb across my cheek as he studies me. "You're weird. You know that, right?"

"Yes." I give him another kiss. "I do."

After a while, we end up lying next to each other. Wade wraps his arm around me, and I rest my head on his chest, listening to his heartbeat. (Trivia fact: in the average lifespan, the human heart will beat over two and a half billion times.)

As we stare up into the fly system, my eyes land on something I've never noticed before.

"Hey," I say, pointing to where a bunch of writing is spray-painted onto the brick wall of the theater. "What's that?"

"The names?" Wade asks. "Those are past students. Seniors used to go up there and add theirs before graduating."

I sit up, trying to make some of them out. There must be dozens. I wonder who those people were when they were students here. And how old they are now. Do they still remember putting their names on this wall?

A chill passes through me. Rationally, I know we're in a drafty old theater. But part of me wonders if Wade was right. Not about the ghosts, necessarily. But about leaving a piece of ourselves behind.

When I leave, will I still be Brady, since that's who most people from the show know me as? Or is Elijah closer to the real me?

Wade sits up. "Hey. You okay?"

Whether I'm Elijah, Brady, or someone in between the two . . . I have time to figure that out. If there's one thing I know about myself right now, though, it's that I'm definitely the type of person who likes being alone with Wade Westmore in the fly gallery after prom.

"In case this wasn't obvious," I say, turning to face him. "I like you, too."

We're so close, I can't see his smile. Only the crinkle in his eyes.

"I was hoping you'd say that," he whispers.

I pull him into me again. And even though the show is over, and most of my friends are graduating, and I don't know what's going to happen when Wade heads to college this fall, it doesn't feel like an ending when our lips touch.

It feels like that moment when the houselights start to go down, and the audience grows quiet as the conductor taps their baton on the music stand, and you lean forward in your seat and take a quick breath . . . waiting for the overture to begin.

Acknowledgments

As someone who's watched every telecast of the Tony Awards since around the time I was in high school, I like to think I know a thing or two about acceptance speeches. Speaking from the heart—passionately, as you clutch your trophy and fight back tears—is more compelling than reading off a list of names. However, having put two books out into the world now, I also know that creating a piece of art or entertainment is rarely a solo endeavor.

Which is to say . . . I have a list. And there's no conductor to play me offstage. So get comfortable.

My editor, Kristin Daly Rens. Thank you for giving me the time to try to get this story right. You pushed me to become a better writer, which is a gift I suspect you give all your authors. I'm still in awe of the amount of time and care you put into this book. And just as important, that you love old musicals as much as I do.

My agent, Lauren Spieller. Thank you for helping to foster my writing career long before I had a book deal. Your passion for your clients is one of your many strengths, and I'm extremely lucky to have you in my corner.

Alessandra Balzer, Donna Bray, and the entire team at Balzer + Bray and HarperCollins. I'm still pinching myself at being at such a wonderful, daring, author-loving imprint. Standing ovations for the people who make the magic happen behind the scenes: Shona McCarthy and Mark Rifkin in managing editorial. Danielle McClelland and Melissa Cicchitelli in production. Shannon Cox in marketing and Taylan Salvati in publicity. Patty Rosati and the team in School and Library. Kerry Moynagh, Kathy Faber, Jen Wygand, and the team in sales. And Christian Vega in editorial. (Christian—have you watched *My Fair Lady* yet?)

To have one cover illustrated by Betsy Cola is a dream. To have two is an embarrassment of riches that I'm very grateful for. Thank you to Betsy, along with designers Chris Kwon, Alison Donalty, and Jenna Stempel-Lobell for bringing Wade and Elijah to life in way that makes my musical theater–loving heart sing.

Brandon Powell, thank you for reading an early draft and assuring me I wouldn't be booed off the stage. Sophia Babai, Mey Rude, and Sydnee Thompson, thank you for providing insightful feedback that helped strengthen my characters. Erik J. Brown, Sophie Gonzales, Rachael Lippincott, and Adam Sass: Asking authors you admire to read your work is scarier than a trust fall. Thank you for your time and generous words.

Emily Helck, Katie Henry, Siena Koncsol, and Michelle Rinke. After a decade together, calling you my "writing" group no longer feels like an adequate term. Thank you for being my support group. My friend group. The group of people I can always trust.

Erik J. Brown, Anna Gracia, Naz Kutub, and Susan Lee. You probably see the most insecure side of me—and you *still* choose to be my friend. Thank you for keeping me grounded and making me laugh. Publishing would be a lot less fun without you by my side. Kevin Christopher Snipes, thanks for putting up with my insecurities in person and for always splitting the bill.

I'm extremely grateful for my family—Mike; Ellen; Maddie; Tori; Molly; Ann; Brian; Ethan; Declan; and my parents, who sat through many high school and college performances, watching me stand in the background with the rest of the ensemble. Thank you for always being proud of me. Especially during the bad shows.

My husband, Danny, who deserves his own special award for the number of times he had to hear the *My Fair Lady* soundtrack (among others) play on repeat while I wrote. Thank you for your patience, love, and support. My life is fuller because of you.

Okay, here's the part where I clutch my metaphorical trophy and fight back tears.

It might be too dramatic (even for me) to say that doing theater saved my life, but it definitely changed it. I was a shy, awkward, closeted teen. The theater was the first place where I felt like it was okay to be different. The first place where I felt like I could belong.

Thank you to all the other theater kids—*especially the weird ones*—who did a show with me. And to Gary Gisselman, my theater professor in college. Gary taught his students that we each had our own perspective. That no one saw the world the same way we did. Gary believed in me before I could believe in myself. And in doing so, he gave me the permission to take myself, and being an artist, seriously.

To any young artists out there—*especially the queer ones*—I hope you already know that you're allowed to take yourself seriously. Don't listen to anyone who tells you you're not good enough, or that your dreams are too big. There'll be time to figure that out later. For now, if it makes you happy, if it fulfills you in some way . . . that's all that matters.

So keep going. I can't wait to see what you create.